Bonny *wanted* to become his wife

If she could but marry the duke and love him to completion, surely she could earn his love. She tossed back her head, causing her hood to fall, and smiled up into his face. "Do you think we could wed before Mama dies?"

Radcliff cupped her face in his hands.

She felt the scrutiny of his all-knowing eyes, and for the first time, she sensed a passion beneath his pensive countenance. He lowered his head, crushing his lips to hers.

Bonny felt bereft when he pulled away. She had never been kissed before, and she was surprised at the power of one kiss. And now she knew the desire for something more than a kiss. Something more intimate.

"I think a hasty wedding is an excellent idea," he said flatly. "Else I should ravage you here on the moors."

Dear Reader,

March is the time of spring, of growth, and the budding of things to come. Like these four never-before-published authors that we selected for our annual March Madness Promotion. These fresh new voices in historical romance are bound to be tomorrow's stars!

Among this year's choices for the month is *The Maiden and the Warrior* by Jacqueline Navin, a heartrending medieval tale about a fierce warrior who is saved from the demons that haunt him when he marries the widow of the man who sold him into slavery. Goodness also prevails in *Gabriel's Heart* by Madeline George. In this flirty Western, an ex-sheriff uses a feisty socialite to exact revenge, but ends up falling in love with her first!

Last Chance Bride by Jillian Hart is a touching portrayal of a lonely spinster-turned-mail-order-bride who shows an embittered widower the true meaning of love on the rugged Montana frontier. And don't miss *A Duke Deceived* by Cheryl Bolen, a Regency story about a handsome duke whose hasty marriage to a penniless noblewoman is tested by her secret deeds.

Whatever your tastes in reading, you'll be sure to find a romantic journey back to the past between the covers of a Harlequin Historical.

Sincerely,

Tracy Farrell, Senior Editor

Please address questions and book requests to:
Silhouette Reader Service
U.S.: 3010 Walden Ave., P.O. Box 1325, Buffalo, NY 14269
Canadian: P.O. Box 609, Fort Erie, Ont. L2A 5X3

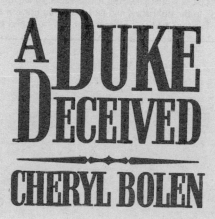

A DUKE DECEIVED

CHERYL BOLEN

Harlequin Books

TORONTO • NEW YORK • LONDON
AMSTERDAM • PARIS • SYDNEY • HAMBURG
STOCKHOLM • ATHENS • TOKYO • MILAN
MADRID • WARSAW • BUDAPEST • AUCKLAND

ISBN 0-373-29006-3

A DUKE DECEIVED

Copyright © 1998 by Cheryl Bolen

CHERYL BOLEN

Two passions—the love of writing and an obsession over all things English—have guided Cheryl Bolen's life for more years than she cares to remember. A former English teacher, Cheryl is currently news editor of an award-winning newspaper in suburban Houston and owns an antiques business specializing in small English antiques. She is married to a college political science teacher, and they have two sons who claim to be grown.

For the man who captured my teenage heart
and who nursed me through my fortieth birthday—
my husband, John Bolen.

Chapter One

"So now you know why I cannot let Mama throw me on the marriage mart, why I can nev-never marry," whimpered Emily, burying her tear-streaked face in her hands.

It pained Bonny Barbara Allan to watch Emily's shoulders bent over the dressing table, heaving in wave after wave of fresh sobs. What hurt even more was Bonny's own powerlessness to help the only two people she cared about. She could no more ease her cousin's acute suffering than she could heal her own beloved mother of the destructive disease ravaging her body.

Bonny's lashes swooped down, clearing tears from her own eyes. "If you shan't marry," she began in a soothing voice, "what will you do? What is it you want from life, Em?"

The question had the effect of renewing Emily's sobbing. "All that I ever w-w-w-wanted has been taken from me." Emily blotted her face with a fresh handkerchief before a new assault of tears gushed forth.

Bonny crossed the carpeted bedroom and stood beside Emily, gently patting her shoulders. Presently, she suggested, "I think you should tell your parents everything."

Emily straightened up, her hands dropping to her lap, her

knuckles whitening as she twisted the handkerchief. She turned frightened eyes on Bonny. "Never! Promise me you'll never tell them—you'll never tell anybody."

"I would never tell anyone," Bonny said reassuringly.

"Especially my mother. You know what she's like. I'm terrified of her."

If the truth be known, Aunt Lucille fairly terrified Bonny, too. "But surely," Bonny said, thinking of the close relationship she enjoyed with her own mother, "you could talk to her at a time like this."

"You're the only one I can turn to since Aunt Camille's gone. I hated to ask you for the money from your grandmother, but there was no one else I could go to. I vow I'll repay you when I get my portion from Aunt Camille's estate."

Bonny waved off her cousin's gratitude. "Pooh, it's nothing. I owe you and your father for coaxing your mother into letting me come to visit here in London." She took a silver-handled brush from Emily's dressing table and lovingly ran it through her cousin's blond tresses.

"Don't pretend that coming here was what you wanted," Emily said, sniffing. "I know you too well, Bonny. You always do everything for everybody else. The only reason you wanted a season in London was to ease your mother's worry."

Seized with a growing sense of grief, Bonny swallowed hard. "I do want Mama to be able to die happy, knowing I'll be taken care of."

Emily, her eyes lowered ruefully, turned from her dressing table to take Bonny's hands. "I've been so selfish talking about my problems, when you've had to watch your mother's life slip away day by day."

"Mama's illness does seem to have devastated me far more than it has her. She continues to say she has had a long, happy life, that all she wants is for me to make a decent match."

"Only decent? With your beauty? Everybody talks of how lovely you are." A feeble smile crept across Emily's somber face and an impish twinkling sparked her reddened eyes. "Which, of course, makes Mama seething mad, but even Mama would have to admit that you could have any man you choose."

Bonny made no attempt to deny her own beauty. That she was extraordinarily beautiful was as much a fact as knowledge that the sun would rise on the morrow. But where nature had been overly generous, circumstances had failed her. "I'm prepared for disappointment since I have no dowry," she said simply.

"With your face, it won't matter."

"Perhaps not to the man, but it will to his family."

"Then you'll simply have to pick one who's already come into his majority."

"I may not have the luxury of selecting a prospective husband."

Emily put aside her drenched handkerchief. "Do you mean you'll take the first one who asks?"

"I may have to. My mother's consumption worsens by the day, and I must assure her that my future is secure."

"Would it not upset you terribly to have a loveless marriage?"

Of course it would cause her a great deal of anguish. How horrid it must be to lie naked with any man, to have him probe one's body, but to lie with a man one didn't love, she thought, must be God's punishment for betraying the sacred bonds of matrimony. Instead of sharing these thoughts with Emily, though, Bonny calmly said, "Haven't your parents had a loveless marriage these last thirty years?"

"I'm quite sure they haven't slept together since I was born eighteen years ago," Emily said matter-of-factly.

"But Alfred's twenty-nine. They must have slept together during the eleven years between your birth and your brother's."

"There would be more than the two of us if they had. What I believe is that they became estranged after Alfred was born. Then I think Papa probably lost himself one night when he was in his cups and made love to Mama nineteen years ago." She giggled. "I believe that's why he no longer imbibes."

If he no longer imbibed, Bonny thought affectionately, it certainly was not because he regretted begetting Emily. She was so much the image of her father—skin the color of butterscotch, small bones, wide blue eyes, blond hair— and only Emily's presence could soften a face hardened by thirty years with a faithless wife. "If you didn't look so much like your father," Bonny said, "I would think..." She hesitated.

"You'd think I was sired by one of Mama's lovers?"

"Then you know about them?"

Emily nodded.

"My mother doesn't approve. I don't think I do, either," Bonny said. "If I should have a loveless marriage, I shouldn't wish to take a lover."

"But lovers can be quite satisfactory. Look at Lady Lynda Heffington. She has the Duke of Radcliff for her lover, and there's not a woman alive who wouldn't swoon over him."

Bonny could understand—understand, not necessarily approve of—lying with a man one was attracted to. "I've heard that the Duke of Radcliff is not nearly as handsome as his heir, Stanley Moncrief."

Emily took a long sniff, patted her eyes one last time with a dry corner of her handkerchief and tossed it on top of her dressing table. "That is true, but there's something about the duke. He's so terribly serious looking. And there's a strength about him. You could picture him slaying dragons with his bare hands for the woman he loves."

Bonny's eyebrows shot up. Such a man held interest for her. "If he loves this Lady Heffington, why doesn't he marry her? Didn't old Lord Heffington pass away some three years ago?"

"Why buy the cow," Emily suggested, "when you can get the milk for free?" As the words fell from her own lips, Emily gasped, and her crying recommenced. "But Harold really was going to m-m-m-marry me."

At precisely this moment, Lady Landis walked into her daughter's room and threw up her arms in indignation. "I simply cannot abide this infernal crybaby business of yours, Emily. Just look at you! That face is much too pretty to go ruining, making it all red."

With a swish of silk, Lady Landis glided across the floor and stood over her seated daughter, glancing at her own face in the looking glass hanging over Emily's dressing table. Tendrils of hair, a subtle mixture of red and gray, curled about her still-pretty face. Her neck had thickened, like her waist, but because of her huge, cat green eyes, her face remained something out of the ordinary. She blinked into the mirror, opened her eyes even wider, gave her reflection a satisfied smile, then spun round to face Bonny, narrowing her eyes.

"My daughter needs to rest for tonight's fete. Please remove yourself from this room, Barbara." Her long fingers raked through her hair. "I refuse to call you that odious name from that terrible ballad. Bonny Barbara Allan, indeed! Your father must have been half-mad to have named you that. And the viscount's sister, too, for allowing her baby to be called such a silly, common name."

Emily grasped Bonny's hand and held it tight, her eyes

beseeching her cousin to stay. "But, Mama, I can't go to-night. I'm too distraught over…over Aunt Camille's death. We—you and I both—should be in mourning."

"After all the money I've spent on your gowns—" Lady Landis glared at Bonny "—and gowns for your penniless cousin, I can ill afford to allow you to go into mourning. You'd surely be a different size next year."

"We could have them cut down later," Emily proposed. "I do seem to be getting thinner."

The viscountess's eyes narrowed again. "It's no wonder, the way you hardly touch your food. You have been so changed ever since you came back from Spain. At first I was so pleased. You'd turned into such a lovely woman. Your breasts were so full. I fancied you beautiful enough to become a duchess." She glared at her slender daughter and spoke with contempt. "But now you're withering away, making yourself a disgusting watering pot."

Emily squared her shoulders and faced her mother, pleading, "Think of Aunt Camille—your only sister."

Lady Landis's artificially darkened lashes lowered, a look of pain sweeping across her face. "Need I remind you," she said, her voice shaking, "how much I miss Camille? And truly I am mourning her even though I'm not wearing black. Remember, almost no one is leaving the Peninsula in the thick of all this dreadful war business. No one in London has heard of her death yet."

"But you can't expect me to smile and be pleasant to any gentlemen in my state of grief?"

Lady Landis crept toward her daughter like a tiger toward its prey. "I can, and you will."

Emily threw a panicked glance at her cousin as Bonny slipped quietly from the room.

Lady Lynda Heffington looked into the distracted face of Richard Moncrief, the fifth Duke of Radcliff, and followed his gaze ten feet across the wooden ballroom floor. There stood perhaps the most beautiful woman she had ever seen, a raven-haired beauty who was surrounded by men. Even from this distance the young woman's long eyelashes and perfectly white teeth could be observed. Though Lady Heffington did not at all like what she saw, she managed a smile, thrust out her ample bosom a bit farther and said in the sweetest of tones, "Will you escort me to dinner tonight, Radcliff?"

The duke did not respond. His eyes were riveted on the lovely creature while his mind absorbed every aspect of her. Her woman's body in the soft white dress. Thick black hair swept back loosely from the smooth perfection of her china-doll face. Eyes that were neither blue nor green but a curious mixture of the two. And a smile that erased all the world's pain. God's eyes, but she was gorgeous, he thought.

And to think, he would not have been here at all had the hostess not been one of his late mother's dearest friends. He had grown so bloody tired of the balls and routs, the gaming hells, the heavy drinking, the excesses he and the other bloods had enjoyed these past fifteen years.

It was time he settled down. He thought of how happy his parents had been in their marriage. A sadness nearly overcame him as he pictured them sitting before a fire, reading by candlclight, utterly content with only each other's presence. That is what he had come to long for.

But, of course, he was not likely to find his life's mate in one of these chits just out of the schoolroom who could talk of nothing but the weather and the latest fashions.

"Radcliff?" Lady Heffington tapped her foot impatiently.

He turned to the coppcr-headed woman, lifting a single eyebrow. Perhaps he should marry a more mature woman. A widow. He eyed the lovely widow at his side. It was certain that she wouldn't do at all back within the comforting walls of Hedley Hall. Lady Heffington gained her sustenance from elaborate ball gowns and admiring glances.

"I asked if you would escort me to dinner later." Her voice was smooth and rich, like good cognac.

"I'm not sure I'll be here."

She pouted. "You will claim me for a waltz?"

His eyes sparkled. "But, my dear Lynda, if I am to hold you that close, I'd infinitely prefer to be in the horizontal position."

Lady Heffington slithered closer. "You're so naughty, Radcliff."

"I endeavor to please, madam."

She slapped her fan against his velvet sleeve.

"Thank you for standing up with me," he said with finality, moving away from her and across the crowded ballroom toward the card room. After taking but half a dozen steps, he was stopped short of his destination.

"There you are," said James Edward Twickingham, who had answered to the name Twigs since his Eaton days. "I say, Radcliff, everyone here tells me the horse you bought at Tatt's today went for four hundred guineas. Why would a horse fetch so much?"

"Because it's the most perfect piece of horseflesh ever to set foot on English soil."

"You rode it here tonight?" Twigs asked hopefully.

"No, my friend, but I'll show it to you tomorrow."

Smiling, Twigs pulled his lanky body face-to-face with the duke and lowered his voice. "Devilishly dull here, old boy. Interest you in a game of whist?"

The duke's gaze once again darted to the dark-haired beauty. "I don't think it's dull at all, Twigs. It looks to be a most interesting night." He leaned closer to Twigs and spoke in low tones. "Do you know who that beautiful woman over there is?"

"Beautiful woman?" Twigs's head bobbed from one point of the ballroom to the other. "Where?"

"Where are all the men gathered?"

"In the card room, naturally."

"In this room, you idiot." Since Twigs was not only his best friend but also his oldest friend, Radcliff could take liberties in his address. "Where do you see most of the men flocked?"

Twigs pondered this for a moment, then ventured, "Over there by Alfred Wickham's cousin."

"Do you mean to say that black-haired lady is Wickham's cousin?"

Twigs's eyes shot to the woman in question. "Hair is black, I do believe. Yep, that's Wickham's cousin. Name's Bonny Barbara Allan. Like the song."

The duke recited the first stanza of "Barbara Allan" to himself.

In Scarlet Town where I was born
there was a fair maid dwelling.
Made every youth cry Well-a-way!
Her name was Barbara Allan.

"Barbara Allan." The words fell off his tongue like precious poetry. "Could you introduce me?" He moved toward Bonny.

"Would if I knew her. Fact is, I don't."

They were within five feet of her now, and the duke noticed that his own cousin, Stanley Moncrief, had found his way to the beauty's side. What a good-looking pair they made, he thought. Stanley, with his coloring like hers and his almost-too-handsome face, was nearly as exceptional as she.

A sudden longing to hear the Incomparable's voice, to shut out all the noises of merriment in the crowded room overwhelmed the duke, and he moved closer to her.

"Miss Allan," he heard Stanley say, "may I have the honor of calling on you at home tomorrow?"

Bonny gave him a mischievous look. "You may, but I will not be there, sir."

The men circling her chuckled at her flippant reply.

Radcliff's eyes twinkled. This was no simpering miss, throwing herself at Stanley's feet as all the other women did. The duke's hand stopped Twigs from advancing, and the two of them stood a few feet from Bonny, watching as Stanley maintained his perfect smile and exited the group, his face flaming.

Stanley's gaze swung up to meet the duke's. "Richard, I had no idea you were here. I thought you were still at Hedley Hall. Is all well there?"

"Yes. I'm taking very good care of Hedley Hall, but don't depend upon it just because you're next in line. I plan to outlive you."

Stanley smiled graciously, a dimple creasing one handsome cheek. "I'm sure you will. After all, you're only my senior by a mere five years."

The duke glanced at Bonny. "And I may still marry and produce an heir."

Stanley looked from Radcliff to Bonny. "Do you know the lovely Bonny Barbara Allan?"

"Not yet."

"But I'm sure you will, cousin. You have such an infamous appreciation for beautiful things." Stanley looked at Lady Heffington and took his leave to dance with her.

"I've got just the ticket!" Twigs announced to Radcliff.

"For what?" the duke inquired.

"To meet the Bonny gel. Get Wickham to introduce you."

"I regret that I haven't seen Wickham tonight."

"Pity. Neither have I. Oh well, shall we go to the card room?"

Emily moved to Bonny's side and whispered, "If you'll look straight ahead at the two men walking from the card room, you will see the Duke of Radcliff. He wears a royal blue velvet coat."

Bonny turned to watch him. He stood under six feet in height and at first seemed nothing but ordinary. Average height, build only a little more muscular than average, wavy hair the color of honeyed toast. But there was something in his craggy face that suggested an inner strength that knew no equal. Perhaps it was the way the corners of his firmly set mouth tugged downward that gave him a sense of omniscience. Bonny studied his face as he politely listened to whatever it was his friend was saying, his eyes holding a hint of insolence.

A Lord Something-or-Other came to claim Bonny for the next dance. Bonny learned the young gentleman's name was Reginald Keating, but the quadrille offered no further opportunity to converse. As they danced, she felt the eyes of the Duke of Radcliff on her, but she avoided his pensive gaze. Though she felt uncomfortable knowing he watched her, she wanted to perform her dance steps flawlessly. She wanted the duke to find no fault with her.

When the dance ended and Keating escorted Bonny from the dance floor, the Duke of Radcliff approached them.

Her heart hammering, Bonny still avoided the duke's gaze. Why did the man have such an effect on her?

"Keating," the duke said, eyeing Bonny, "might I commend you on your selection of dance partners? Pray, make me known to this lovely lady."

Keating, his cheeks turning red, stammered, "C-certainly, your grace." He stepped away from Bonny and presented her. "Miss Bonny Barbara Allan, the Duke of Radcliff." With a half bow and the utterance of "Your very obedient servant," Keating took his leave.

Radcliff peered into Bonny's eyes. "Bonny doesn't suit you. You were born to be a Barbara."

She cocked her head and said challengingly, "Why doesn't Bonny suit, your grace?" She hoped her response concealed the tremors within.

"Because it implies a lovely, rosy-cheeked child. Not a woman with regal bearing."

She could feel the sweep of his gaze, and she could not have felt more undressed had he removed her gown. Color flooded her face.

"Would I be too much the fool to hope you could save one dance for me tonight, Miss Allan?"

The only dances still open were waltzes. Aunt Lucille had told Bonny she was not to dance the waltz until the patronesses at Almack's accorded her permission. But she had been waltzing back at Milford for the past two years, and she was quite good at it. "My card is full, save for the waltzes, your grace."

"A waltz will do very well."

While the duke and the beauty engaged in discourse, Stanley Moncrief eyed the pair from beneath lowered brows. It was not the first time he had studied Bonny Barbara Allan. Since first laying eyes on her a week before, he had contrived to reacquaint himself with Alfred Wickham, to learn where Wickham's lovely cousin would be each night, to dance the maximum two dances with her on each occasion and, simply, to join her court of admirers.

Did she not realize how fortunate she was to receive such homage from one whose blood was far more blue? From one to whom any number of women in this very room would readily surrender their virtue? To think he had relaxed his own rule of courting only heiresses to pay such marked attentions to this country miss, who had returned the privilege with the utmost discourtesy.

Only steam shooting from his ears could have accurately portrayed his thunderous mood as he watched Bonny treat his cousin with such civility. Did she not know Richard could not ride nearly so well as he could? And did she not observe that the duke's dress was not of the latest order of fashion, as was his own? Why, just look at Richard's cravat! Had his own man created so simple an effect he would have turned him out without a reference! And Richard's address was not as generally commended as his own. He was the one who had patiently cultivated Bonny's acquaintance, yet Richard—not following the proper, if unwritten, rules of the ton—had blatantly introduced himself to the unworthy chit and now enjoyed the fruits of what Stanley could only perceive as the advantage of his cousin's rank.

Well, he was not going to let the chit make a cake of him. Stanley strode across the room to an assemblage of young women, with a flicker of his eyes detected the loveliest one and begged the pretty thing to stand up with him.

The girl's widened eyes sparkled when the handsome Stanley distinguished her with his notice, and she floated with him to the dance floor on a cloud of her own self-importance.

When the duke claimed Bonny for a waltz, he slipped an arm around her, finding her size much to his liking. She was neither short nor tall but just right. "Is this your first journey to London, Miss Allan?"

"Yes, your grace."

"And how do you like it?"

"I know I'm supposed to say I'm in raptures, but actually I find myself quite uncomfortable."

The duke's step slowed, and he shot her a concerned gaze. "How so, Miss Allan?"

"Being country bred, I find so many rules a bit stifling."

"Well put!" he exclaimed. "I confess to such feelings myself." The girl must be referring to Almack's, he thought. "Tell me, have you been to Almack's?"

"Not yet, your grace."

He made a mental note to get Lady Jersey to send a voucher to the remarkable Barbara Allan. But, of course, others in her party would have to be included. "You stay with your family, Miss Allan?"

"With my uncle, David Wickham, Viscount Landis. I am to be presented along with his daughter, Emily."

Two vouchers, he thought. "Where, then, are your parents?"

"I'm from the North Country, your grace." She hesitated. "My father, who has been dead six years now, was a country vicar and something of a scholar."

He liked her even better for her honesty. Most maidens avoided mentioning vicar fathers—and hence a lack of dowry. In no way did the lovely Bonny Barbara Allan act like a girl straight from the schoolroom, as he knew she must be. Even her full, rich voice sounded like a woman's.

"Did your father's sons inherit his scholarly interests?" the duke asked.

She lowered her head. "Unfortunately for him, your grace, he had no sons. In fact, he and Mama were married some twenty years before they had a child, and they had to settle for one disappointing girl, whom I fear my father raised very much like a boy."

"I find it very hard to believe they were disappointed in you and even harder to believe you are anything like a boy." His eyes whisked over her entire body. "Did you inherit the scholarly pursuits?"

"I regret to say I wasn't a very good student, though Papa did try."

"Then you've read the classics?" he asked.

"Yes, your grace," she said shyly.

This beautiful creature he held in his arms must know a great deal more than all the other silly girls, he thought with appreciation. "Funny that you should say your parents had no children for twenty years. It was the same with my parents."

"Then you are an only child, too?"

"Yes. In fact, now I'm the only Moncrief left—save my second cousin, Stanley."

"I am so sorry for you, your grace." In a hoarse whisper, she added, "I will soon be the same."

"Your mother is ill?"

"Gravely."

By God, that's why the girl was in London. Soon to be orphaned with not two guineas to rub together, she would probably accept the first offer she received. The thought was like a blow to his windpipe. A surge of protective tenderness toward her washed over him.

And—against all logic—he vowed to be the first to make her an offer.

Chapter Two

Her legs spread wide over the Duke of Radcliff's muscled torso, her bare breasts brushing against the patch of hair on his chest, Lady Heffington softly brushed her lips across his damp forehead. "Oh, *mon chéri,* but I had to do all the work tonight." She slid off Radcliff to lie beside him in her regal-size bed. "Did you have a long workout with Jackson today?"

"How well you know me," he lied. How could he tell her he would not have been in her bed this night had he not promised her earlier? How could he tell Lynda she had been unable to arouse him as she usually did by merely removing her clothing? How could he tell her his mind was full of a raven-haired miss swathed in white?

"I know you so very well. In fact," she said, reaching across his chest to stroke his arm, "we suit most agreeably. And, of course, our backgrounds are so similar. You do remember my grandfather was the Duke of Hargrove."

"How could I forget, lascivious Lynda."

"I do love it when you say these things to me, Radcliff. I love you much too dearly. You have made me lose my pride. For the pleasure of your touch, I forget that you ignored me earlier tonight. Not one waltz!"

"But don't you agree this is infinitely superior to dancing?" He removed her hand from his arm, kissed it, sat up and got out of the bed.

"You're not going to stay the night?" She sounded disappointed.

"We must consider your reputation, my dear lady."

She moved to a sitting position on the bed. Muted light from the tall casement nearby illuminated her full breasts. "You never worried about that before."

He stepped into his breeches. "I have an early meeting with my solicitor in the morning." Another lie.

What a contrast bustling London was to the loneliness of Milford, Bonny thought the next day as she took in the capital city's ever present activity. The boot-clad matron with mismatched clothes who sold posies on the street, the nuts warming over a small fire while the barker yelled, "'Ot chestnuts," the constant clopping of horses' hooves colliding with stone streets.

Bonny and Emily entered the hack waiting outside Bonny's old servant's house on Kepple Street and settled back in its plain seats, which were not nearly as plush as those in Aunt Lucille's barouche.

"Were you not pleased with Mrs. Davies?" Bonny asked Emily.

Emily sniffed and dabbed at her eyes with a handkerchief. "Oh, she is all that you said she was, and her lodgings are far better than I had hoped for," Emily replied with feigned enthusiasm.

"And we can count on her discretion. In my entire life I've never known her to betray a confidence."

"That is most reassuring."

As much as she abhorred lying, Bonny settled back in the coach and concocted stories that would explain to an enraged aunt what two young ladies of quality were doing in a rented hack. For herself she would not lie, but she would to protect Emily.

Of course, the likelihood was slim her aunt would discover their clandestine journey, but in the event she did, they needed a satisfactory explanation. Perhaps they could say Em became too exerted from their long walk through Hyde Park to make it back to Cavendish Square on foot. Any account they devised would be far superior to the truth.

When the coachman, at Bonny's instruction, brought the hack to a stop a block away from Cavendish Square, the two women disembarked and Bonny paid the driver from the remains of the money her grandmother had left her. They walked briskly in the afternoon sun, much too warm now in the merino cloaks they had needed when they left the viscount's slumbering household that morning.

A placid Styles met them in the marble entry hall and informed the young women that her ladyship was most desirous of communicating with them.

Before they could put up their cloaks and reticules, an overdressed and highly agitated Lady Landis swept into the foyer, her heavily perfumed scent permeating the room. "Wherever have you been?" she demanded.

Emily gave a start, slowly removed her cloak, faced her mother and calmly announced, "Why, Bonny and I wished to have a nice long walk in the park."

Lady Landis glanced disapprovingly at them. "I can see that neither of you has any idea how ladies of fashion are to behave on the day after a rout. Did you not know gentlemen would begin calling?"

"We will freshen our toilets at once, my lady," Bonny said, moving to the wide staircase.

"It's much too late!" Lady Landis glared at Emily. "Are you aware of whose personage called here this hour past?"

Emily looked down at the gilded baluster. "No, ma'am."

"None other than the Duke of Radcliff," her mother announced smugly.

Bonny felt a flutter in her breast at this announcement.

"But, Mama, I didn't even dance with the duke last night," Emily said, brushing a blond ringlet from her face.

"Of course you didn't. You had every dance promised. You did quite well for yourself," said a beaming Lady Landis. "There's just one thing. We must get Martha to sew lace around the neckline of your dresses. Your endowments are a poor match for Barbara's." Lady Landis shot an angry glance at Bonny's generous bosom.

The door slammed open, and Lord Alfred came strolling in. "Let me look at you two," he said heartily, smiling with pleasure upon his sister and cousin. "All I've heard from my chums is how bloody lucky I am to live with the two prettiest girls in London."

"Pray, don't look at them now," Lady Landis said. "They've exhausted themselves walking for hours, but you should have seen them last night, Alfred." She attempted to give him a reproachful look but instead slyly smiled at her son, whom she quite adored. "Where were you last night? I did so want to show off my two children, for even though I do say it myself, your father and I produce the most attractive offspring!"

Alfred ignored the compliment. "Those affairs ain't for me and well you know it, Mother."

"I am sure I don't know why not. All of the young beauties would probably fight each other over you, Alfred," his proud mother said.

Color flushing his face, Alfred made eye contact with Bonny. "Pray, pay no attention to my mother, Bonny. You know how mothers are."

"I do indeed," said Bonny, smiling.

"Tease about me if you like, but we'll see how the girls

will set to blushing when they lay eyes on your handsome features,'' his mother said.

Though Lady Landis's affection for her son might blind her a little, Bonny had to admit her remark about her children's attractiveness rang true. The tallish, brown-haired Alfred certainly could be described as handsome, though he was totally unaware of it and cared only for the sporting pleasures and the company of other young bucks.

''Come now, sweetheart,'' Lady Landis said to Emily, ''we must select your gown for tonight. You have to look your best for the duke.''

Lady Landis had never before called Emily sweetheart, thought Bonny as she climbed the stairs, her own thoughts turning to the duke's earlier visit. With a catch in her breath, she wondered if he had come to see her. For reasons she could not understand, it now seemed very important that she look her best tonight.

Bonny wore another white dress, this one trimmed in blue ribbons. Much of the evening's activities seemed to her a repeat of the previous night's. How dull it would be to go to these affairs night after night, doing the same things and seeing the same people. She smiled, thinking of how correct Alfred had been in his assessment.

But where the previous night's affair had been enjoyable, tonight's was not. Emily looked so terribly forlorn it quite worried Bonny. Bonny also fretted over the absence of the Duke of Radcliff and chastised herself more than once for searching the dance floor for him.

Lady Lynda Heffington's absence afforded Bonny as much pleasure as the duke's absence gave disappointment. Then the thought of the two being together hit her, making her even more upset, which made her mad at herself all over again.

Why on earth, she asked herself, would a duke be interested in the daughter of a lowly country parson? What a foolish girl she was to fill her head with him. All of these musings made her very poor company for the group of young men who gathered around her. An earl whose name she couldn't remember came to claim her for the promised dance. His boyish face beneath a mop of blond hair had won Bonny's immediate favor.

Since the dance was a waltz, it afforded them the opportunity to talk. "And what did you say your name was, sir?" she asked.

"Henry Blackburn, Earl of Dunsford."

That name, she thought. Emily's Harold had the same name. Could the earl possibly be related to Harold? she wondered. "Is Harold Blackburn related to you?" she asked casually.

He stiffened. "That was my brother."

"I'm terribly sorry," Bonny said softly. "I understand he fought very bravely at Badajoz."

"How did you know?" he asked in a suddenly pained voice.

"My friend knew him there." For some reason, she chose not to reveal her friend was her cousin.

"Did your friend serve with the Light?"

"My friend's a lady."

"God in heaven! Would her name be Emily?"

"Why, yes," Bonny said hesitantly.

"You don't know how I've longed to find this Emily my brother wrote me about. But I didn't know her last name."

Bonny withheld Emily's name. Emily might not want the Earl of Dunsford to find her. "You and your brother must have been very close."

He did not answer for a moment. Finally, he spoke in a choking voice. "We were only a year apart, and as our mother died shortly after giving birth to Harry, there were just the two of us. We were as close as two brothers could possibly be." His shaky voice stopped, and his grip on Bonny's hand tightened. "I refused for the longest time to buy his colors. I'd had a terrible feeling he would die on a foreign battlefield. He insisted, and eventually I gave in—" He fought to control his emotions.

"My lord, please don't blame yourself. Know that your brother died doing exactly what he wanted."

"Somehow that doesn't lessen the pain." He drew in his breath. "I have to talk to this friend of yours. May I call on you tomorrow, Miss Allan?"

Better to keep him away from Emily's house until she better knew how Emily would react to his presence. "I will be riding in Hyde Park tomorrow morning. Perhaps you could meet me there, my lord."

"That would be most agreeable."

The waltz soon ended, and Dunsford began to lead Bonny from the dance floor, when the Duke of Radcliff approached them, nodding to Dunsford, who, assuming the duke was Bonny's next partner, promptly took his leave.

The duke must have just arrived, Bonny realized as she found herself searching his masculine face, which never smiled. What was there about him that invaded her thoughts all day and made her as nervous as a French noblewoman around a guillotine now? Certainly not his rank. She was enough of her mother's daughter not to be impressed by that, and to tell the truth, she had neither the background nor the desire to be a duchess.

Something in the duke's manner told her that she could trust him. That he could be counted on for wise counsel and unwavering support. But it was more than that, she thought, feeling a lump in her throat and a stirring deep within her as her eyes flitted over his sturdy body.

"Would you honor me by dancing the next dance with me, Miss Allan?" the duke asked.

"I should be happy to do so, your grace."

The country dance did not afford them the opportunity to talk but caused her considerable loss of composure every time their hands touched. And to make her even more uncomfortable, she felt Lady Landis's disapproving glare throughout the dance.

When the orchestra stopped playing, a winded Bonny determined to find Emily to see if her spirits had lifted. She located Emily fifteen feet away, in time to see her pale cousin swoon.

Emily, in her butter-colored dress, collapsed in a heap on the dance floor.

Bonny shrieked and ran toward her, but Radcliff and Lady Landis got to her first.

Paying more notice to the attentive duke than to her daughter, Lady Landis said, "Your grace, I don't know what's got into my silly daughter, but I'm sure this will bring her round." She held the vinaigrette under Emily's nose.

Bonny threw herself on the floor beside Emily, took Emily's slim hand and spoke in a quavering voice. "Em—Em, are you all right?"

Emily's lids slowly uncovered lively blue eyes that peered into Bonny's. "I saw Harold," Emily said in a hoarse whisper.

Her poor cousin was delusional, Bonny thought. Then she remembered Henry, Harold's brother. Could Emily have mistaken him for his dead brother?

"I daresay it's far too hot in here for someone as delicate as my Emily," said Lady Landis, smiling at the duke. "Perhaps, your grace, you could assist my daughter out to the balcony for a bit of fresh air."

"I think we should take her home, Aunt."

Emily sat up straight, eyeing her mother. "No! I'm perfectly all right."

Radcliff helped her to stand. "Your mother's right," he said in a gentle voice. "You need a bit of fresh air."

Lady Landis watched angrily as Bonny accompanied her daughter and the duke to the balcony. Bonny stayed with Emily while Radcliff went to get the ladies ratafia.

"I don't understand it, Bonny," said Emily, shivering from the cool night air. "I kissed Harold's cold lips before they buried him, yet I swear I just saw him. Do you think my broken heart has turned me mad?"

"Not at all. I suspect you saw Harold's brother, Henry, who is just a year older than Harold." Bonny placed gentle hands on her cousin's slender arms and began to rub warmth into them.

"How do you know this?"

"Because I danced with him."

"Then Henry must look just like Harold," Emily said sadly. "As painful as it would be to look upon the brother's face, I have a strong desire to do so." A flood of tears erupted.

When the French doors to the balcony opened, the two cousins looked up, expecting to see the duke with their ratafia, but instead they saw Alfred and the empty-handed duke, their faces grim, and Lady Landis on their heels.

"It is my mother," Bonny said shakily, despair in her eyes.

"A letter addressed to you and marked Urgent arrived just after you left," Alfred said kindly. "I took the liberty of opening it."

Bonny closed her eyes. "When did she die?"

"She hasn't!" Alfred said. "At least not yet. Doctor says she's near the end and calling for you."

"Then I must go to her," Bonny said simply, striding toward the door.

"Allow me to assist," Radcliff said. "I can have my

coach at Cavendish Square within the hour to take you home.''

"How very kind, your grace,'' Lady Landis said. "Were it not for you, my poor niece would have to wait for the stage tomorrow.''

Bonny did not like accepting the duke's offer, but she knew there was no time to waste, and it looked as if her aunt would not do without her own chaise and four for the several days' journey to the North Country.

"I will accompany them to expedite matters,'' Radcliff said, his commanding gaze meeting Lady Landis's. "I hope you will allow your daughter to accompany Miss Allan on this sad journey.''

"But of course.'' The woman's sparkling eyes betrayed her somber countenance.

Chapter Three

Before an hour had passed, portmanteaus had been packed, Emily's abigail, Martha, had been roused from her sleep to accompany them on the journey, and the Duke of Radcliff appeared at their door, his crested coach awaiting them. Bonny and Emily had changed to traveling clothes and wore over them hooded capes. The duke personally assisted the ladies into the carriage while Lady Landis, still dressed in her turquoise sarcenet ball gown, stood shivering beside him.

"I hope my daughter will be a good traveler, your grace," Lady Landis said. "She has such a delicate constitution."

"Have no fears, ma'am, for I will personally see to every comfort for the young ladies."

"You are so very kind, your grace." Lady Landis fluttered her eyelashes. "Do you not desire to bring your servants with you?" She looked to see if there were any more coaches.

"I shall be able to make out without my man." *If Evans is still my man when I return.*

The obstinate valet had been unable to disguise his anger at being left behind. "It is hoped your grace sees no one of consequence in the hinterlands," Evans had said haughtily.

"As it happens," the duke had told Evans, "someone of the most important consequence will be with me, but it is my hope that I will not be judged by the tie of my cravat."

Just as Bonny was taking her seat inside the carriage, she remembered she had told the Earl of Dunsford she would be riding in Hyde Park in the morning. The poor fellow could wander around for hours looking for her. There was only one thing she could do. She would have to send a note to him. She leapt from the carriage and met the duke's quizzing gaze.

"Your grace, there is something of the utmost importance that I must do. I will be back in just a moment."

She ran straight to her aunt's writing desk, grabbed a piece of vellum, dipped the pen in Lady Landis's gilded inkwell and scribbled a note to the earl telling him she had suddenly been called out of town. She sealed it with candle wax and wrote his name on the front. She got Styles to wake up the page, for she wanted the note sent round that very night.

While she waited for the page to get dressed, she went back to the coach, letter in hand, and leaned into the carriage. "Em, do you know the direction of the Earl of Dunsford's London home?"

Emily gave her cousin a searching look.

"I must cancel my morning meeting with the earl," Bonny said to a still-puzzled Emily.

"Their—I mean, his—home is on Half Moon Street."

When Bonny turned around, not only was the page waiting for her, but the duke gazed at the letter in her hand, his brows creased and the corners of his mouth sloping downward more than normal.

She quickly looked away from him and leaned down to the lad. "This letter must be delivered to the Earl of Dunsford on Half Moon Street tonight.'' She reached into her reticule to find a coin, but before she could, the duke placed two shillings in the boy's hand.

A huge smile illuminated the boy's face. "Much obliged, your highness," he said, then skipped off.

Bonny turned laughing eyes on the duke. "Your highness?"

He shrugged, his face still grave, then took her hand and assisted her into the carriage.

She thought perhaps he held her hand a second longer than necessary, and she gloried in it. Feeling intoxicated, as she did every time she was with this enigmatic man, Bonny took her seat inside, sliding over to make room for him, happy that Martha had chosen to ride next to Emily.

Before Radcliff got in, he accepted a letter from Bonny's distracted uncle, who leaned into the carriage and said, "Please deliver this to my sister."

Bonny could not remember ever seeing the viscount look happy, but tonight must be one of the blackest nights of his unhappy life, she thought, knowing how close her uncle had been to her mother when they were young.

"I beg you will not judge our family by Miss Allan's simple home, your grace," Lady Landis said to Radcliff. "My husband's—the viscount's—sister, Barbara's mother, could have married better, but there you are." Lady Landis had no message for her sister-in-law, no farewell for Bonny, but once again ran on about how very obliged she was to his grace.

"I am happy to be of some service," Radcliff said stiffly. Then he climbed into the carriage. As the coachman closed the door, Radcliff sat next to Bonny, rendering her a simpering, blathering idiot again. She never felt quite herself when she was in his presence. She could think of nothing clever to say and felt totally inadequate.

Though Bonny had not yet been presented, she had for

the past few years been the object of men's adoration. There had been the assemblies at Milford, followed by the routs in London. She had met many a noted Corinthian of exalted peerage, but no one had ever affected her as Radcliff did. With the others, she could act perfectly natural, even flirty. But with the duke, she only acted shy.

While it would have been perfectly natural for him to speak to Emily, who sat directly across from him, the duke spoke instead to Bonny. "Since your home is so blasted far away, my plan is to travel as far as we possibly can each day. I propose to travel all night tonight, switch horses, then keep going until the sun goes down tomorrow night. I regret that riding for that many hours will be quite uncomfortable."

"I daresay I am used to the long ride, having made it only just recently, but I fear my cousin may not hold up as well as I do," Bonny said, thankful that words had sprung to her suddenly insipid mind.

Emily's voice came to life. "Nonsense. You've been listening too much to my mother. As long as we can stretch our legs once in a while, I'll do remarkably well." She stifled a yawn.

This was followed by a long yawn from Bonny.

The duke pulled out his watch and held it toward the window, where light from passing street lamps allowed him to read. "It's past two."

Bonny thought back to see how many hours it was since she had risen the previous morning. They had not gone to bed until four, then got up at nine-thirty to sneak off to Kepple Street. No wonder she was so tired.

Radcliff turned to Bonny. "When I called today, your aunt said you and your cousin had left quite early."

"Yes, your grace," Bonny said, "and I fear we won't be good company for we are so very tired."

"We have the next few weeks for good company. For

now, we must try to sleep." He patted his shoulder. "May I offer you a shoulder for your pretty head, Miss Allan?"

How she wished she could see his face, to read his expression, but the carriage was much too dark. She was in a dilemma to know how to respond. Should she shrug off his invitation? Or would that offend him? She decided to say nothing and gently laid her head on his shoulder.

But going to sleep was quite another thing. Her mind kept reeling with thoughts of this quiet man beside her. His shoulder—indeed his whole body—seemed so much larger now in this small carriage. She very much liked the solid feel of his man's body and the masculine smell of his Hungary water. She knew she had been correct about him earlier in the evening when she had been able to look into his warm green eyes and detect a softness that lay beyond the stern cut of his jaw. He was solid in body and in mind. A great support. And much more than that, but she could not allow herself to harbor such hopes.

It did not take long to get through London because few carriages and horse carts impeded their progress at this hour. Their only interruption was for the tollgates, which seemed to be all too frequent. Never had Bonny ridden in so fine a carriage, the ride as smooth as sitting in the drawing room. She could have served tea without spilling a drop.

Radcliff told himself he could not sleep because he was protector to these young maidens. But had they been in the comfort of his ancestral home, sleep still would have eluded him. Nothing in his heretofore predictable existence had been the same since he had set eyes on the ravishing Bonny Barbara Allan. He—Richard Moncrief, the fifth Duke of Radcliff—had for the past dozen or more years been quite content with the carefree life of a bachelor. The sporting. The bedding of beauties. Running with other like-minded blades who happily performed any number of foolish deeds at his behest.

Now, though, his hedonistic life seemed strangely empty. Memories of his parents and their devotion to each other and to him flooded his thoughts these past two days and left him bereft. Until Barbara, no other woman had ever evoked these emotions. What was there about her that made him forget her extraordinary beauty and long to hear the gentleness in her voice when she spoke of her mother or see the love in her eyes as she fretted over her frail cousin?

Never would he have believed he would willingly give up his comforts to undertake a round-trip journey of more than a month along rugged roads just to be near a girl fresh from the schoolroom. He who had always loathed traveling, whether it be stifled in a crowded carriage or riding outside in the foul weather until his very bones throbbed in pain. Yet here he was in a traveling coach as content as a kitten basking in the sun.

He gathered Barbara against him, a gentle smile settling on his face. That he had determined the first night he met her that Bonny Barbara would be his bride seemed not at all foolish. His attraction to her lay not only in her beauty but also in her refreshing honesty, her humility, her exposure to the classics.

She possessed all he could ever want in a bride. And he wanted her more than he'd ever wanted anything in his privileged life.

This time, he feared, his good fortune would fail him.

Once they were out of London, the coach proceeded at a monotonous pace, which, along with the steady clopping of horse hooves, lulled Bonny to sleep.

The carriage was still quite dark when she woke to find the duke's arm hooked around her, pulling her rather into his barreled chest. And to her utter embarrassment, her right hand reposed on his muscled thigh. She listened to the steady thumping of his heart beneath her ear, and she could never remember knowing such utter contentment. She pretended to sleep still, enjoying the feel of being so close to him, but she slowly put her hand back in her own lap.

As daylight began to filter into the carriage, she sat up quite straight, not wanting Emily and Martha to see her in so familiar a position with the duke.

The duke politely removed his arm from around her and sat erect, also. She turned toward him. He looked very tired. "I'm very much afraid my own comfort has been at your expense," she whispered.

The corners of his stern mouth lifted ever so slightly to reveal a dimple in his tanned cheek. "Actually, Miss Allan, I don't know when I've ever been more comfortable."

As the days of the journey stretched onward, they fell into a regular pattern. The duke rode a horse most of the day, leaving the women to the coach. Each evening they would stop at an inn, where he arranged for them to eat in a private dining parlor and where he would procure rooms for each of them.

The last night of their journey, they stopped at the Blue Cock Inn, where Radcliff informed the cousins there were not enough available rooms. Emily and Bonny would have to share.

While their things were being taken to the room, the duke escorted the ladies into the private dining parlor, where he had ordered ale and kidney pie. Though it had turned beastly cold outside, a fire nicely warmed the darkened room. The duke sat on one side of the table, which was but a short distance from the hearth; Emily and Bonny sat on the other side. Bonny welcomed the musty scent of a rich peat fire, the first she had smelled since she left Milford.

"I feel such a burden, your grace," Bonny said.

"You've had nothing to do but ride and ride for eleven long days. How deadly dull it must be for you."

"It hasn't been dull. I've never been north before, and I'm enjoying new scenery. There's a gentle beauty about this country with these long stretches of lonely moors."

Gentle beauty. That was exactly how she felt about the moors. Most Londoners cursed them, but Bonny had always loved to wander by herself along the moors. Nothing gave her so great a feeling of inner peace as walking through the mist here in Northumbria, where the land gently sloped into shrouded skies. "I find it so myself, your grace," Bonny said with a funny little catch in her voice. For once, she did not avert her eyes from his but looked at him full force, drawn by his penetrating gaze, which made her feel he knew her every thought.

She wondered how long they would have looked into each other's eyes had not the innkeeper's wife chosen that moment to deliver their ale. The kindly woman, not used to having so grand a personage as a duke, could not do enough for them.

During these evening meals, Emily and Bonny had learned more about the duke. That his seat was in Kent, that he appreciated beautiful things from horses to snuff-boxes, that he preferred the country to the city.

And Radcliff had learned more about them.

"I must confess I enjoy going where I've never been before," the duke said, glancing at Emily this night. "Is that what took you to Spain, Lady Emily?"

"That and the fact I'd be with my aunt Camille. I was much closer to her than I am to my own mother. Maybe because she never had children of her own. She spoiled me greatly."

"Her husband served with the Peer?"

Emily nodded agreeably. "Yes. Uncle Trevor's a colonel."

"I suppose not having children made it much easier for your aunt to follow the drum," Radcliff said. "Did you enjoy it, Lady Emily?"

Emily's eyes sparkled. "It was the greatest experience of my life." She lowered her lashes as well as her voice. "It was also the most sorrowful."

Bonny met the duke's awkward gaze. "Emily's aunt Camille took a fever and died not two months ago. In a French farmhouse. I regret to say my aunt Lucille, Emily's mother, wanted to put off the mourning until Emily was presented. You see, few people know yet of her sister's death."

He nodded. "And if Emily was not presented this season, you, too, would have had to wait another whole year."

"Exactly," Bonny said, her lips firm. "For they were to present us together, and because of my mother's situation, waiting another year would not have been acceptable. So you see, I am a burden to everyone."

"No you're not!" Emily protested.

"Your cousin's quite right, Miss Allan. It is obvious you two are quite fond of each other, and I would guess that Lady Emily most certainly prefers being with you than with anyone else."

Emily nodded at this.

Then the duke turned his eyes on Bonny. "And as for myself, I find it an honor to be able to spend so many days in your agreeable company. I daresay, there are a score of men who would happily join me in paying court to your beauty." The duke stabbed his fork into his pie to avoid making eye contact with Bonny.

Feeling flushed, Bonny poked her own fork into the steaming pie and took a bite. It bothered her that he always brought up her beauty, especially now that she knew of his love of beautiful things. Was she to be treated like just another object? Something to be admired, then put on a shelf? As attracted as she was to him, she knew such a relationship would not satisfy her. She wanted a man of passion and feeling.

"It is still very kind of you, your grace," Emily said in her wispy little voice, "to oblige my cousin so. You are very gallant."

Bonny looked up into his face, the soft candlelight on it, and felt a tightening in her chest. His eyes met hers. "You are indeed gallant," she said softly.

In their room later, the ladies lamented the lack of a fireplace, kept on a good deal of their clothing under their nightgowns and climbed beneath the several counterpanes the innkeeper's wife had piled on the double bed.

"I will be so glad to be at your house tomorrow," Emily said through shivering teeth. "To be warm through and through. It's so bitterly cold up here."

"I very much fear you will take a cold in your weakened state, Em."

"Quit worrying about my health so much."

"Oh, very well, I'll worry about Mama. I do hope she is still alive." Bonny's tone was as forlorn as the wind howling outside their window, and her insides churned with sickening grief.

"I do, too," Emily said. "I think she needs to meet Radcliff."

"Why, pray tell, do you think she needs to meet Radcliff?"

"Think how happy she would be to think him your future husband!"

"He's no such thing! The duke is merely a kind man. He has no interest in me. He could have any lady he wants. It's not likely he would choose one with no dowry, or someone as unsatisfactorily prepared to be a duchess as I."

"He's one of the richest men in all of England. He

doesn't need to marry money. And it's my opinion he means to marry you.''

"That's absurd. It's obvious by his refusal to call me by my first name that he wants to maintain a detachment.''

"He doesn't have to say it, you goose. He shows it. In every moment of the day, in every action, and when he looks at you, he positively drips with adoration.''

"Pooh!'' Adoring looks, indeed. Coolly appraising gaze, more likely. Nothing in the man even hinted at passion, Bonny thought, turning her back to her cousin. She pulled the blankets to her chin, thinking she should have worn gloves to bed, worrying Emily would catch her death of cold, worrying about her mother.

But most of her thoughts centered on Emily's words. If only they rang true. For despite the disparity in rank between Radcliff and herself, and against her own reasoning, she had indeed fallen in love with him.

The duke lay awake, tormented with thoughts of Bonny. Every night since he had left London he'd lain awake thinking of her. Of how badly he wanted her. In his mind's eye he would see her lovely face with those incredible eyes rimmed in long black lashes, see the silkiness of her fair skin and the luster in her thick black hair. He could almost taste her perfect little mouth on his. And he would imagine how glorious it would be to feel her soft body beneath his.

He had been unable to ride inside the coach since that first night, giving up the relative warmth to ride along the lonely country roads, the wind and cold making him shiver through every limb. All in an attempt to purge Barbara from his thoughts. Being so close to her and not being able to take her in his arms and thoroughly love her, to have her take him inside her, had driven him half-mad. He could not trust himself when he was with her. He would know nothing but misery until he could make her his own.

But each night, the same memory came back to him. The memory of Barbara sending a farewell message to the Earl of Dunsford. He grew to hate his old school chum with a fierceness that scared him. But above all, he grieved that Barbara had lost her heart to Dunsford before that night he had first seen her across that dance floor and fallen hopelessly in love with her.

Chapter Four

Radcliff watched with worry as Bonny ran into her mother's house, and his step quickened to catch up with her. He remembered his own mother's death and wanted to be with Bonny if grim tidings awaited.

The poor girl had been too anxious to wait for the housekeeper to answer the door. Holding her skirts in front of her and taking the stairs two at a time, Bonny had hurried to the second floor and come to a sudden stop in front of a butter yellow bedroom. Radcliff eyed her solemn face as she stood at the doorway looking into the unoccupied room.

By this time a middle-aged woman whom he judged to be the housekeeper came panting from the stairway, put her hands on her stout hips and addressed Bonny. "Aye, 'tis Miss Bonny."

Radcliff knew when he saw a pleasant look on the woman's face that Bonny's mother must still be alive.

"If ye be lookin' fer your mama, ye be lookin' in the wrong place. She couldn't be a-takin' them stairs with her poor lungs, so we moved her bed into your papa's library."

"Then she's—" Relief flashed across Bonny's face.

"She's still alive, but don't be gettin' yer hopes up.

Dr. 'oward says she can't last much longer. I believe she be 'angin' on to see ye one last time.''

Bonny's long black lashes lowered and she swallowed hard, then hastened back down the stairs, taking a piece of Radcliff's heart with her. If possible, she was even more beautiful when she suffered, he thought.

Emily, who had not made the trip upstairs, stood on the first floor looking up at Bonny with a questioning gaze. ''Is she—?''

''She's in the library.'' Bonny hurried past her cousin.

Emily, the housekeeper and the duke followed Bonny to the library. Though it was much smaller than his library at Hedley Hall, Radcliff thought the Allan family library fit its name far better. The Hedley Hall library housed no less than two couches, two fireplaces, a goodly sized gaming table and attractively bound classics of literature that showed little sign of use. But this was indeed a book room. The many shelves were crammed with well-worn volumes, and still more towers of books filled every tabletop and nook the small room could yield.

In one corner of the room reposed a daybed next to a window where red velvet draperies had been pulled back. And from that bed came the sound of Mrs. Allan's hacking cough.

''Mama!'' Bonny exclaimed as she ran to take her mother's hand.

The elder woman's face brightened when she looked up at her daughter, but she withdrew her hand.

Bonny turned to Emily, who was at her side. ''Mama won't let me touch her, you know. She thinks I will get the consumption, too.''

''As well you could,'' Emily reproached her.

Bonny frowned. ''I am far too healthy, but I don't think you ought to be here in your weakened state.''

''But, I—''

"Please." Bonny gave her cousin an imploring gaze.

Emily nodded and moved to leave the room. "Though you know I don't care if I live or not."

Wondering why so lovely a young woman would want to die, Radcliff silently moved behind Bonny, hoping she would not ask him to leave as she had Emily. He felt a need to be here with her.

Mrs. Allan tried to speak, but talking was difficult.

"Yer mama was mad at Dr. 'oward," the housekeeper said, "fer sendin' fer ye. She sent another post tellin' ye not to come. 'Course, I told 'er ye would be on yer way. I knows our Bonny."

"Yes, Mrs. Melville, you do," Bonny said.

"I'll be off now to prepare the tea and see to the fires," Mrs. Melville said.

Bonny turned back to the sickbed. "Mama, don't be mad at me for coming," she said softly.

"When have I ever been mad at you, love?" Mrs. Allan whispered.

Bonny reached into her reticule. "I have a letter for you from Uncle David. Shall I read it to you?"

Mrs. Allan's gray head nodded.

Bonny unfolded the letter and began reading.

Dearest Cynthia,
It pains me exceedingly to know how ill you are and to be powerless to aid in your recovery. But I am not powerless to ease some of your worry. Please know that for as long as she needs it, Bonny Barbara will have a home with me and will be treated as I treat my own dear Emily. With the money our mother left her, you should not need to worry about her future. While my wife has done little to endear herself to either you or to Bonny Barbara throughout the years, please know that I will not tolerate anything less than the

most cordial treatment of your daughter from my wife henceforth.

Your most affectionate brother, David

"Such a sweet little brother—" Mrs. Allan began to cough.

Her face pained, Bonny moved closer to her mother.

Radcliff wanted to pull her away from the menacing cough, to protect her from the disabling disease, but he forced himself to hold back.

Finally, Mrs. Allan stopped coughing and spoke again. "But he would have you for love of me." The older woman stopped and took a deep, rasping breath before continuing. "I want to know that when I'm gone, there is someone who loves you as your father and I have loved you." She gasped for more breath, holding up her hand, a sign that she was not finished talking. "Someone you will love as I loved your father." The woman's eyes filled with tears.

The old woman put to words what Radcliff felt in his heart toward Bonny. Drawn to Mrs. Allan by the deep affection they shared for her daughter, he stepped forward, sucking in his breath and trembling, fearing he would make an utter fool of himself but knowing what he must do to allay the woman's worries, to free himself of this obsession over Bonny.

"I will love your daughter, Mrs. Allan, if you will do me the honor of allowing her to become my wife."

Bonny spun round, alarm in her eyes as she faced him.

Cursed, but he had not done that very well, he chided himself. Such a shock it must have been out of the blue to lovely Barbara, who was already in such a distraught state. He should have spoken to her first, which he would have done had his declaration been planned. Whatever had possessed him to rattle off so to the sweet old woman?

But just as Barbara had been unprepared for his offer, he had been unprepared for the glare of rejection he saw on her face. Did she love Dunsford so? He knew he was taking unfair advantage of her sorrowful circumstances to usurp the Earl of Dunsford. And he knew if given the chance to do so again, he would. Never had he wanted anything as much as he wanted Bonny Barbara Allan, and he would do anything to win her. He vowed to earn her love if she would but give him the chance. He held his breath as he watched her face, trying to gauge her reaction. Was it anger or was it shock?

He smiled and spoke with a calmness he was far from feeling. "Aren't you going to introduce me to your mother, my love?"

Bonny stood frozen with her back to her mother, her face impassive.

Hoping that Bonny would not betray him, he looked into her mother's blue-green eyes, eyes that forty years before must have looked like Bonny's. "I fear you have done too good a job instilling proper manners in her, ma'am, for she still feels awkward addressing me by my first name." He stepped closer to the bed and bowed. "I am Richard Moncrief, the fifth Duke of Radcliff, your most obedient servant."

The old woman looked from him to Bonny and back to him. "I have never tried to speak for my daughter," she managed to say before another outburst of coughing. When the coughing stopped, she added, "Ask Bonny. Not me."

Radcliff's eyes searched Bonny's inscrutable ones. "I beg to speak to you privately after you have visited with your mother." He left the room.

When the door closed and no one remained with Mrs. Allan except Bonny, the older woman said in a feeble voice, "Surprised you, didn't he?"

Bonny nodded.

"Gentlemen don't make so far a journey out of kindness. Did you not guess why he came?"

Still stunned by the duke's proposal, Bonny shook her head. She could not believe that was why he had come all the way to the North Country. It couldn't be for her. He couldn't possibly love her as he had told her mother. She would know it if he did. There would have been some kind of intimacy, even if it were just calling her by her first name. But there had been nothing.

Could it be that he offered for her because he was so moved by the sight of her emaciated mother lying on her deathbed? But surely a man would not throw away his future to comfort a dying stranger.

Whatever his motivation, she could not allow him to make so noble a sacrifice.

Mrs. Allan's rumbling cough commenced again, but this time lasted longer than the previous bouts, upsetting Bonny.

"You're talking too much," Bonny said when her weakened and shaking mother finally stopped coughing. "I've tired you."

The old woman's heavy lids began to fall. "You're in love with him, aren't you?"

Bonny did not know what to think. First, Emily foolishly supposed Radcliff in love with her. Now, her mother surmised she was in love with Radcliff. She froze. Her mother had never once misjudged her feelings.

She looked into her mother's expectant face. "I'm desperately fighting it, Mama," she admitted. Her mother's face softened, and she nodded off.

When Bonny left the sickroom, she found Emily and Radcliff in the parlor sitting before the fire, with Emily serving tea.

"Are you finally warm?" Bonny asked her cousin.

"Finally."

"I know the trip's been hard on you," Bonny said in a tender voice, much as if she were addressing a child. "After your tea you need to get under your counterpane and take a long nap. I've instructed Mrs. Melville to see there's a fire in your room at all times."

"I wish you wouldn't worry so about me."

"It seems to be Miss Allan's pleasure to carry the burdens of the world on her very lovely shoulders," Radcliff said.

Color flooded Bonny's face. No man had ever remarked about a part of her body before.

"Your grace, I thought perhaps we could bundle up and walk among the moors for that private conversation you sought."

Radcliff got to his feet. "I am at your service, Miss Allan."

As Bonny went to get her merino cloak and gloves, she caught sight of Emily's smiling face.

The vision of Bonny in the hooded blue wool cape with its white fur trim framing her beautiful face made Radcliff catch his breath. Today her eyes matched the lapis blue of the cloak, and the white of the fur matched her perfect teeth. He offered her his arm and led her outside beneath the gray sky. "Your mother is resting?" he inquired.

"Yes, your grace." She wrapped the cloak tighter around her. "I fear my visit was very hard on her."

"Stop blaming everything on yourself. Did it not occur to you that your mother would prefer to expend the little breath she has left on you rather than expel it into a lonely sickroom?"

"I had not thought of it that way, your grace."

"Please call me Richard, Barbara." As surely as the wind pierced his chilled bones, he knew she would try to decline his offer. And just as surely, he knew he would do everything in his power to make her agree to become his wife. If he could but make her marry him, he would wrap her in so much love she would have to love him one day. And he could wait. As long as he could be with her.

"When I said you were gallant last night, I had no idea the extent of your gallantry. To offer for me to please my dying mother was—was wonderful of you. But, of course, I cannot accept."

Had she kicked him in the pit of his stomach, he could not have felt worse. "You make a grave mistake if you think I offered for you because of your mother. Did it never occur to you that I want you for my wife?"

"Quite honestly, no, your grace. Before this journey, we had scarcely spoken to one another. I could hardly expect that you could want to spend your life with me."

"But I assure you I do. Perhaps we did not know each other well before traveling north together, but you cannot deny that we have come to know each other during the journey. I realize there is much more to you than a beautiful face. You are extremely well read and have a keen mind. You worry excessively over those you love. And you don't like marmalade."

She ignored his amused expression and pressed on with more serious matters. "We spoke to each other across tavern tables. That is quite a different setting than a duke's drawing room. I am ill prepared to be a duchess."

"You're the granddaughter of a viscount, Barbara." He covered her gloved hand with his own. "I've seen you grace ballrooms of the best houses, and none could compare with you. I would very much like to behold your lovely face across the breakfast table for the rest of my days."

"That is hardly a reason to propose marriage, your grace. You have seen my mother. The fact that she was a noted beauty does little for her appearance now. A face does not stay flawless as the decades advance.''

''I have other reasons to seek a wife,'' he said in a more formal tone. ''I have a very strong desire to settle down. I am four and thirty years. If I don't start a family soon, I will be as old as my parents were when I was born. And I shouldn't like that at all.''

Bonny watched a stunted fir tree that had permanently bent with the winds, and she tried to speak casually. ''Then you have been considering marriage for some time, your grace?''

''Blast it all, Barbara, stop calling me your grace!''

Her lips curved into a smile. ''Yes, Richard.''

''I'm not proud of the way I've lived for the past ten years.'' Avoiding her gaze, he kicked at the ground. ''I admit I gave no thought to marriage. But as of late, I have decided I very much desire to marry and have children and live at Hedley Hall, to enhance the lands that have prospered under my family for generations. And besides, I want to keep my cousin, Stanley Moncrief, from getting his hands on my estates. He would but lose them at the gaming tables or use them to keep himself in the latest dandified apparel.''

What the duke had told her put a different complexion on his offer, she thought hopefully. If he, indeed, had determined to take a bride, she had to accept before he offered for someone else. But the thought of being a duchess scared her. She feared she would be an embarrassment to Radcliff.

Marrying the duke, Bonny knew, would please her mother, now that she knew Bonny's feelings for him. But above all, Bonny *wanted* to become his wife. If she could but marry him, and love him to completion, surely she could earn his love.

For she was convinced he did not love her. He had said he wanted to gaze upon her face. He had said he wanted to have a family. He had said he wanted to keep Stanley from inheriting his estates. But he had not said he loved her.

She tossed back her head, causing the hood to fall, and she smiled up into his face. "Do you think we could wed before Mama dies?"

Radcliff cupped her face in his hands.

She felt the scrutiny of his all-knowing eyes, and for the first time, she sensed a passion beneath his pensive countenance.

He lowered his head, and she smelled his Hungary water, felt his warm breath, then his lips crushing hers. He enfolded her in his strong embrace as the intensity of the kiss deepened.

Her arms reached for him, tentatively at first, then firmly as she prolonged the kiss.

When finally he did pull away, Bonny felt bereft. She had never been kissed before, and she was surprised at the power of one kiss. And now she knew the desire for something more than a kiss. Something even more intimate.

She lingered within his embrace and kept her arms about him. He freed one hand to brush away windblown strands of rich black hair from her cool face, then he lifted her chin. "I think a hasty wedding is an excellent idea, my love," he said flatly. "Else I should ravage you here on the moors."

She could have stood forever on the hazy moors within his arms. The wind stung her face, but she basked in the warmth of his body, dazed by the passion of his kiss. And to think she had thought he lacked passion! He had even called her "my love."

He pulled away from her, took her hand in his and began to walk back to the house. "I shall ride to Lambeth Palace for a special license. I'll leave immediately. It is my intent to have your vicar perform the ceremony at your mother's bedside.''

Within the hour, she watched him ride off toward London.

Chapter Five

Radcliff sat in the sitting room adjacent to the countess's sleeping chamber. He knew the news he was bringing Lady Heffington would be most unwelcome. She had made no secret of her desire to be his duchess.

"Mon chéri," she greeted him, gliding into the room in a black lace negligee. Were it not for his Barbara, he would have thought the lascivious Lynda of the ivory skin and voluptuous body extraordinarily beautiful.

"You have been away far too long," she said.

He stood up, and she swept over to him, linking her hands behind his neck. She tossed her head back to gaze at him.

"It has been three weeks since anyone has seen you, *mon chéri.* I've been most dreadfully worried about you. That odious Lady Landis said you had taken her daughter to Northumbria, but of course I knew that couldn't be so. Why, her thin little daughter would no more turn your head than a charwoman."

Removing her hands from his neck, Radcliff frowned. "But I regret to tell you another woman has, indeed, turned my head."

Her eyes filled with tears, and her normally rich voice

shook. "I knew it. It is that cousin of Lady Emily's, is it not?"

"It is. I have a special license in my pocket."

She gasped but did not speak for a moment. When she did, her voice was soft, almost a whisper. "You make a great mistake, Radcliff. You don't know the girl. She's but a child. She will never love you as I do. And she will never know how to please you as I do."

"Nevertheless, she will be my duchess." A grim set to his mouth, he picked up his gloves. "I wanted to tell you before you read it in the papers, Lynda." His voice softened. "I owed you that." He walked toward the door. "I bid you good-night, madam."

"'Tis a beautiful bride ye'll make," said Polly, the maid, as she placed the last pin in the dress she was sewing for Bonny's wedding.

Lifting the train of her gown, Bonny moved back to gaze into the mirror. The embroidered ivory muslin made a lovely dress for a country wedding, but of course it never would have done for marrying a duke, had they been back in London.

"Radcliff will love it," said Emily, who had removed herself from a seat before the fireplace in Bonny's room to circle around Bonny approvingly.

The ease with which her mother and Emily had accepted her forthcoming marriage to Radcliff surprised Bonny, since she herself was still plagued by fears that something would prevent so agreeable a union.

"While ye've got me sewin', ye might as well have me make a mournin' gown, Miss Bonny," Polly said.

Bonny whirled round and snapped, "My mother is still very much alive."

A dejected Polly, hanging her head like a scolded child, helped Bonny out of the gown.

After Polly assisted Bonny into a printed muslin day dress and left the room, Emily said, "I know it was a thoughtless thing for Polly to say, but she was right, you know."

Bonny lowered her head and spoke softly. "I know. I'm just not myself lately."

"You've had time to prepare for your mother's loss. Aunt Cynthia would not want you to be melancholy. Think of your future with Richard and how happy you two will be."

"You sound so confident of my happiness."

"That I am. As I've said all along, he adores you."

"I wish I had half so much assurance of his attachment." Surely Emily was mistaking the generous man's excessive kindness for love. Because he was so very good to her did not mean he was in love with her. After all, he had never said he loved her.

"You're a goose if you can't see what's as plain as the nose on your face."

"Then a goose I am." Bonny's eyes scanned her cousin. "But I'm happy to see the color coming back to your face, Em. I think these cold old moors must be just what you needed to get back your health."

"More likely it's the absence from my dear, well-meaning mother. Then, too, my body's healing. It's been ten weeks since my precious Harriet was born."

"Now, don't you start getting melancholy. Your baby's in perfectly good hands with Mrs. Davies."

"I know. It's just that it seems so wrong that I must be ashamed of the only things in my life that have given me joy."

"Harold and Harriet?"

"Yes. I love them both so much. And I could never be ashamed of loving Harold." Emily retied the satin ribbon adorning her dress. "I'd do it all over again. Part of Harold lives on. I see him every time I look at Harriet's sweet face."

"I worry what life holds for little Harriet."

"If only Aunt Camille had lived. After Harold got killed, she vowed to raise our child and say it was hers."

"It's not fair that society prevents you from raising her, but, alas, both of you would be horribly branded."

Emily nodded.

"I want you to know you'll always have a home with me and Richard. Harriet, too."

Emily sighed. "Sooner or later I'll have to return to Mama, and I do so long to see Harriet."

Bonny, nodding sympathetically, heard the clopping of horse hooves from outside and ran toward her second-floor window. It was not the first time in the past several days she thought she had heard the sound of a lone rider and expected to see Radcliff, only to be disappointed. This time, her heart hammering ever faster, she wiped the pane clear and saw him seated on his stallion, galloping into the hollow where her house was located, the capes of his coat flapping behind him.

"It's Richard," Bonny happily announced, running to the stairs. She wanted to run to him, to throw her arms around him, but when she got to the front door, she held back.

He strode through the door, already divesting himself of his greatcoat, and her breath caught at the sight of him. He looked incredibly handsome dressed casually in his riding clothes, mud splattered on his Hessians. His rugged hand pushed stray strands of his toast-colored hair from his forehead as his warm green eyes flickered at the sight of her, the hint of a dimple in his cheek twitching.

All she could think to say was, "You have the license, your grace?"

He slammed the door behind him. "Confound it, Barbara! We'll be married on this very day and still you cannot call me Richard.'' He moved closer. ''Could you at least welcome me back with a kiss, my dear?'' He lowered his head to her.

Her heart fluttered as she brushed her lips across his, eyeing Emily and Mrs. Melville coming down the stairs.

''His grace is back,'' Mrs. Melville said. ''And he'll be wantin' a nice spot of hot tea.''

''What I desire first, madam,'' Radcliff said kindly, ''is for you to dispatch a messenger requesting the vicar's attendance here today.''

The old woman's face brightened. ''I'll do that as quick as a wink, your grace.''

Radcliff took Bonny's hand in his, a gentleness coming over him. ''Your mother?''

Bonny's lashes lowered. ''She lives still.'' Biting her lip, she looked back at Radcliff. ''You look so very cold, your—Richard. Come sit before the fire and have some tea.''

The crackling fire warmed the cozy morning room. Bonny took a seat on the sofa that faced the fireplace and motioned for Radcliff to sit beside her. She poured his tea and handed it to him, her hand shaking.

She noticed his hands cradled the cup for its warmth. ''Three times while you were gone, we thought we had lost Mama, but each time, she rallied back.''

''So she could make it until today,'' he said softly.

Bonny nodded, offering him a scone but taking none herself. The sad vigil at her mother's side these past days had greatly reduced Bonny's appetite. Radcliff's nearness distracted her from all the things she had been thinking of to say to him.

''I confess I am very hungry.'' He took a big bite out of the warm scone. ''I wanted to arrive in time to get the vicar and marry today and had to forgo my meal.''

Bonny jumped to her feet to summon Mrs. Melville to prepare his grace something more substantial.

"Quit worrying about me, Barbara," Radcliff instructed. "I believe you should be dressing for your wedding, and I, my love, need to clean up."

With Dr. Howard and Emily as witnesses, Bonny married Richard Moncrief, the fifth Duke of Radcliff, at her mother's bedside. As Radcliff placed the emerald ring on her finger, Bonny looked into her mother's faded face. Though tears raced down Mrs. Allan's cheeks, the dying woman's face was placid, only her lips touched by a wan smile.

When the ceremony was over, Mrs. Allan spoke not to her daughter but to her new son-in-law. "Take care of her," she said weakly.

Radcliff drew his arm around Bonny and gave her a loving glance. "I will do everything within my power to make her happy, ma'am."

A wide smile crossed the old woman's face, a face still pretty despite networks of wrinkles and years of ill health.

And the breath Mrs. Allan had so painfully strived for these past few years finally came to an end.

The doctor felt for her pulse, then looked into Bonny's pained face and nodded. "I regret to say the parson will have to perform two ceremonies today."

Bonny gasped and started to sob. Radcliff's arms closed around her, pulling her against his chest. She found the steady thumping of his heart beneath her ear strangely comforting. She cried against his shirt for a long while.

Later, Emily coaxed Bonny upstairs to change clothes while Radcliff assured his bride he would see to all the arrangements.

When Bonny came back downstairs, her husband brought her wool cloak and gloves. "Come, my love, we'll walk along the moors. They will suit your melancholy mood." He gently placed her cloak around her, lifted the hood over her black ringlets, then outlined her face with his finger.

The gray moors and the eternally cold winds of Northumbria very much suited her mood, Bonny thought as they walked along in silence, her mind whirling with emotions. Here in this land of mists her parents had lived, loved and died. And nothing of them now remained. Save her. She thought of the quiet man at her side—her husband now— and wondered if she would bear his children, and if those children would have a part of her cherished parents in them.

She and her husband came to a stop atop the knoll where first he had kissed her. They stood amid a bed of wild crocuses that failed to die, despite the wind and ice that unrelentlessly surrounded them.

She felt the whistling winds sting her face as she raised it to meet Radcliff's gaze. "The ring—my wedding ring—is lovely."

"It was my mother's."

She eyed the cleft in his chin. His somber face reflected her own mood. "It seems you remembered everything when you went to London."

"Which reminds me. I placed the notice of our nuptials in the papers."

"I am most gratified." She still could barely believe Radcliff had gone through with the marriage, let alone had taken pains to inform the ton of his intentions. She should feel elated, but she didn't. She could not entirely blame her mother's death for her lack of enthusiasm. Her discomfort with Radcliff stemmed from the distance between herself and her husband. There was no easy intimacy between them. No words of love. Not that she could fault him for that. No woman had ever married a more compassionate, unselfish man than her Richard. She had observed so many of his kindnesses during their long journey to Milford. He had made her mother's final days very happy ones. And with every action and every gaze at his bruising masculinity, he stole another piece of her heart.

If only he could love her with the depth of emotion her father had felt for her mother. If only he cared for more than a lovely face and young body to bear his children.

She looked into his weathered face. "What a wretched wedding day for you," she said shakily.

"Quit worrying about everyone else, Barbara. It's all right for you to hurt for yourself."

"You've been in my shoes, haven't you."

He nodded solemnly. "When I was three and twenty, my father died. Less than a year later, my mother joined him."

She swallowed hard, tears once again springing to her eyes. "How did you handle your grief?"

"I thought getting foxed would lessen the pain, and the habits I adopted after my parents died very nearly had me joining them."

"You must have felt so terribly empty."

"Utterly."

The thought of him lonely and suffering nearly overpowered her. She wanted to love him so thoroughly he would never know pain or loneliness again.

They stood facing each other, the wind slashing its chill into their very bones. She raised her head to kiss him, her arms slipping under his greatcoat to pull him into her as his arms encircled her. The feel of his lips on hers was just as powerful as before, but this time he did not pull away. And this time she parted her lips. When she had heard of the French custom of kissing with tongues, she had been horrified, but now she couldn't get enough of him as they exchanged hungry, wet kisses, her breath coming in ragged gasps.

She no longer felt chilled, but rather fevered, as she clung to him, the evidence of his own ardor swelled against her skirts.

He pulled away ever so slightly, his hands brushing stray strands of hair back from her damp temples. "What a passionate little baggage you are, my love, but I shall wait to take you in the marriage bed at Hedley Hall."

"When will that be?" she asked, her voice barely above a whisper.

"We shall leave tomorrow." He pulled her cloak tightly about her, lifted her gloved hand and kissed it.

Walking back toward the hollow, her hand in his, Bonny said, "But I need to go through the things here."

"This is not a good time for you to do that. We will come later—after you have had time to heal—and my servants will help you pack and go through everything. In the meantime, I have arranged for Mrs. Melville to stay on here."

God, but he was glad to change to talk of the mundane. He had already revealed to his wife far more than he had ever revealed to anyone, telling her of the suffering when he had lost his parents. He had never admitted the pain to anyone before. Only a weakling let people see his wounds. Just as weak was letting those he loved know how deeply he cared.

He remembered setting off for Eaton like a miniature man, hearing his mother's soft cries in the distance, while he willed himself not to break down and run back into her secure embrace and admit how desperately he wanted to stay back with her.

But always his father urged him to behave like a man. And a man did not give in to weakness. A man concealed his deepest emotions.

With a grim set to his mouth, he remembered how he had sat beside his mother's grave and spoke of his love for her—words he had never been able to tell her while she was alive.

Before the dim sun went down that night, Bonny, her husband and cousin, along with a couple dozen villagers, buried her mother in the kirkyard beside her father's grave. As she stood within the confines of the low rock wall that surrounded the yard, listening to the lonely whoop of the wind and the words of the vicar, she wiped but a single tear from her eye. She remembered the smile on her mother's face as she breathed her last breath. And Bonny knew her mother had joined her beloved husband.

After the ceremony, Bonny turned to her own beloved husband. He raised her chin with his knuckle. "Tomorrow, my love, we go to your new home."

Chapter Six

On this day Radcliff had chosen to ride in the carriage with the ladies, for they would soon arrive at Hedley Hall and he wanted to see his bride's face when she first set eyes on her new home. Throughout the journey he had continued his practice of riding by himself, rather than undergoing the torture of being so close to his wife, whom he still had not made truly his own.

When he told Bonny on their wedding day he would wait to take her in the marriage bed at Hedley Hall, he had meant it. Making love to her on their actual wedding night was out of the question. She had just buried her mother that very evening. After she was dressed for the night in an embroidered white muslin gown, he had entered her chamber with a sleeping draft and coaxed her into bed, gently pushing the glorious black hair from her beautiful face. "Here, my dear, this will help you sleep," he had told her.

She looked at him curiously and obeyed. "You are not sleeping here, sir?"

"We can wait until we get to Hedley Hall. We'll have the rest of our lives. Tonight, we will show respect for your

mother." He had brushed his lips across hers and left her
room.

Consummating their marriage in a drafty inn along the
way held no appeal to him. Bonny deserved far more grand
surroundings, as well as privacy not afforded in the close
quarters of the country inns.

Bonny would truly become his wife on his mother's bed,
the bed where he was conceived and born, the bed where
his heir would be conceived and born. He had written ahead
to his capable housekeeper, Mrs. Green, to redo his
mother's room for his bride. He instructed her to have the
room done in a turquoise blue to match Bonny's eyes.

He turned away from the coach window and took
Bonny's hand in his. "I had best warn you, my love," he
said, "that Hedley Hall is a bit, how should I say it?—
awesome for a residence."

Her eyes flashed. "How so, Richard?"

"I am given to understand the first duke was close to
Queen Elizabeth and welcomed her at Hedley Hall, so he
wanted it to be quite as magnificent as a palace. Actually,
it looks rather like a Tuscan palace. In fact, Cosimo de'
Medici visited Hedley Hall in the sixteenth century and said
as much."

"Oh dear, I assure you I will not know how to act."

"You will make it a home once again, I am sure. My
staff will be at your complete disposal to show you the
linen closets and—well, all the things a mistress of the
house knows about." He shifted his weight on the soft
squabs of the carriage. God, this was far more comfortable
than his mount. He had ridden enough these past few weeks
to last a lifetime. It was a wonder he was not barrel-legged.

"I hope your servants don't find me meddlesome,"
Bonny said.

"They will love you." He lifted her hand and brought
it to his lips. "In truth, Hedley Hall is more cozy to live

in than one might think. During my parents' time, they took up residence chiefly in the west wing. That wing, which was added later, has less marble and more wood and seems to me more English. The main building is rather grand and is only used now for large assemblies—of which there have been none since my parents died.''

"You don't want to open your house to friends?''

"As soon as you are out of mourning, my dear, I want to have the biggest ball ever thrown at Hedley Hall to show you off.''

The duke knew the road well, and as they neared their turnoff, he tried to calm the rapid beating of his heart. "After the next turn, my love, you will see your new home.''

She moved to look through the window. The road they traveled split into two long roads that approached the magnificent Hedley Hall from either side and formed a semicircle which met at the pedimented portico entrance of the symmetrical three-story building. The afternoon sun struck the building in such a manner that the stuccoed brick walls looked golden. The building stretched across a neatly mowed park, and chimneys and dormers jutted from the roofline.

"It's so beautiful,'' she said softly, squeezing his hand. Her reaction pleased him very much.

In anticipation of meeting their mistress, the liveried servants lined up inside the grand marble entrance hall. Her husband had informed Bonny he kept but a skeleton staff, so she was quite surprised to find that staff numbered more than twenty servants, including a new girl, Marie, whom he had instructed Mrs. Green to engage as Bonny's personal maid.

As she stood in the massive entry hall with its thirty-foot ceiling and chandelier with hundreds of lights, Bonny's chest tightened. She had never felt so insignificant, so lost.

A vicar's daughter was as ill prepared to run this...this palace as a stable lad to become a king. She had made a terrible mistake. She would bring embarrassment to her husband. Her eyes scanned the thick scarlet carpet that ran up the broad marble staircase. She looked at the French tables with porcelain vases and the Carrara Roman statues. She knew so little of such treasures. Why couldn't she have fallen in love with a simple country squire?

She looked at her husband and swallowed hard.

The upper servants—Carstairs the butler, Mrs. Carstairs the cook, Evans the valet, Mrs. Green the housekeeper—were introduced by name; the others merely smiled politely.

After introducing the new duchess to her staff, the duke said, "And this is the duchess's cousin, Lady Emily."

"Lady Emily! We received a post for you," Mrs. Green exclaimed. "It's right over here." She fetched the letter and gave it to Emily, who took it with shaking hands and read.

"Mama demands that I come home at once." Emily's voice revealed her agitation.

Bonny stepped toward her cousin, and Emily handed her the letter. Written immediately after Lady Lucille read the duke's marriage announcement in the *Gazette,* the hastily written missive accused Emily of failing to suitably impress the duke and ordered her to come home to try to repair her situation.

Radcliff watched Emily look entreatingly at Bonny, then he asked Mrs. Green, "What room have you made ready for Lady Emily?"

"The green room, your grace."

He dismissed the servants, then offered his wife his arm as he led her toward the west wing. "I will show you the main house later, my dear." Turning to Emily, he said, "When would you like to return to London?"

"As soon as possible."

Their voices echoed in the vast room.

"My carriage is at your disposal."

"That is very kind, your grace. I should like to depart early tomorrow, then."

"Oh, Em, are you sure?" Bonny asked disappointedly. "You're welcome to stay here, isn't she, Richard."

"For as long as she likes," he said.

"No. I really do need to get back." Emily's eyes held Bonny's. "I have a very strong longing to get back to London. There are things there I miss very much."

They walked along a broad marble hallway, lit by a row of sashed windows.

"If you will just show me to the green room, I shall rest," Emily said. "I'm quite tired from the journey."

Bonny moved to Emily's side and slid an arm around her cousin. "I am so very vexed with myself for allowing you to make such a long journey in your weakened health."

"Pooh!" Emily said.

The marble floors ran into the newer west wing, but this wing looked cozier because oriental carpets in deep reds and blues covered much of the floors, and the rich dark woods of the wainscoting and balusters added a warmth that was lacking in the opulent main house. As they mounted the stairs, Richard pointed out portraits of various ancestors.

The duke showed Emily to her room, which was near the top of the stairs. Bonny entered the room to satisfy herself that a fire had been laid.

Next, Radcliff walked his wife to the end of the broad hallway to his own chamber, where deep reds covered the bed and windows, and dark woods gave the room a masculine look. Opened draperies offered light from the many windows of this corner room.

Bonny's eye fell on the large tester bed, but her husband was already walking toward the adjoining dressing room.

"Our rooms connect through this room," he told her.

She joined him and found the chamber as large as most sleeping chambers.

"Now you will see your room," he said softly. "It is where I was born. In my mother's day it was pink, but I had Mrs. Green oversee having it decorated for you." He opened the door to her room. "I wanted it the color of your eyes."

Sun bathed the large room from at least ten tall windows, where aqua draperies opened beneath gold cornices. The aqua damask walls and silk bedspread matched the rose-patterned carpet.

The duke watched his wife's face brighten as she surveyed the room, then turned to him, her eyes twinkling with excitement. "It's the most beautiful room I've ever seen."

He kicked the door shut behind him and closed the short gap between them. "I'm glad you like it, for this is the most important room in the house, my love." He gathered her into his arms. He could hear the rapid thumping of her heart as he held her, cherishing the feel of her, his wife.

He lowered his head to kiss her and was pleased with her hungry response. His hands moved over her back, her hips, pressing her ever closer. Her breath, like his, grew harsh and labored as the kiss deepened. His lips trailed from her mouth to the hollow of her neck, and down the slope of her chest. He reached into her bodice and cupped a breast, while his other hand worked in a frenzy to free her of her dress. When it fell to her waist, his mouth closed over a pink nipple.

Her eyes darted to the window. "We'll be seen."

"No one will see us, my love," he said softly.

She backed away from him. "I would feel better if you drew the draperies, Richard."

"But I want to see you."

Color rose to her face. "I would rather you didn't."

A smile curved his mouth. "Very well, my love." He strode to each of the windows and pulled the draperies together, turning to her when he finished, longing in his eyes.

She modestly held her dress over her breasts, her eyes on him as he crossed the floor to her and drew her to him. The top of her dress fell down as she closed her arms around him.

"Don't be shy, Barbara, for I am your husband. I will know your body as well as you do, and you will know mine. We belong to each other now." He tugged gently, and the rest of her garments slid off.

He took her hand and led her across the darkened room to the big tester bed. She lay on the bed, pulling part of the spread to cover her nakedness while her husband threw off his own coat and cravat and kicked off his boots. Wearing only breeches and an open shirt, he came to lie beside her, lifting away the blue bedspread to gaze upon her.

Catching his breath, he swallowed hard as his eyes lingered over her lovely milky white body. God's eyes, but she was incredibly beautiful! He reached to cup her full breasts, kissing her feverishly until she arched against him, her breath ragged.

Pleased beyond measure at his wife's hungry response, he slid his hands along her satin curves until his fingers moved into the soft join of her thighs, and she sucked in her breath. After she became accustomed to the gentle movement of his hand, she widened her legs and his stroking eased into her wetness, making her breath come even faster.

She pressed into him, urging him with her movements to continue whatever it was he was doing to her.

He had kept on his breeches so she would not see his enlarged need and be frightened. When he could stand it no longer, he eased open his pants and brought her hand to stroke him. Her hand did not enclose him but petted him as a frightened child might pet a dog.

"It's all right, my love. This was made to fit perfectly in you." He gently guided her to lie on her back and withdrew his luxuriously wet finger, replacing it with himself.

She gasped, but it was a gasp of pleasure rather than pain, he discovered as she parted her legs ever wider, raising her hips to meet him.

Mindful of his wife's innocence, he went ever so gently, savoring the incredible feel of being sheathed within her. As she lunged against him with urgency, he began to plunge deeper and deeper, his mind incapable of anything save the utter joy of his wife's compliance.

He felt her warm breath and held her tighter as she began to shudder beneath him in wave after wave of wrenching spasms that perfectly matched his own release. Then he collapsed over her.

He had never felt so utterly satisfied with a woman, but he had never lain with a woman he truly loved. His love for Barbara nearly overpowered him with its intensity. Nothing in her statuesque demeanor would ever have told him she could be so receptive to his lovemaking, though he'd known of her warmth by her affection toward Emily and her devotion to her mother.

Bonny told herself she should be ashamed over her wanton behavior. Wasn't a lady supposed to recoil from such intimate acts? But she couldn't seem to get enough of this man who was now her husband. She had not even felt any of the pain a virgin was supposed to feel. Was that because Richard was so skilled a lover? She wondered if what happened between them was just another physical act to her experienced husband. Was she just another body he could use for his own pleasure? Could he possibly feel half of what she was feeling?

She lay in his arms a long while, feeling utterly complete

while wrapped in his embrace. She lost all track of time. It occurred to her she should be embarrassed, were the servants to guess what they were doing, but her pride was not as great as her pleasure.

Richard propped himself on one elbow to trace with a finger her cheek, her nose, her mouth as his eyes studied hers. "Do you hurt?"

She shook her head, the vestiges of passion still in her eyes as she raised her head to kiss him.

"Oh, my love, you will get me started all over again, and we cannot spend the day in bed—much as I would love to."

"I did not realize this—what we have done—happens in the daytime."

He laughed a hearty laugh. "Oh, what an innocent you are, my dear." He brushed back stray strands of black hair from her damp temples. "But very satisfactory in bed, I am happy to say."

Words of love would have pleased her more, but those words would have to hold her. "I feel like an utter harlot, I assure you."

He laughed again. "Please don't. Remember, all married persons do what you and I just did."

"And a lot of persons who aren't married. You most certainly must be considered a skilled lover, my husband."

"My love, if I have intimately known women in the past, I must assure you none have been nearly so captivating as you."

Those words gave her great comfort. She had felt her lack of experience would render her unpleasant in his bed, since she had been told men placed great importance upon the pleasures of the flesh. She was gratified to know he found her adequate, and she decided to learn to pleasure her husband in every way.

Radcliff kissed the tip of her nose, rose from the bed and

went into the dressing room. She heard the sound of trickling water. A minute later he reappeared with a wet handkerchief and sat on the edge of the bed. "There is blood the first time, you know."

Her face grew red as he brought the cloth between her legs. "Let me do that!" she said, taking it from him. "And please turn your head, sir. This is most embarrassing to me."

He refused to turn his head. "Your body will be as mine and mine as yours, as I have said." He watched her wipe between her legs, and when she finished, he took the blood-stained handkerchief and tossed her chemise to her. "I apprehend you would like to dress. I will see to the bedspread."

Averting her gaze from his, she did as her husband instructed, but conflicting feelings battled in her mind. During the lovemaking, her nakedness seemed comfortable, even pleasing. But now it was embarrassing, though not nearly so embarrassing as the idea of him wiping between her legs. Only her husband's calm reaction prevented her total humiliation. He seemed so thoroughly comfortable it quite convinced her that all married people shared such intimacy with regularity. She thought of his words. *Your body will be as mine and mine as yours.*

She truly belonged to him now.

Chapter Seven

Casting a rueful glance at her sleeping husband, Bonny reluctantly left her warm bed as dawn's hazy glow slipped into her room the next morning. Remembering his lips and hands exploring every inch of her during their night of lovemaking, she fought the desire to climb back in bed with him. She must see Emily off.

Not having alerted Marie that she would rise so early, Bonny was glad to dress herself. She was not accustomed to having a maid, nor was she comfortable allowing that maid to find a man in her mistress's bed. Bonny wondered how other married women handled such a situation. She had so much to learn. About being a married woman. About Hedley Hall and being a duchess. About her enigmatic husband.

Fastening the last button of her long-sleeved mourning dress, she quietly left the room and walked down the cold hall to meet her cousin.

Emily's room smelled of a wood fire. Her bed was already made and her valise and hatboxes stacked one on top of the other near the door. Emily stood fully dressed in a muslin day gown, directing her gaze out the window.

Bonny entered the warm room, pleased that her servants

had taken such good care of her mending cousin. "You're all dressed, and Martha's even done your hair." Her voice cracked with emotion. "Oh, I do so hate to see you go."

"But I really must. Not just because of Mama sending for me, but I long so to see Harriet, to take her in my arms."

Bonny nodded knowingly. "I am persuaded your mother will once again throw you on the marriage mart."

Emily placed her gloves in her reticule. "I know, and I've decided to be very complacent, and if some poor unfortunate man should offer for me, I will merely decline and tell Mama he did not suit. Eventually, she will have to accept that I shall be a spinster."

Bonny thought of how full and rich her own life had become because of Radcliff and felt terribly sorry for her cousin. Walking to the door, she said, "You don't think you could ever love again?"

"I could know no greater love than already I have shared with Harold."

Her hand on the doorknob, Bonny said, "I understand since I've met his brother. Lord Dunsford is not only very attractive, but sensitive, too."

Emily nodded sadly and whispered, "Then he is very much like Harold."

Her heart heavy for her cousin, Bonny walked into the hall and saw the door to her husband's chamber close.

In the magnificent dining room, a fire blazed and the smell of freshly brewed coffee greeted them. Though the room was extravagantly large, it was surprisingly warm. Atop salvers on the sideboard Bonny discovered hot scones, steamy porridge and crisp kippers, which she began to put on her porcelain plate as a solemn footman entered the room.

"Allow me to serve you, your grace."

Exchanging a bemused glance with Emily, Bonny took a seat at the long table.

As they were finishing their meal, Mrs. Carstairs brought Emily a lunch basket. "His grace asked me to make this lunch for you and Martha," the plump Mrs. Carstairs told Emily.

Bonny fairly glowed over her husband's thoughtfulness as she and Emily slipped on their cloaks and left the room.

"I fear I have already blundered," Bonny whispered. "Duchesses, apparently, are not permitted to serve themselves." Though she made light of it, Bonny worried she would be the laughingstock of the servants' hall.

They walked to where the coach and four waited. Her husband, dressed and shaven, also awaited them. At the sight of Radcliff, Bonny drew in her breath.

He met her gaze with a softness in his eyes, a flicker of a smile and a slight nod, but it was to Emily that he spoke. "Lady Emily," he said, taking her hand and assisting her into the carriage, "I regret that you must leave so quickly, especially since my poor wife will sadly lack for female companionship."

"Then you will have to bring her to London, your grace," Emily said, climbing into the carriage.

The duke's brows lowered. "London during the season is no place for one in mourning."

"I don't think I can wait until her mourning is over to see Bonny again."

"We will not wait that long," Bonny said cheerfully as the horses began to kick up gravel from the driveway.

Radcliff hooked an arm around his wife and spoke to Emily. "Please know you will always be welcome here at Hedley Hall."

Emily's eyes glistened with tears as she said her farewells and the carriage pulled away.

The duke and duchess watched the carriage until the

sound of hooves against the pebbles could no longer be heard. Then Radcliff looked down into his wife's face. "Your home, Hedley Hall, my dear, is in need of a woman. Mrs. Green is very competent—been housekeeper since I was a lad—but she is unused to making decisions, and her eyesight is not what it once was."

They strolled back into the house, Bonny feeling quite regal as she passed between two liveried footmen with her handsome husband at her side.

"I regret to say that I have taken no interest in the place since I assumed the title, therefore much needs to be done," Radcliff said.

"I cannot believe Mrs. Green would welcome my interference in what has been her domain for so many years, sir. And you must perceive I am completely unprepared to run such a mansion."

"You have excellent judgment and good taste. You will do a fine job, I am sure. And I trust you, my dear, to know how to get what you want done while making Mrs. Green think it was her very own idea."

A grin turned up the corners of her mouth. "Yes, that might answer very well, sir."

He took her hand and pressed it between his. "You are at liberty, my dear, to make all the changes you desire. I have conveyed as much to Mrs. Green."

"And her reaction?"

"She was actually quite pleased. Today, she will give you the grand tour."

Bonny was disappointed her husband was not going to escort her through the rambling house. Surely he would know the history of the Moncrief family—her family now—better than a housekeeper. "And what do you do today, sir?"

"I will check my lands with my steward and visit tenants. Tomorrow, I should like you to accompany me fishing. We can have Cook prepare a picnic."

"I shall look forward to it very much."

They strolled through the opulent salon. "I should warn you that today will exhaust you. Hedley Hall is quite vast. In earlier days it took one servant all day just to open and shut all the casements."

She had no problem believing that. There must be more than three hundred windows in Hedley Hall.

In London, Lady Lucille was not the only person to read with indignation the *Gazette* announcement of the forthcoming nuptials between the Duke of Radcliff and Bonny Barbara Allan. Stanley Moncrief, his head not well from overindulging the previous night, read the unwelcome announcement as he partook of strong morning coffee.

"The bloody bastard cannot do this to me!" he shouted.

His man, Wilcox, bringing his master the day's post, came to stand placidly at his side. "Is there a problem, sir?"

Stanley just sat, staring at the announcement. He had read it twice in the hopes he had read it incorrectly the first time. But there it was. "The fifth Duke of Radcliff has announced his intention to marry Bonny Barbara Allan of Milford."

"Yes, by God, there is a bloody problem. It seems my dear cousin Richard has decided to wed. Just when I had come to anticipate being the sixth Duke of Radcliff. Damn him! When a man gets to four and thirty without marrying, wouldn't you say he would be a bachelor for life, Wilcox?"

"I couldn't say, sir."

"Well, I bloody well could. But I hadn't counted on that blasted Bonny Barbara Allan." He thought of her Roman countenance and grew rigid. "Hers is a face that has cost me a dukedom."

Wilcox placed his master's letters on the breakfast table. "Will that be all, sir?"

Distracted from perusing the day's post, Stanley merely nodded, tossing aside first one, then another piece of correspondence without opening it. *They are all the same,* he thought, *tradesmen demanding payment.* Suddenly, an idea came to him. "Wilcox," he yelled. "Pack my things. We're going to Kent. I have a keen desire to see my dear cousin."

As the frail, white-haired Mrs. Green guided her through the vast rooms of the main house, Bonny kept thinking about the long-ago servant whose sole job was opening and closing all the casements. If that servant walked as slowly as the elderly Mrs. Green, Bonny thought with amusement, one day would not be enough.

She tried to imagine these echoing rooms filled with voices and laughter, but the musty smell of disuse was stronger than her imagination. To bring life back to these cold rooms would indeed give her pleasure.

She regretted that Mrs. Green was unable to enlighten her on the history of the fine paintings by Italian masters or the gilded French furnishings draped with costly silk brocades. Why, the contents of only one of these lavish rooms would cost more money than her father had possessed in his long lifetime.

"His grace tells me he wishes you to redecorate these rooms, for he plans to entertain now that he has so lovely a wife to display," said Mrs. Green, her voice trembling with the unevenness that comes from decades of use. "Now that I've seen you, I understand completely. Even as a boy, his grace always had an eye for what was of the best quality, what was most beautiful."

Bonny felt the color rise to her face. Was that why Radcliff had married her? Was she to be an ornament? Another beautiful possession?

"You will want to modernize," Mrs. Green said. The old woman stopped and looked at Bonny.

"I have no wish to change what is quite lovely as it is."

Bonny perceived a satisfied twinkle in the old woman's eyes.

"The draperies have faded and will have to be replaced," Bonny said. "What do you think about having the new ones made exactly as the old ones?"

"I think that is an excellent idea, your grace." The stooped Mrs. Green ambled across the marble floors of the grand salon and into the dining hall.

Looking up at rows of massive crystal chandeliers, Bonny wondered if lighting all their candles was the sole task of still another servant. "I realize my husband has not retained adequate staff to keep the main house cleaned. Perhaps we could hire workers to do the heavy cleaning. Do you think the chandeliers might need polishing?"

The old woman looked up and agreed.

Bonny eyed paint peeling near the ceiling some twenty feet above them. "And what do you think about having the rooms repainted—in the same colors, of course?"

"To tell you the truth, your grace, my eyes aren't what they used to be. I daresay you can tell better than I."

Mrs. Green saved the lived-in wing until last. By this time, Bonny fairly shivered from the coolness of the unused rooms of icy marble, where closed draperies hid even the sunlight.

In the warmer west wing, Mrs. Green showed Bonny the linen rooms, the butler's pantry—all the rooms not normally viewed by a visitor.

Bonny especially enjoyed the nursery. She smiled when she found a primer in which Richard's name had been printed in a shaky, youthful script. Being here, Bonny now felt even closer to her husband. How she longed to fill this room with their children.

She also enjoyed Richard's study, where fires blazed at two hearths. On a table beside one of the sofas, a collection of snuffboxes caught her attention. She picked up one, a blue Sevres porcelain with elegant gilding. Another was of gold encrusted with diamonds.

"His grace is noted for his collection of snuffboxes," Mrs. Green said. "It is said to be the finest in the world."

Bonny placed the box she held back on the table ever so carefully. "They are so beautiful."

"Yes. His grace loves beautiful things."

There it was again. His reason for marrying her. If only he loved her as she loved him. But even last night, when he whispered words of adoration, he never said he loved her. But had she told him? No, she could not possibly be the first to say that. Then he'd likely be compelled to say he loved her, whether he meant it or not.

Bonny glanced at Mrs. Green. "You've known the duke all his life?"

"Oh, yes."

"What kind of boy was he?"

The old woman's face softened. "Well, he worried his poor mum to death. Never afraid of anything. He would get on the fiercest horse and take those fences when he was just a wee one. And I will never forget when he jumped into the lake—before he ever knew how to swim. He was a wild one. Then, when he went to Oxford! Well, I'm just glad his poor mum, rest her soul, did not know half of what he did.

"But he was a good boy. A very loving son. And very kind to the tenants. Generous." Mrs. Green gazed off into the distance, her voice low and tender. "I remember how he loved to go in his mother's room in the mornings. It was pink in those days. The most beautiful room you ever saw—still is, even though it's a different color."

"Yes, I quite agree."

"He loved his mum's beautiful room. As rough and tumble as he was, he appreciated beauty."

"Yes, I do," said the duke, walking up and kissing his wife on the cheek.

Bonny turned glad eyes on her husband and tried to calm the rapid beating of her heart. "You're back earlier than I expected, sir."

"It is not really that early, my dear. We keep country hours, which barely gives me time to clean up for dinner. Since there will be just the two of us, I beg you wear something colorful. No mourning garb."

She followed him up the stairway, playfully mocking an obedient servant. "Yes, Richard."

"How do you find your maid?"

"She seems to be very competent. I'm told she is handy with a needle, and I intend to employ her talents on my mourning clothes."

"Did she arrange your hair today?"

"Yes, I was quite pleased. Do you like it?"

He stopped at the top of the stairs and studied her. Ringlets fell on her face from the swept-back arrangement. "I do."

She lowered her lashes and a contented smile played at her lips. "Do you now have your man back?"

He chuckled. "Yes, Evans entered my chamber as soon as you left yours this morning. When I heard him busying himself in my dressing room, I called out for him to come into my wife's room. He barely spoke to me. He hasn't got over my going off for a month without him."

They arrived at her door, and the duke followed her into her room.

"When he saw the condition of my clothes and boots,

he got all puffed up with self-importance. Now, I think, he feels needed again.''

Radcliff shut the door behind him and walked toward her, desire burning in his eyes.

It was hard for her to try to make conversation with him when she could think of nothing except falling into his arms and feeling his lips on hers and his hands stroking her bare body. ''I cannot think but that Evans must resent your marrying.''

''He will get used to it.'' Radcliff's voice sounded raw.

She found herself meeting him, wrapping her arms around him and kissing him hungrily. It no longer mattered to her that the draperies were open or that he could look upon her nakedness. All that mattered was this moment and the exquisite feel of her husband against her. She moaned as his hand slipped into her bodice, and later, when her gown crumpled to the floor, she felt only a sense of pleasure when his eyes lingered over her body.

Her hand cupped the swell in his breeches, and he soon pulled them off. Now it was her turn to gaze as her hand rounded his hardness.

''I told you this could give you pleasure.''

She answered him with a dazed smile. She had not felt anything like this since she had tasted her first champagne.

''Come, my love, for I cannot wait.'' He took her hand and crossed the floral carpet to the bed. Their bed.

Again, they did not remove the spread but lay atop it, Radcliff spreading his wife's legs and positioning himself between them while his gentle hand worked its magic on her.

She called out his name, raising her hips to him, burying her face in the hollow of his neck, sucking in the smell of his Hungary water.

Soon he was plunging into her with a maddening rhythm until they both cried out a frenzied, joyful wail of utter pleasure. Then he collapsed on her, his body—like hers—wet and exhausted.

He stayed within her for a very long time before he pulled away and gazed into her face. Brushing back damp strands of hair from her forehead, he whispered, "Your body is less resistant to me now. I am so very pleased I married you." He gathered her into his embrace. "You are everything I could ever want in a wife."

But there was one thing more he desired from her. Her love. Her passion for him had given him a false confidence in her affection. Then, this morning, as he walked back from instructing Cook on Lady Emily's lunch, his wife's words—spoken behind her cousin's closed doors—shattered him.

Lord Dunsford is not only very attractive, but sensitive, too.

Chapter Eight

"Would you prefer to walk or ride to the lake, my love?" Bonny's husband asked, looking down at her. His voice was gentle and concerned when he added, "Are you less sore?"

She squinted, for the overhead sun struck her eyes, but she did not avert her gaze from his close scrutiny. She knew she should blush over his second question, but talking of their intimacy brought them closer and she couldn't seem to get close enough to this man she loved so fiercely. Boldly matching his gaze, she answered: "Let's walk." She took his hand. "It seems my body has grown quite used to yours now, sir."

"I am very glad to hear that." Radcliff walked with her across the park, a wren's trill crescendoing in the cool air around them.

"Where are the fishing poles?" she asked.

"I had my groom take them to the lake and set them by the water's edge. He also took the picnic basket."

Her eyes twinkled. "Does he also hook the worms for you?"

"Do you imply that others do my unpleasant work?"

Her smile widened. "To be sure."

"You must know about fishing, then. Do you fish?"

"Not since I was a child, since my father died."

"Did you like it?"

"I liked being outdoors and I liked being with my father. The same two reasons I am here today." This time she did turn her gaze from his.

He brought her hand to his lips and softly kissed it. "I am gratified to know you desire my company outside your bedchamber."

His words irritated her. Did he think her so lacking in feeling that she gave herself to him only for the joy of physical pleasure? "You sound as if you have more confidence in your lovemaking than in your personal charms."

He did not answer, and they walked on in silence. After a while, the neatly mowed grass gave way to pasture, and the land began to slope. Some distance off they could see the small lake.

"Steps are being taken to hire villagers to begin the cleaning and painting you spoke of to Mrs. Green."

"You are most efficient, sir."

"And you have won Mrs. Green's wholehearted approval, my dear. She's already encouraging us to begin the nursery while she's still alive to enjoy a babe."

Bonny turned to her husband and drew in her breath. "Should you like that?"

Wind tousled his hair and his eyes narrowed from the sun, but his mouth lifted into his far-too-infrequent half smile. "Very much."

She squeezed his strong hand. "Me, too."

As they got closer to what her husband called the "lake," Bonny could see that a stream actually widened in the valley between the sloping hills. A wooden hump-backed bridge spanned the lake near the mouth of the stream, and woods bordered it on the opposite side.

"Is this your very own private lake?"

"It is, but I have special days for my tenants to enjoy it."

They found the poles, one large and one small, beside the bridge, where a small rowboat was moored. Radcliff lifted his wife into the boat to keep her skirts dry, then he handed her the poles and buckets before unfastening the boat and climbing in.

"Do I put your worm on for you?" he teased.

"But of course. Ladies don't soil their hands with worms."

He set about the task of baiting their hooks while she rowed toward the center of the lake, the oars slapping at the water in a rhythmic pattern.

"By the way," he said, not removing his eyes from his task, "I am glad you have only the one cloak, the blue one you're wearing. I don't like you in black."

"When it is just you and I, I will wear what pleases you," she said.

"When we go to London, I want you to have all the latest fashions in every color imaginable. You must be the best-dressed woman in London."

"First, I shall need more mourning clothes, sir."

"Then you'll have black cloaks and black muslins and black gloves. I hate to think of it," he said, shaking his head. His eyes raked her from head to toe, then he spoke softly. "You were made to smile and laugh and wear beautiful gowns."

"There will be time later."

Radcliff handed her the small pole, and the two of them cast their lines into the placid lake. Sitting in silence in the gently swaying boat, they waited for a fish to bite. Though it was a cool day, there was no wind. So unlike Northumbria, Bonny thought, remembering the ever present whooping of the winds in her land of moors.

From time to time she would steal a glance at her hus-

band, his face so much as it had been the first time she set
eyes on him at the rout, his mouth firm in its straight line,
tugging down ever so slightly at the corners. Such a rugged
face it was, she thought. Tanned from the sun. A cleft in
his square chin nearly matched the dimple that would poke
into his cheek if his lips ever lifted into something close to
a smile. And right now, loose strands of wavy, honey-
colored hair dipped onto his forehead.

"I think, sir, you lead a charmed life. Do you always get
what you want?"

His chest tightened. If only she knew the doubts clawing
their way back into his mind. He kept telling himself Barbara was his. Hadn't she shown it in every way? But then
he would remember what an obedient, loving daughter
she'd been. It was just like her to offer herself in marriage
to a man she did not love to please her dying mother.

But what of her lovemaking? How could she be so warm
and open to him if she indeed loved the Earl of Dunsford?
"I am not above altering the playing field to give myself
the advantage. Why do you ask?"

"I was thinking about the sun today," she said, the boat
rocking on the gently swelling waters. "I haven't seen it
in a month, and the one day you choose to go fishing, it
pokes its head through a sky of clouds."

"I was quite lucky." His pole bent and tugged, and he
brought in his first catch of the day.

He was to catch three more while Bonny still waited for
her first bite.

"I think I could use some lunch now," he said, lying
down his pole and taking up the oars. When they got to
the water's edge, he leapt from the boat, rope in hand, and
tied it to the bridge, then lifted Bonny from the boat and
carried her to dry land.

The picnic basket yielded boiled eggs, fresh loaves of
bread, slabs of cheese, two apples and a bottle of Madeira

the duke had thrown in. They ate and drank their fill. When Radcliff offered Bonny a third glass of wine, she refused. "I had best not. I feel giddy."

Her husband lay back, chewing on a blade of grass and feeling the sun's warmth, the blended smell of woods and daffodils stirring an erotic mixture of emotions deep within him.

"I shall take off your boots so your feet can dry," a light-headed Bonny informed him while pulling off first one, then another boot.

"Would you care to take off anything else?" he asked.

She cocked her eyebrows and glared at him. "I think not. Not in broad daylight."

"But you were most bold in broad daylight in your bedchamber yesterday." His hand closed over her thin skirts and fastened on her thigh.

"You cannot seduce me out here, sir."

"Just lie here with me, Barbara. Feel the warmth of the sun."

She nervously complied, lying on her stomach a forearm's length from her husband's side.

He shielded his eyes to gaze into her face, catching his breath at her loveliness, the length of her long black eyelashes sweeping down over those beautiful eyes, the soft mouth beneath her aquiline nose.

"I hope the sun will not spoil your lovely white skin," he said.

"Pooh. It feels too good to worry about."

"Being beautiful doesn't seem important to you."

"It is a trial."

"How so?"

"Can you imagine what a dilemma it is to receive flowers from eight different men, all begging you to wear theirs that night to show your affection?"

"What other problems does a beautiful woman encounter?"

"Well, I cannot tell you how many terrible poems have been written in my honor. My eyes have been called faded ink pools, my hair has been likened to lumps of lignite, and I have been told I have the body of Venus—which did not please me at all, since all the Venuses I've seen in my father's books are quite disrobed."

Radcliff laughed at the images she drew.

She touched the dimple in his leathery cheek with a finger. "I love to see you smile. You seldom do so."

He brought her hand to his lips. "You do have the body of a goddess, you know," he said, his voice throaty.

"Then you, sir, have the body of a god."

He saw desire in her eyes and pulled her to him for a hungry kiss, his hands moving over her back, her hips, pulling down the hood, which still covered her head, then running his fingers through her hair, sucking in the light floral scent of her perfume.

His breathing quickened and his heart beat so loudly it almost covered the sounds of his wife's soft moaning. He felt himself grow hard. God, but he wanted her even more than ever, so badly it hurt.

Firm arms drew her against his body, and she melted into him. He heard her heart pounding against his own. His hands moved to stroke her skirts and cup her where her thighs joined. Her breath came faster. He began to pull up her skirts until his fingers reached her and she gasped with pleasure.

Soon, the two of them lay on the grass, facing each other, clothed at the back, but joined in the front only as two lovers whose hearts pumped to the same beat.

During the fevered frenzy of their union, Radcliff lost all sense of time and place, knowing only that what he shared with Barbara was bliss beyond measure.

He loved her so totally he would love her if she lay in his bed like a fireplace poker. Never would he have imagined that beneath her cool beauty she was possessed by such passion. He held her close, savoring the feel of being within her. In a thousand years, he could never find another like his Barbara. His wife.

Her mind fogged with pleasure, Bonny could scarcely believe one week ago she had never seen a man's naked body and now she craved one. She craved the very sight of Richard. The commanding sound of his deep voice. The feel of him. His touch had the power to unleash her soul. Lying there on the sloping meadow with skirts hiked up and a man's sex plunging deep inside her was something a lightskirt might do, not a lady, not the Duchess of Radcliff, but it was the Duchess of Radcliff who lost all sense of propriety when she was with her very virile husband. She knew a hunger greater than any shame.

What happened between her and her husband was not shameful. There was too much affection in his voice, too much satisfaction in his eyes when he looked upon her after their lovemaking.

She knew men kept mistresses. Her chest constricted at the thought of him lying with another. She held him close, intoxicated by the feel of him, by his male scent, and determined to bring him such pleasure he would never seek a mistress.

He withdrew from her, gently smoothed her skirts back down, tucked himself in his breeches, then lightly kissed the tip of her nose. "You drive me mad, wench."

Was that all he could say? If only he could tell her the words she hungered for.

Chapter Nine

The country life suited her husband very well, Bonny reflected as he strolled into the dining room dressed simply in country clothes and smelling of fresh shaving soap. That first night she had seen him she had not thought him particularly handsome outfitted in pants and coat of blue superfine with flounced lace shirt cuffs and an elaborate cravat with diamond pin. But in country clothes that matched the shades of brown in his hair, buff cloth breeches and Hessians, he looked ruggedly handsome.

Radcliff looked her over approvingly before lifting the coffee cup extended him by a footman, whom he immediately dismissed. "Marie does admirably with your hair."

Bonny lowered her lashes and smiled. "I am quite pleased with her."

Taking a seat across from her, Radcliff shot Bonny a contented gaze. "I am happy to see no dark circles under your eyes, my love. I know I kept you from sleep the greater part of the night."

She thought of how she had thrown off all covers, how his lips and hands moved over her body, how she hungrily stroked him and lashed about wildly beneath him. Her breath grew short at the memory. And she could not meet his gaze in the morning's bright sunlight. "Pray, sir, I cannot discuss that in the breakfast room."

He tossed his head back and laughed. "You passionate baggage. If I wanted to, I believe I could have you writhing with pleasure beneath me in this very room in a very short span of time."

She took a sip of the now cooling coffee and diverted her gaze. "I daresay you could. You do seem to have that effect on me."

The lopsided grin appeared on his face as he broke open a scone and spread a thick layer of marmalade on it. "But, alas, I must spend the day with my steward."

"You are so very much at home in the country, I wonder why you spent so much of the year in London."

"Before you, the company was awfully thin here." He bit into his scone.

"None of your friends live in the area?"

He shook his head. "I met my closest friends at Oxford, including old Twigs. He's quite my best friend. You haven't met him, have you? James Edward Twickingham?"

"No. I suppose he is a bachelor."

Her husband chuckled again. "I cannot even fathom Twigs noticing a woman, unless she were mounted on an exquisite bay. He cares for nothing except the sporting pleasures."

"Does he not even know bits o' muslin?"

Her husband cocked a single brow. "My sweet wife knows about those? Have you not been told that ladies do not discuss such things?"

"Pooh. It is different with you. You are my husband. And you have told me any number of times that nothing between us should ever be embarrassing." She dabbed a chunk of the warm scone in clotted cream, eyeing Radcliff. "When you were at Oxford, surely you and your chums learned from buxom serving wenches, right along with Homer and Aristotle.''

His eyes twinkled mischievously. "In my case she wasn't a serving wench, but the upstairs maid of a country squire. There was a little ditty we sang of her.'' Lifting his voice to a merry tenor, he sang.

"She'll show you her breast,
She'll lift her skirts,
That's our fair Denise.
And when you are through,
She'll yell like a shrew,
Next gentleman, please!''

Bonny attempted to scowl, but a faint smile played at her lips. "I shall pretend I did not hear that outrageous verse and return to the subject we were discussing. You have no good friends in the area?''

"No male companions. Our family has always been close with Squire Carlisle.''

"Has he no sons?''

"None that lived past infancy, poor man. Perhaps that's why he frequently solicited my company when hunting and fishing. I really must call on him. Perhaps this afternoon I could present you to the Carlisles.''

The idea of meeting her husband's friends appealed to her. More than that, though, she welcomed the opportunity to spend time with Radcliff. "I should like that. While you are with your steward this morning, I had planned to call upon the vicar. What is his name?''

"Philip Widdington.''

"Is there a Mrs. Widdington?''

Radcliff set down his porcelain cup, the corners of his mouth lifting. "There is. She is twice the size of her husband and quite dominates the poor fellow.''

"And are there little Widdingtons?"

"I should say so. Must be a dozen of them. The rotund Mrs. Widdington is a good breeder. Has stout, healthy children."

How Bonny longed to be a good breeder and have Richard's stout, healthy children.

"And how do you propose finding the parsonage, my love?"

"I thought you could tell me how to get there. It will be a lovely day for a walk."

"I will not have you traveling about the unfamiliar countryside unattended. My groom will drive you."

Bonny rose from the table and crossed the room, stopping by Radcliff's chair to lightly brush his leathery cheek with a kiss.

"I'll have Rusty bring the phaeton around for you," he announced.

She longed for more endearing words. So many times during their night of lovemaking she had bitten back her declarations of love. He must be the first to say it. But would those words ever tumble from her husband's lips?

After one hour in the Widdingtons' chaotic household, Bonny was not so sure she wanted to be *that* good a breeder. The house was hopelessly cluttered and smelled of an unpleasant pet odor, Mrs. Widdington had scarcely been able to get the hair out of her eyes, and shrieking, crying babes vied with one another for their harried mother's attention.

But one of the babes made the nerve-splitting hour worthwhile. His name was Jonathan. Not quite old enough to walk, the chubby fellow with deep blue eyes and an adorable giggle bounced happily on Bonny's knee and thoroughly enjoyed her making a cake of herself over him. With reluctance, she gave him back to his mother at the end of the hour. "It was so very good to meet all of you, but I must get back to Hedley Hall."

Mrs. Widdington pushed her light brown hair from her brow. "Our pleasure, your grace."

At that second, two-year-old Anna collided with the tea table, sending the teapot and teacups clattering to the floor.

Bonny stooped and gathered the broken pieces of glass before Anna could cut herself, and the vicar found tea towels to wipe up the spill.

"Oh, your grace, I am so very sorry," Mrs. Widdington said, color rising to her already rosy cheeks as she slung Jonathan halfway over her shoulder. "Pray, don't clean that up. Philip will get it."

Bonny placed a chunk of broken china in her palm. "It's nothing. I was afraid Anna would get cut."

"She's seen worse, that one has," her father said, crouching to the floor and relieving Bonny of the broken porcelain. "She's a right whirlwind, she is."

Having watched her climb on top the piano, pull the cloth off the table and poke Jonathan in the eye, Bonny could not deny the parson's remark. She hoped poor little Jonathan would not emulate his sister's behavior when he got older.

On the lane leading to her phaeton, Bonny met an extremely well dressed young lady whose eyes swept over her, and a flicker of emotion—was it envy?—crossed her pretty face. She stopped in front of Bonny, smiled broadly and extended a gloved hand. Her pink glove perfectly matched her gown and pelisse, and she wore a rose-colored bonnet trimmed in the same pink. "You have to be the new duchess. You are just as beautiful as they said." She smelled of rose-scented perfume and spoke in a girlish voice.

Bonny took her hand. "You're very kind...and correct about me being the Duchess of Radcliff."

"I'm Cressida Carlisle."

"Squire Carlisle's daughter!"

"Richard's mentioned us?"

"Indeed he has. In fact, we had planned to pay you a call this very afternoon."

"You make me ashamed we have not called on you."

"Pooh. I daresay you had no way of knowing before yesterday that we were even here."

"True. I heard that your cousin was with you. Will we have the pleasure of meeting her?"

Bonny frowned. "I am sorry to say she has returned to London."

Bonny felt the young blonde studying her. "I fear you will sadly lack female company," Cressida said.

"I do miss my cousin, but I'm enjoying getting to know my husband."

Cressida coughed. "Well, I shan't keep you, since we will have the pleasure of a nice, long visit this afternoon. My parents will be delighted—and I will, too."

On the way back to Hedley Hall, Bonny struck up a conversation with the freckled groom as they bounced along the bumpy country road. "How old are you, Rusty?"

"Fourteen, your grace."

"Do your parents work at Hedley Hall?"

"I 'aven't got no parents, your grace."

"How is it you came to be employed by his grace?"

"I would 'ang around his grace's town 'ouse 'opin' to earn me a shillin' watchin' 'is grace's 'orses. The duke could see I loved me 'orses, and 'e asked me if I would like to come learn 'ow to take care of 'em. Now I got me a regular post, a roof over me 'ead, three meals a day and the best master in all of England."

Her dear Richard had obviously taken pity on the poor orphan and had wanted to ease life's cruel harshness for the lad. Bonny fixed a smug smile on her face. *And I have the best husband in all of England.*

When she got back to Hedley Hall, Bonny went first to check on the cleaners. Mrs. Green was overseeing the removal of the old draperies in the musty banquet hall. Their absence brightened the room with undiluted sunlight, but as the drapes came down, clouds of dust rose, causing Bonny and Mrs. Green to start coughing.

Alarmed because of the elderly housekeeper's frailty, Bonny led her from the room. "Come, Mrs. Green." She coughed. "We shouldn't want your lungs to take a disease."

The old woman issued no protest as Bonny escorted her from the room.

"I must commend you on the progress being made at Hedley Hall," Bonny said when they reached the ballroom.

"Thank you, your grace." Mrs. Green sneezed. "Did you have a nice visit with the vicar's family?" Mrs. Green's lips twitched mischievously.

"Why, Mrs. Green, I believe you know how very unpleasant those children of theirs can be—all except for the precious baby boy."

"Indeed. They're a wild bunch. Unfortunately, the poor little babe will probably turn out like all the rest."

They walked across the ballroom's parquet floors, which were in need of a good polish. Mrs. Green took a dust cloth from her pocket and ran it over the gilded frame of a massive painting of the Spanish Armada. "This place is sadly in need of a great deal of work, I'm sorry to say." Mrs. Green's thin, shaky words echoed in the vast room.

"With the extra day help, it will be done before we know it," Bonny said reassuringly.

Mrs. Green sniffed away the last of the dust. "I do hope your visit to the rectory wasn't altogether frightful."

"Oh, no. In fact, as I was leaving, I had the good fortune to meet Miss Cressida Carlisle."

Bonny detected a slight stiffening in Mrs. Green's manner at the mention of Cressida. "'Tis a pity that one never married," Mrs. Green said. "She had many offers during her season in London but turned them all down. I always felt she was holding out for his grace."

Bonny thought of the lovely young woman and swallowed hard. "For Richard?"

"Yes. They were the best of friends as children."

"Then she's past thirty?"

Mrs. Green nodded. "Though she's younger than his grace. She rather followed him around like an adoring pup."

Bonny's chest tightened. "Did he return her ardor?"

"No. He treated her as a sister, if you ask me."

"Well, I must say she was quite nice to me."

"I feel sure it has been many years now since she accepted that she would never be his duchess."

Bonny left Mrs. Green to supervise the laundry and went to her room to freshen up before Radcliff returned, her thoughts on the unfortunate Cressida Carlisle, who had chosen the lonely life of a spinster.

On the ride to Squire Carlisle's manor in Radcliff's curricle, Bonny inhaled the fresh country air, not objecting to the cool winds, which ruffled her hair and caused her bonnet to flap. This was the first time she had truly observed the green Kent countryside. "I must scold you, Richard, for praising Northumbria when your own Kent is so much more beautiful." The sun shone again today, glancing off the many lakes. Sheep grazed in hedged meadows, and gently rising hills seemed to hunker over the landscape.

"They are different types of beauty."

She watched Radcliff's masculine hands holding the ribbons to the high-stepping bay and spoke in an offhand manner. "Speaking of beauty, do you find Cressida Carlisle beautiful?"

"Cressy?"

Bonny nodded, her eyes on the rugged profile of his unwavering face.

"Never gave it a thought. She's quite a rattlebrain. I suppose she's fair enough, but..." He turned and lifted Bonny's chin to gaze into her aquamarine eyes. "She's no match for the lovely Duchess of Radcliff."

Bonny listened to the steady clop of the horse, glowing over her husband's words.

The Carlisle manor house seemed small compared to Hedley Hall, but the stately redbrick mansion was three times bigger than Bonny's home in Milford.

The Carlisles greeted the Duke and Duchess of Radcliff with enthusiasm. Both the squire and his wife appeared well fed and were much older than Bonny had expected. She soon realized that Cressida was their youngest child, four older sisters having married many years ago and produced a bevy of grandchildren for the squire.

Like so many older men, the squire still powdered his hair as men of fashion had done a dozen years previously. His wife looked much like Cressida but plumper and grayer.

They all took tea in the drawing room, permeated with the scent of a half-dozen bouquets in porcelain and crystal vases. The agreeable Mrs. Carlisle served tea from her silken settee.

Before much time passed, the loud-speaking squire and Radcliff were deep in conversation about sport and farming matters, which the women tried to ignore while they discussed fashion.

"I see that you are in mourning," Mrs. Carlisle said.

Bonny's eyes lowered. "Yes. My mother died just after Richard and I wed."

"How terrible," Cressida said.

"Yes," Bonny replied, setting her teacup back on its flower-trimmed saucer. "What helps most is that she had prepared for her death for some time and went without sorrow."

"And you've got his grace to fill in some of the emptiness," said Mrs. Carlisle.

Such personal observations were generally withheld from unfamiliar acquaintances, but Bonny found the older woman's remarks comforting. She decided she quite liked the entire Carlisle family.

"I hate to bring up fashion since you are in mourning," Cressida said, "but I do long to hear of the latest fashions in London."

Bonny picked up a biscuit. "I'm probably not a good one to ask. I was in London but a month after spending my entire eighteen years at a parsonage in Northumbria."

"You humble yourself," Cressida said. "I am sure you were the picture of fashion when you captured Richard."

Bonny appraised Cressida, who wore her hair in the latest fashion and whose sprigged muslin dress seemed most appropriate day wear. She noted, too, that Cressida had changed from the lovely pink dress and matching pelisse she had worn earlier in the day. "Judging from your short curly hair, Cressida, I would say you have kept up quite well with London fashions."

Cressida shrugged off the compliment. "Is it true that hats are all the rage, even for evening wear?"

"Oh, yes, hats and feathers are on every London woman's head." Bonny wondered why Cressida did not wear the white cap that was expected of women who were past their youth. Is that why Bonny had been so surprised to learn Cressida was past thirty?

"I feel so removed from everything here," Cressida complained.

"Richard admitted company could be quite thin, which explained why he spent so much time in London," Bonny said. "But we expect to spend more time here now that he intends to settle down."

A smile broke across Cressida's face. "It will be perfectly wonderful to have another woman around."

"Then maybe you'll get your head out of those books," Mrs. Carlisle told her daughter.

Cressida gave an exasperated sigh. "Mama just doesn't understand how truly wonderful the books from the Minerva Press are. Have you read the latest?" Cressida asked Bonny.

"Because of my religious upbringing, my father discouraged me from reading stories of that nature." Never mind that her father had shared with her his own eclectic library, which included works of a quite pagan nature.

Mrs. Carlisle poured more tea. "When you are finished mourning, your grace, we shall have to have a ball."

"I shall look forward to it."

As the duke and duchess departed, Cressida and her mother announced they would pay Bonny a morning call.

Bonny was relieved to know that Cressida had so well accepted the fact that she would never be the Duchess of Radcliff.

Chapter Ten

Stanley had ridden hard all day, and he was bloody glad to see Hedley Hall's dormers and chimneys lining up across the gray horizon as he humped over a gentle Kent hill. He stirred with envy when he beheld Hedley Hall spreading its magnificent proportions across the countryside. Richard did not deserve such splendor. He cared nothing for entertaining. Why, he had scarcely used the ancestral home since Uncle and Aunt died so many years before.

What grand entertainments he would have if he were master at Hedley, Stanley thought. An invitation to Hedley Hall would be coveted by the noblest in all of Europe. Each guest room would be fit for a king, and only the finest meals would be served in the great dining hall. The best musicians in Europe would entertain his guests. Why, his own consequence would be second only to the regent's.

Dismounting from his stallion once he reached the imposing entrance, Stanley felt mist on his face and eyed the dark clouds. "We barely miss a thorough drenching," he said to Wilcox. He handed his reins to a footman and ordered, "Do see to my horse and to my man's."

He strode into the palatial entry hall, looked Carstairs up and down, then said, "Announce me to your master. I'm his cousin, Stanley Moncrief, in case the years have erased your memory.''

"I am sorry to say his grace is not home at the present.''

Stanley's eyes narrowed. "Not here? Then where is he?"

"He and the duchess have gone to pay a social call.''

"The duchess!'' Stanley's heart sank. He had hoped to get to Richard before the foolish deed was done. The stories he had planned to tell on the fair Bonny Barbara Allan! By the time he finished, Richard would have fled the country to avoid linking his life to hers. But, alas, the vows must have been spoken. He swallowed hard. "Then, they have already married?''

"To be sure, sir.''

Things were not totally lost. At least Richard was here. He had not ridden to Kent for nothing. It might not be too late. He turned on his most charming smile, one that never failed to melt one of the gentler sex. "Please show me to my room and have someone bring my things.''

"I shall have to consult with the housekeeper to determine which room will be most satisfactory, sir,'' Carstairs announced, pivoting stiffly and striding toward the west wing.

A few minutes later, Mrs. Green escorted Stanley to the green room Emily had occupied. The housekeeper informed him that country hours were kept, that the room had been thoroughly cleaned—including fresh bed linens put on this very week—and assured him a fire would be lit in his grate in a thrice.

After he settled in his chamber, he began to pace on the green carpet. Fortunately he had another plan up his sleeve, a plan he hoped would cause an irreparable rift to the marriage of the Duke and Duchess of Radcliff.

Carstairs forgot to inform the duke his cousin had arrived. The butler had other things to worry about when his master, soaking wet from encountering a rainstorm on the way back from Squire Carlisle's, came flying into the hall barking orders left and right.

"Her grace needs a hot bath in her chamber as soon as possible. See that there's a fresh fire in my chamber and her grace's. Send Evans up immediately. And Marie, too."

The duke had pulled his drenched wife into his embrace and shot a worried look at her before mounting the stairs and ensconcing Bonny in her dry room.

From behind her screen, Bonny threw off wet clothes while a procession of servants carried pans of hot water to her room. Marie assisted Bonny with her bath, then Bonny slipped into her shift and sat at her dressing table while Marie worked wonders with her hair, pinning it back into a Grecian style that hid its wetness. Marie curled little ringlets to frame Bonny's face, and by the time she assisted her into a rose-colored gown, the ringlets had dried.

Marie stood back to survey her mistress. "I am so very glad that his grace likes ye in colorful gowns. Mourning don't suit one as pretty as yer grace." Her eyes darted to the low-cut neckline. "His grace may want ye to wear a pelisse. He seemed sorely worried ye would take the death of cold. The duke is most surely a man in love."

Bonny dabbed perfume behind her ear. If only those words were true. She could understand why Marie suspected Richard of caring. In truth, he really did care about her. But he cared for his horse, his groom, his snuffbox collection. And now that she was his wife, he seemed over-solicitous of her. A smile brightened her face. Perhaps those feelings were deepening to love.

"I had best get ye a shawl to keep his grace from worrying so." Marie found one of ivory cashmere and draped it across her mistress's shoulders as Bonny absently stroked its softness.

From the mirror on her dressing table, Bonny saw Radcliff steal into her chamber, and a quick smile lit her face. Dressed for dinner, he held a large velvet box. "That will be all, Marie," Bonny said, her eyes fastened to her husband's.

Marie turned to face the duke and curtsied.

"You are free the rest of the night, Marie," Radcliff said. "The duchess will not need your assistance getting ready for bed."

A knowing smile swept across Marie's face as she left the room; color rose to Bonny's cheeks.

"How very embarrassing, Richard." Bonny tried to sound annoyed. "You might as well have told her you planned to undress me."

He reached her in two long strides, threw her shawl to the ground and bent to gently kiss her neck. "Very well, I will next time."

"I beg that you don't."

His lips moved up to her ear and he whispered, "As lovely as you look, my dear, I fear something is missing."

She slowly swiveled to face him, her expression puzzled.

He opened the velvet box and withdrew an elaborate diamond necklace. "These. The Radcliff Jewels."

She had never seen so many diamonds in one place. "Oh, Richard, I should be afraid to wear anything so valuable."

He unfastened the clasp and draped the heavy necklace around Bonny's neck. "Nonsense. They are yours. They belong to the reigning Duchess of Radcliff."

As thoroughly as she belonged to Richard, Bonny still had a difficult time believing she *was* the Duchess of Radcliff. Her fingers traced the larger stones. Would the necklace pass to the wife of their son? If only she could give Radcliff a son.

After he fastened the necklace, her husband proffered his crooked arm and escorted her to dinner.

* * *

From the drawing room Stanley had a view of the foot of the main stairway. A man of excellent taste, he appreciated the magnificent grilled ironwork of the balusters. The first duke had found a Parisian artisan to create and carry out the pattern for him. While Stanley was contemplating the artistry, he heard his cousin's voice and soft female laughter. When the duke and duchess came into view, he quite caught his breath, his eyes lifting from the soft sweep of Bonny's breasts, up her elegant ivory neck to her incredible face. God's teeth, but she was beautiful. He rose to his feet to meet them.

Radcliff saw him first and halted on the oriental carpet at the foot of the stairs, a puzzled look on his face. "Stanley? What a surprise to see you here."

"Carstairs did not tell you?"

"Tell me what?"

"That I came when you were out this afternoon."

Radcliff hooked his arm around Bonny. "I regret to say I did not allow the poor fellow a chance to speak." He gazed into Bonny's face. "That sudden storm this afternoon drenched the duchess and me. Allow me to introduce my wife—"

"But I have met Mr. Moncrief," Bonny said, directing a smile at her husband's cousin.

Stanley bowed. "Your most obedient servant, your grace."

"Come, let us eat," Richard said. "That storm made me hungry. I daresay if my household knew you were here, they set a place for you."

The staff had, indeed, set three places at the long table. Richard sat at the head, with his wife and cousin on either side and two footmen seeing to their every need.

"I thought from her grace's elegant appearance that more than just the three of us would be here," Stanley said.

"The duchess dresses thus to please me."

Stanley's eyes flitted from Bonny to Radcliff.

"And," Bonny added, separating her pheasant from its skin, "we are not given to entertaining because I am in mourning."

"Her grace's mother died immediately after we married," Radcliff explained.

Damn his luck, Stanley thought. If the old woman had only died a day earlier, the mourning daughter would have been forced to postpone her wedding. "How very surprised I was to learn of your marriage, which actually I did not learn of until today. The announcement in the *Gazette* was hard enough to believe."

"The reason for the haste was that Barbara's mother desired to see us marry before she died."

So that explained the hurried ceremony, Stanley thought. "I was also surprised because I did not think you well acquainted with Miss Allan." He held up his empty wineglass as a silent command to the nearest footman, who readily refilled it.

The duke's knuckles whitened around his fork and he spoke defiantly. "You forget, cousin, my wife is no longer Miss Allan."

Stanley turned on one of his dazzling smiles. "To be sure."

Radcliff relaxed and spoke more kindly to Stanley. "What brings you to Hedley Hall?"

"There is a private matter I wish to discuss with you, and I also wanted to offer my congratulations."

"Anything you have to say can be said in front of my wife."

God, but he must be besotted with her to give the chit that kind of trust. Stanley only hoped it wasn't too late. If she were with child... Well, it did not bear thinking of. One thing perfectly clear was that Richard must be in love.

But what of his young bride? "I would rather not discuss it in female company. What I have to tell you could offend female sensibilities."

"Very well," the duke agreed. "We'll take brandy in the salon once we have finished dining." His eyes darted to his wife.

"I will select a book from your library while you speak with your cousin," Bonny told her husband.

Stanley was rather proud of his ability to adjust to shattered plans. His goal now was to keep the duke and duchess apart, to do what he could to prevent conception of a sixth Duke of Radcliff, while at the same time attempting to separate the duke and duchess in a permanent way. And he had been able to think of a plan to set his scheme in motion without uttering a single lie.

In the salon after dinner, Radcliff refused to sit down but instead paced the patterned carpet, sipping brandy and smoking a cigar.

The duke's almost hostile treatment of him angered Stanley. Richard never had liked him. Well, he would show him.

"And what is this matter that might offend my wife's delicate sensibilities?" Radcliff spun around to glare at his cousin.

"Knowing what a particular friend, James Edward Twickingham—Twigs—is of yours, I thought you would want to know what has happened to him."

"To Twigs?" the duke said, his eyes rounding. "He's not—"

"No, my dear fellow, he's not dead. At least he wasn't when I left London."

Radcliff's voice when he spoke was filled with concern. "What has happened to him?"

"He has suffered a great many broken bones and is currently laid up at his town house. There are those of us who fear he is not being seen to adequately. He won't allow his parents to know what has happened. They have been out of charity with him for quite some time, I understand.''

"Damn it, man, how did he break these bones?"

"That is the delicate subject I wish to impart to you. It seems one night Twigs and many of your crowd were rather deep in their cups and made a wager that Twigs would not swim naked in the Thames. To which Twigs bet he would.''

"In the dead of winter?"

"Just so.''

The two men exchanged amused grins.

"But that is not what caused his injuries. It seems he sustained the injuries as he got out of the water, naked as a nymph, just as the carriage bearing the Duke and Duchess of York drove by. I myself was not there, but I have been told that Twigs moved faster than one chased by a swarm of bees and leapt over a brick wall—the result of which was a broken leg, broken arm, broken rib and a multitude of bruises.''

"All of this certainly explains why he doesn't want his parents to know.''

Stanley looked into his brandy snifter. "As I understand, his parents have been most displeased with what they consider his immaturity.''

"I am not privy to his parents' likes and dislikes.'' A deep frown furrowed Radcliff's brow. "You say he is at his London address?"

"Yes, with only his man to look in on him. From what I have heard, he is most subject to taking a dangerous infection and dying. And he is also very lonely. He does not know I am here, but I believe your presence in London is what he needs to begin the mending process.''

"By all that's holy, I'll move him to my place in Berkeley Square, and Barbara and I will do our damnedest to nurse him back to good health.''

A smug, satisfied smile spread across Stanley's face. It was a start.

Bonny selected Dante's *Divine Comedy* in Latin and took it to her chamber. Since her husband had told Marie not to come, she dressed herself for bed in a soft white muslin nightgown. She put the Radcliff Jewels back in the velvet case, sat at her dressing table and began to brush her long tresses, which by now had dried thoroughly.

Through her mirror, she saw her fully clothed husband enter from his dressing room. He pressed a kiss on top of her head. ''I did not at all like you wearing that indecent gown tonight,'' her husband said. ''Why did you not at least wear a shawl?''

''You, sir, threw it off.''

''I did not know at the time another man would be raking his eyes over you.''

Bonny's own eyes twinkled.

Richard turned his back to her, folding his hands behind him as he began to pace. ''I fear we must go to London tomorrow, my love.''

She turned round to face him, frowning. She had begun to feel secure here with just the two of them. London and its myriad attractions could take her husband from her. ''Why?''

''Twigs is very much in need of me. How would you perform as nursemaid, my dear?''

She swallowed. ''I will do whatever you desire, sir.'' He nodded absently but was not looking at her. She could tell his mind was on other matters. ''Is your friend sick?''

''He has suffered many broken bones and may have taken a fever to boot.''

''Is no one looking after him?''

"Only his man."

"Then we must go tomorrow."

"Yes. I shall alert Evans." He turned on his heel and left.

After he was gone, Bonny lightly smoothed perfume over her pulse and on her throat, thinking of Richard's face buried in its scent. She daringly stroked a dab between her breasts.

When she finished at the dressing table, she brought the candle to her bedside and, climbing on the bed, began to read by its light, propping herself up on lacy pillows and draping her coal black tresses over her shoulder. She must look wide-awake when Richard came back. Kind soul that he was, he would not want to disturb her if she seemed tired.

Richard's presence in her bed could never be unwelcome. She had grown to love their intimate encounters and waking to the heat of him beside her.

The candle burned steadily as she read words that no longer had meaning for her. Her mind was engaged with thoughts of Richard, listening for his footsteps, hungering for him.

When the candle burned out, she turned her head into the pillow, an emptiness deep within her.

He would not come tonight.

Chapter Eleven

Viewing her new town house after a long day's travel did not diminish Bonny's first impression of the stately home at the head of Berkeley Square. After the liveried footman assisted her from the traveling coach, Bonny stared at the white mansion illuminated by a half-dozen gaslights. It was as large for a town house as Hedley Hall was for a country home.

"All this for just one person?" she asked her husband.

He waited several seconds before answering. "Two now." He never responded to anything without carefully developing a reply and delivering it in his most serious manner. Why couldn't levity come more easily to her husband? Bonny wondered, gazing at the stern cut of his face, the corners of his wonderful mouth tugging southward.

"And what rooms have you had redone here, sir?" Bonny asked.

"I had thought to have yours done before we came to London, but since I decided only yesterday to travel here, your chamber remains as it was in my mother's day." He ushered her through the double doors.

A thousand candles in crystal chandeliers and gilded sconces around the damask walls lightened the broad hall.

A flurry of impressions hit Bonny. The attentive servants in the same crimson livery as at Hedley Hall, the checkered floor of alternating black and white marble, the huge ancestral portraits staring down at her from beside the baroque staircase.

She met her husband's steady gaze. "You sent someone ahead to announce our arrival."

Her husband's harsh features softened slightly. "To be sure, my dear."

He introduced her to a whole new staff headed by Mandley, the butler, and Mrs. Henson, the housekeeper, who looked remarkably like Mrs. Green.

"I hope I don't call you Mrs. Green," Bonny said. "You resemble very much our housekeeper at Hedley Hall."

The woman's shriveled face brightened, and her faded eyes flickered with mirth. "But Sarah's my sister, your grace."

"Ah, lovely! If you are half as capable as your sister, I shall count myself most fortunate," Bonny said.

"The duchess is tired from the journey," Radcliff said. "You can show her around tomorrow, Mrs. Henson. I shall take her to her chamber. Perhaps you could send up a small repast."

"Cook's already taken care of that. It will be up momentarily. I also saw to it that the linens were changed in the old duchess's chamber, and there's a fire in the hearth."

Upstairs, Bonny appreciatively eyed the old duchess's room of ivory and gold. It did not at all appear to need updating. "Oh, Richard, I think it's charming just the way it is." She went to pull off her black pelisse, and he came to assist her, the corners of his mouth turning up ever so slightly.

"But you know I prefer that you are surrounded by color, preferably the color of your eyes."

The feel of his strong hand brushing across her shoulder had the power to make her knees cottony.

"And if you must wear that blasted mourning, we'll have Madame Deveraux make up some for you. She is all the rage with women of fashion."

Bonny's stomach sank as she wondered if he had ever taken Lady Heffington to Madame Deveraux.

A soft knock sounded at her door, and she opened it to Marie, who went straight to her mistress's portmanteau and began to unpack.

Radcliff strode toward a doorway on the other side of the room. "Like Hedley Hall, my dear, my dressing chamber connects our rooms here. I will divest myself of these riding clothes."

The next caller at Bonny's door proved to be Mrs. Henson bringing up a tray, which she set on a small table between two French chairs. Bonny noted with disappointment there was only one glass. Was her husband not going to join her?

When Marie finished unpacking, she helped Bonny into a nightgown, then removed the pins from her hair and brushed it out, babbling on the whole while about her excitement over London. Bonny only half listened. Her mind was on Richard. Why hadn't he returned to her room? He had avoided her last night and had chosen to ride his horse today rather than share the coach with her. And now she was left in a strange room to eat alone.

Evans hovered around his master. "Your grace's complexion has become unfashionably dark from spending so much time in the outdoors of late. It is most agreeable that you have returned to town life."

Radcliff cocked an eyebrow at his valet. "I find I prefer the country life."

"Do I understand that the country life you always found

so sadly lacking now has an appeal for you?'' Evans assisted Radcliff from his jacket, fashioned by Weston himself to fit the duke's muscled torso to perfection.

"Things are different when one has a family. I am too old to continue with the young man's pursuits that have occupied me these last dozen years.''

Evans stiffened and proceeded to brush his master's coat. "It is regrettable the old duchess is not here to instruct her grace in the ways of the nobility.''

"The new duchess will do admirably.'' The duke took a seat and began to loosen his Hessians.

With no need for words between the two, Evans came and helped Radcliff remove the boots.

"Quite so, but her grace does seem rather young.''

Was Evans jealous of Barbara? Radcliff remembered the mornings when he would share his day's plans with Evans, and sometimes lament the activities of the preceding night. But Barbara had usurped Evans. She had become his closest friend as well as his lover. It was she who now shared his mornings. He thought of her black hair fanning across the silken sheets, of her waking in his arms, a smile on her gentle lips. And a knot of emotion unraveled deep within him.

After Marie left, Bonny approached her husband's dressing chamber nervously. He wasn't there. She opened the next door—the door to his room. On a small table she saw his untouched dinner.

"Richard, I thought perhaps you could join me for din—'' she announced as she walked into her husband's chamber and confronted a stern-faced Evans, who was in front of her husband. She stood there blushing in her nightgown before she gathered up the presence of mind to turn her back to the unfriendly valet and return to her chamber.

"I'll be there in just a moment, my dear," her husband called.

He soon joined her, bringing his tray with him, and fell into a chair. "I'm awfully fatigued."

"If your muscles are sore from riding Sultan all day, I am glad," Bonny said poutingly. "Leaving me to ride in the lonely barouche."

He tore off a chunk of the cold mutton on his tray. "So you missed my company?"

"Today—and last night."

A crooked smile crinkled his tanned face. "I can assure you that I will not allow you to spend your first night in a strange new bed alone."

On his way out the following morning, the duke paused at the sideboard in the entrance hall to look over the calling cards that had been left in his absence. Most of them were from other bucks who comprised his set. No doubt they wanted to announce Twigs's unfortunate accident. But one card caused him to stiffen, and an earthquake rumbled and surged and cracked his insides. Addressed to his wife, it was from the Earl of Dunsford.

Returning to her aunt and uncle's on Cavendish Square, Bonny was seized with a sense of unreality. Only three months before, dressed in a severely wrinkled and outdated dress, she had stepped off a crowded stagecoach, utterly alone, to face for the first time the thriving city known as the capital of the world. Now, a stylish barouche pulled by matching bays and sporting the crest of the Duke of Radcliff drew up to Wickham House, and a driver, a coachman, two outriders and a tiger—all in the crimson livery of the Moncriefs—danced attendance on her. In the span of twelve weeks, she had leapt from frightened schoolgirl to contented woman, from modest virgin to passionate wife.

Bonny's altered circumstances failed to win her aunt's approval, though.

"Forgive me, Barbara," Lady Landis remarked in cool tones as the three women sat down on a silken sofa for tea in the drawing room of Wickham House, "for not calling you 'your grace.' I know you truly are, but I cannot bring myself to address you thus. It seems like only yesterday you were nursing at Cynthia's breast."

"Pray, don't think of me any differently. I'm still the same Bonny Barbara, only now it's Bonny Barbara Moncrief, who happens to be a duchess." Bonny, too, had a hard time believing she was, indeed, a duchess. She directed her gaze at Emily and her heart plummeted. The color was once again gone from her cousin's pale cheeks. Her swept-back blond hair seemed as lifeless as her thin face. Like a funeral wreath, sorrow hung around her.

Lady Landis poured steaming tea into heavily gilded porcelain cups and handed one to Bonny. "So sorry about your mother. David took it very hard indeed. Of course I tried to console him by telling him how very happy Cynthia must have been at her passing to know that a duke had married her cherished daughter—for to know Cynthia was to know how she positively doted on you, Barbara."

"Then if you knew Mama so well," Bonny said stiffly, "you also know that she didn't give a button for rank."

"Certainly not for herself. David tells me any number of peers offered for her when she was presented. She was still beautiful at thirty when I met her."

"But she never wanted to be the wife of anyone except Papa, even though he was only a country vicar."

Lady Landis poured a second serving of tea into her own cup, having impatiently gulped down the first. "Very noble of her, I'm sure," she said without conviction, holding her chin in such a manner so as to tighten the sagging flesh beneath it. "Of course, Ronald Allan was awfully handsome."

"No wonder Bonny's so beautiful, with both her parents so uncommonly good-looking."

Lady Landis ignored her daughter's comment. "Despite what you say about your mother's indifference to titles, as a mother, I know she had to be thrilled with your match."

Bonny's smile widened. "She was." She remembered how acutely her mother was aware of her feelings for Richard.

"As I will be if ever my very unobliging daughter would give encouragement to any of the circle of men who pay court to her," Lady Landis said. "Do you know she actually turned down an offer from the Marquis of Eden!"

"Mama!" Emily protested. "He was older than Papa and as round as a billiard ball. I'd kill myself before I'd marry him."

"Pray, don't talk about killing yourself," her mother commanded. "Your father and I will not force you to marry."

Emily left her biscuits untouched. "I am most grateful to hear that."

Lady Landis's bejeweled hand swept back the loose tendrils of her silver-threaded auburn locks. "I am convinced you nearly won the hand of a very handsome peer, only to lose him to a scheming country miss."

"You may be sure I have no notion what you're talking about, Mama," Emily said, her cheeks hot.

Bonny's cup clattered as she set it down firmly on the table. "I would like Em to accompany me to Madame Deveraux's today. Richard insists that I purchase more fashionable mourning wear." Bonny knew her aunt would not object to her daughter being seen in the establishment of the most fashionable modiste in London.

Eyes narrowed, Lady Landis said, "Allow me to suggest

that you put yourself in the duke's hands, Barbara, since you know nothing of the ways of the exalted. And, of course, I will be most happy to assist you in any matters of judgment.''

Bonny got to her feet. "How very kind of you," she said dryly.

As pleased as Bonny was to see Emily again, she longed even more to see baby Harriet. Once inside the Radcliff barouche, the two young women could speak in private.

"To be perfectly honest, Em, I'm quite mad to go to Kepple Street and play with Harriet."

"You will not believe how she has grown. She quite babbles all the time now and plays with her feet and giggles over them." Emily's whole demeanor changed when she spoke of her child. Liveliness lit her eyes and a smile transformed her solemn face.

How Bonny wanted her own baby, and how she pitied Emily for having to hide what she loved most.

The ride from Cavendish Square to Kepple Street was accomplished in mere minutes. When the driver came to a stop in front of Bonny's former servant's house, Emily exclaimed, "But Bonny, you cannot risk someone of the ton seeing your coach here."

Bonny had not thought about the Radcliff crest mounted on the barouche, announcing to everyone that the Duchess of Radcliff visited these quarters. That would never do! What if her husband questioned her about it? She had sworn not to reveal Emily's secret.

The coachman came to open the door.

"Please tell the driver I was mistaken in the address," Bonny said. Remembering a square they had passed a few blocks before, she instructed the driver to take them there.

The ladies got out and strolled through the park of the square, then headed to the Kepple Street house, where they visited with the baby for half an hour before hastening back to the barouche and making a quick trip to Madame Deveraux's.

At Madame Deveraux's, Bonny told the modiste she wanted mourning gowns in muslin and in sarcenet, with matching pelisses. She also ordered a hooded black cloak trimmed in black fur with a muff to match.

As Bonny and Emily were leaving the shop, Lady Lynda Heffington entered. A pang of jealousy seized Bonny when she looked at the beautiful woman, whose rust-colored dress and matching pelisse and hat fit to perfection and complemented her milky skin and copper hair.

The older woman glanced at Bonny, went white and came to a sudden stop. "Why, you're...you're the Duchess of Radcliff," Lady Heffington said, fixing a smile on her face.

Bonny drew up stiffly. They had never been introduced, so Bonny decided to act as if she did not know who Lady Heffington was.

Lady Heffington regained her composure. "Allow me to introduce myself. I'm Lady Lynda Heffington, and Richard is a particular friend of mine."

More than a particular friend, Bonny thought. They had been lovers. Had Richard known her body as he knew Bonny's? Had he traced his fingers over her lovely cheeks and nose and mouth and breasts as he had Bonny's? Had he ever called her the names he whispered to Bonny when she lay silently against his bare chest? Wretched emotions surged through her. She swallowed the lump in her throat, extended a black-gloved hand and tilted her head slightly toward Emily. "And this is my cousin, Lady Emily Wickham."

Lady Heffington nodded at Emily, then turned back to Bonny. "I see you are in mourning."

"Yes. My mother died immediately after Richard and I

wed. It had been a last wish of hers to see us marry before she died."

"So that's why you married in such haste." Lady Heffington pushed forward. "You'll tell Richard you saw me?"

Her cheeks hot, Bonny replied, "What was your name again?"

Lady Heffington's eyes narrowed. "Just say Lady Lynda."

"The nerve of that lightskirt!" said an outraged Emily once they were in the carriage. "Calling the duke by his first name. Has she no manners? I must say, I quite reveled in the way you pretended not to know her."

"In truth, I never have met her. And Richard has never spoken of her."

"I should hope not!"

The Radcliff coach deposited Emily back home before returning to Berkeley Square. Bonny had barely removed her pelisse before Mandley announced that the Earl of Dunsford awaited her in the drawing room. She had forgotten all about him and his desire to meet Emily.

Bonny swept into the dark room at the front of the house, which was shuttered for mourning, and held out her hand. "How very nice to see you again, my lord."

"It's very kind of you to see me, your grace. May I offer you my felicitations on your marriage?"

"Thank you. Please sit down. I've ordered tea."

He folded his long legs and sat upon the satin settee, nervously turning his signet ring. "I am glad we are alone," he finally said. "For what I have to say is of a private nature."

She shot him a puzzled glance.

"I do not know the identity of your friend who was my brother's lover, but I do know this about her—she is the mother of my brother's babe."

His words slapped Bonny, leaving her dazed. How could she respond to him? She had given Emily her word never to discuss the baby with anybody.

"There's no use denying it, your grace. And I assure you I harbor no malice toward your friend. Quite the contrary. Harry loved her very much. He wrote me of how he planned to marry her. And if she loved Harry, I would have to look favorably on her. As for the babe, I want to know if I have a niece or a nephew."

"My lord, you can't know of what you speak!"

"Oh, but I do," he said firmly. "You see, my brother's man imparted to me the particulars. He was with Harry on the Peninsula, you know."

The tea was brought in and Bonny served the earl, punctuating the silence with inquiries as to whether his lordship cared for sugar and cream or if his lordship would like a scone.

Her duty done, Bonny got to her feet and began to pace the room. She stood before the tall window that looked out over Berkeley Square. She watched a nurse wheel a baby through the park. And she thought of baby Harriet. Of how Emily professed that she was the image of her father. She remembered the earl dancing with her and speaking of his dead brother, his voice cracking with emotion. She remembered him telling her there were just the two brothers. Then she knew what she must do.

She turned to face the earl. "You have a niece. Harriet. Named for her father."

His face cleared, his eyes softening. "Have you seen her?"

Bonny nodded. "I am told her resemblance to your brother is remarkable."

"She is in London?"

"She stays with my old nurse on Kepple Street. No one knows, save her mother and I."

"I must see the babe."

Bonny turned back to gaze out the window. She saw her husband's coach and four coming up Berkeley Street and her heart swelled with love. "You must go now," she said, facing the earl. "I shall ride in Hyde Park in the morning. If you meet me there in a coach, I will take you to Kepple Street."

With his heart constricted, Radcliff watched the Earl of Dunsford's lanky legs skip down the steps of Radcliff House. The lout had wasted no time in renewing his friendship with the duchess. The very thought of Dunsford with his wife made the duke want to run his fist through a wall.

Chapter Twelve

Before the patient arrived, Bonny went to inspect the room Twigs would occupy. On her orders, the morning room had been converted to a sickroom. A half tester bed now occupied the center of the brightly lit room. On either side of the bed, tables of substantial size featured any number of conveniences: a bell to summon servants, copies of the *Morning Post, Royalist* and *Gazette,* playing cards, pen and paper and a water pitcher and drinking glass.

When Bonny heard her husband enter Radcliff House, she hastened to meet him, but the troubled look on his face alarmed her. Had Twigs died? Slowly, she approached her husband and placed a tender hand on his arm. "Has something happened to Twigs?" she asked softly.

Her husband's gaze moved from her hand, resting gently on his arm, to the worried look on her face, and he spoke without emotion. "His man and Evans are assisting him in now."

"Thank heavens! From your grave face, I thought—well, it does not signify." She dropped her hand. "Are you all right, sir?"

His eyes darted to the drawing room. "I get along tolerably."

"I thought we would put Mr. Twickingham in the morning room. We've moved a bed and everything there for him, and it will be much easier than carrying him upstairs on a stretcher."

"A very good idea." Radcliff began to stroll toward the sickroom. "And when he is able to get about a bit he won't have to maneuver the stairs."

"Exactly." Bonny heard voices and turned toward the front doorway as the two valets angled in the stretcher bearing a solemn James Edward Twickingham.

"Twigs, old fellow," said Radcliff, who had abandoned his inspection of the sickroom to greet his greatest friend. "I would like to present you to my wife." Radcliff moved to Bonny's side.

The infirm young man met Bonny's gaze. He was fair and frail-looking, with light brown hair and eyes that were green at the core and surrounded by pink, and which—like his long nose—had a tendency to water freely.

Bonny wondered if his slenderness was the result of his accident or a lifelong condition. She walked up to the stretcher, displaying her friendliest smile, and held out her hand. "Mr. Twickingham, we are so very happy to have you with us."

Twigs broke eye contact with her and glanced around the room. "You're the duchess?"

"I am."

"Too young. Remember the old duchess. Very old woman. You sure you're the duchess?"

The duke walked up to the stretcher. "She's the duchess, Twigs. Remember, she was Bonny Barbara Allan, Alfred Wickham's cousin."

"'Pon my word, quite taken with her, you were, Richard. So this is the chit you married?" Color rose to his face. "So sorry, your grace," he said to Bonny. "Not a chit. Don't know what I was thinking to say such a thing."

"That's quite all right, Mr. Twickingham," Bonny said. Now he looked behind him.

"She's talking to you, Twigs," the duke said.

"Oh, quite so," Twigs replied, taking a long sniff. "Not used to anyone calling me Mr. Twickingham. Thought me father had come."

Radcliff met his wife's amused gaze. "He's right, my dear. Everyone calls him Twigs."

"Then I shall, too." Addressing the valets, Bonny said, "You may take Mr. Twigs into the morning room."

After the patient was settled in, the Duke and Duchess of Radcliff sat in the side chairs beside Twigs's bed.

Bonny spoke more to her husband than to his friend. "Twigs seems to be quite healthy, apart from his disabilities."

"Yes. I talked with his doctor, and he said he is already greatly improved over what he was two days ago. The fever is completely gone."

"Now we just need to keep him so busy he won't have time to dwell on his inactivity," Bonny said.

Radcliff nodded, his face grim. "I see we had a caller today."

We? she wondered. "Oh, you mean the Earl of Dunsford. An old friend. He came to offer felicitations on our marriage."

"Do you think it's proper for you to entertain male callers with no chaperon?"

Bonny laughed out loud. "Richard! I'm a married woman."

"I must say," Twigs said, "seems quite queer to think of you as a married man, ol' chap. Won't be the same ever again, 'pon my word."

Radcliff spoke to his friend in a tone such as a father might use with a son. "It's time we were settling down."

Mandley entered the room quietly. "Would your grace be requiring any refreshments?"

"Richard," Twigs whispered, "tell him we want brandy."

"I'll do no such thing. The doctor said you need to decrease your consumption of spirits."

Twigs wiped at his watery eye with the back of his bony hand. "Hog's breath. What does that Methodist know?"

The duke dismissed Mandley, reached into the fob of his waistcoat and took out his watch. "You may have a glass of port at six o'clock." He picked up a deck of cards from the bedside table. "I see, my dear, that you have provided us with cards. Piquet, Twigs?"

A smile spread across the patient's face. "A capital idea, ol' fellow."

Bonny rose to leave, and Radcliff held out his arm to stop her. "Do you play?"

"Not in a very long time," she said. "I used to play with my father."

"Watch us to refresh your memory so that you can play with Twigs when I can't be here."

Her husband's touch and his desire that she stay had the power to send Bonny's pulse racing. She quickly sat back down and watched with amusement as Radcliff easily relieved Twigs of his guinea-a-game wagers. Before an hour passed, Twigs's eyelids grew heavy.

"I'm afraid I've tired you," Radcliff said, moving to leave.

Twigs jerked up, then winced from the pain of the sudden movement. "No such thing! Haven't been so amused in weeks."

"Nevertheless," Radcliff said, getting to his feet, "the duchess and I will take our leave." His voice softened and he laid a hand on his friend's arm. "Oblige me by resting."

Twigs pouted.

"And your reward will be a bumper of Madeira," Radcliff promised.

Closing Twigs's door behind them, the duke strode across the marble hall. "I have business to attend in the library, my dear."

"Would it bother you if I come? I should like to write a letter." Bonny wanted desperately to prolong her time with Radcliff, not just because she enjoyed and craved his presence, but because she sensed a moroseness about him that deeply disturbed her.

His face as inscrutable as ever, Radcliff said, "Not at all. Should you like to sit before the fire while I use the desk?"

She nodded, lifting her gaze to his and smiling.

His jaw tightened and he looked away quickly before leading her into the pea green library of dark wood, tooled leather volumes and a blazing hearth.

Bonny took writing paper from her husband's desk, sat beside the fireplace in a club chair and began chiding herself. She was not fit to be a duchess. A well-bred duchess would be sitting upstairs right now in her gilded lady's study penning her letter at the escritoire in front of the rose-moiré-draped window. She wouldn't be foisting her company on a husband obviously occupied with more important matters, obviously not desirous of her presence.

Without speaking, her husband sat at his desk going over some papers for several minutes before he set down his papers and asked, "Do you write to a friend?"

Bonny looked up from her writing. "Yes, I suppose. Cressida Carlisle. She said she would call on me, and since we left without notice the very next day, I thought it only courteous that I write, explaining that we were suddenly called to town."

"Very thoughtful of you, my dear."

"Truth be told, I feel sorry for her. Cressida seems quite

lonely and hungry for the companionship of another young woman.''

The corners of his mouth lifted ever so slightly. ''Young woman? Funny, I more readily accept her as a young woman than I do you, despite that she's more than a decade older than you.''

''I'm wondering if I should be offended by your remark.''

''You may be sure that I find you a mature woman even if you are but eighteen.'' His eyes locked with hers, and the air became charged, then he looked away. ''On the other hand, I shall always think of Cressy as an emptyheaded girl, though she be one and thirty.''

''Do I take it that you prefer mature women, sir?''

His gaze flitted over her body and the dimple reappeared in his cheek. ''To be sure.''

Radcliff had made her a woman, and she wore his brand as proudly as a coronet. Hands trembling, Bonny returned to her letter. A minute later, she said, ''Speaking of mature women, I met a friend of yours this morning at Madame Deveraux's.''

He raised an eyebrow.

''A Lady Lynda...''

''Heffington.'' He picked up his papers again, his face as unreadable as a stone wall.

''She referred to you as Richard. Are you very old friends?''

''We have long been acquainted.'' He put his papers down again. ''How did you find Mrs. Deveraux?''

Bonny would oblige her husband and avoid talk of Lady Heffington. Or was she sparing her own feelings? The thought of him lying with Lady Heffington was torture. ''She assisted me personally and seemed quite happy to have the patronage of the Duchess of Radcliff. I hope I can learn to act like a proper duchess.''

He raised his chin, looked at her squarely, and spoke with authority. "You are a proper duchess."

Whether from the crackling fire or her husband's words, warmth spread through Bonny like brandy.

As she neared the finish of her letter, she spoke again to her husband. "What would you think of my inviting Cressida to London?"

Radcliff closed his account book and chuckled. "The offer would be most generous of you, but, pray, there is a limit to how much dinnertime prattle I can tolerate. How long would she have to stay?"

"Never mind," Bonny said softly. "I shouldn't want to annoy you, Richard."

"I am just as concerned about annoying you, my dear. I'm afraid steady doses of Cressida Carlisle would be quite tedious."

"I shan't ask her."

He shoved his papers aside. "Now you make me feel like an ogre."

"You're not an ogre, Richard," Bonny said in her silken voice. "You're kind and good."

"You, my love, are the kind one. Always worrying about the other person from dear Twigs to Cressy Carlisle."

"Pooh. You're the one who's flown to town to look after a sick friend." She placed her pen on her papers. "What did the doctor tell you about Twigs?"

A heavy frown creased Radcliff's brow. "For now, he needs to stay off the leg, but the boredom has played heavily on him. The doctor gave me to understand that Twigs is threatened by severe melancholy."

"Then your presence has helped already," she said cheerfully, "for he did not seem melancholy in the least this afternoon."

"I hope that you may be right."

"I heard what you said about the drinking of spirits. Is Twigs overly partial to drink?"

"To be sure, but all the bucks of our circle are so inclined."

"Then I am most happy you decided to marry and quit such a silly crowd."

He looked at her with hooded eyes. "Are you, Barbara?"

"Most heartily," she said with determination.

God's eyes, he could not get that odious Dunsford out of his mind. To think that the earl had come calling on his wife her very first day back in London. Could the man not accept that Bonny had married another and get on with his life?

Could he, Richard Moncrief, the Duke of Radcliff, ever have been able to put Bonny out of his life? It would be easier to quit breathing.

He tried for the fifth time to read the column of figures, but again his mind was otherwise engaged. He turned his attention back to his wife. "I recall your mother speaking of your legacy from your grandmother. Would you like my stockbroker to invest it for you?"

"How thoughtful of you," she said with a shaky voice. "I shall see him tomorrow."

"I...I don't know if I'm quite ready yet."

The worry in her face tore at his heart. Rising, he crossed the room to her side and took her hand in his. "My dear, I don't mean that you need your own money for any reason. Remember when I told you my body would be as yours and yours as mine?"

She nodded, her face grave, her eyes downcast.

He swallowed. "Everything I possess is yours, Barbara."

She brought her hand to his cheek, and he fell to one knee before her chair. "You don't have to do anything with your grandmother's money if you don't want to." He trailed a finger across her cheekbone. "I promise you, you will never need it. You might wish to keep it for our daughter—or a second son.''

Her face brightened. ''Oh, Richard, I hope we shall have a house full of children.''

''I shall do my best to oblige you.'' He drew her tightly into his embrace and buried his head in her breasts, reveling in the feel of her arms gathering around him, the brush of her lips on his hair, the sound of her racing heart beneath his ear.

Freeing his hand, he cupped her breasts, reverently stroking the soft muslin that covered them until her nipples went rigid. Then, his mouth closed over them. She gasped with pleasure. He kissed a trail up her neck until he took possession of her mouth. Her breath coming ever faster, she reached to stroke the swell in his breeches.

Without breaking the hungry kiss, he slowly got to his feet, pulling her with him, holding her so close it was as if there were no clothes between them.

When he pulled away, she moaned and met his gaze, her face like one delirious with fever.

''If we stay here another moment,'' he said throatily, ''I shall have your clothes off, and it will never do to have Mandley see the Duchess of Radcliff disrobed. Shall we go upstairs to finish what we've started?''

She answered him with a hungry nod.

If only he had the power over her heart that he seemed to have over her body, he thought.

Chapter Thirteen

Bonny's chamber was more dark than light as she slipped from the bed. Her movements had not disturbed Radcliff, who lay on his side, his breathing heavy. She quickly dressed in a brown riding habit Emily had discarded, glad that her husband could not see her. Of course, he was too kind to ridicule her meager wardrobe, but she hated to bring him shame. Already she felt totally unprepared to be a duchess and feared the servants mocked her. If only she could have fallen in love with a plain mister or even a mere viscount!

When she finished dressing and went downstairs, shafts of hazy morning light angled through the tall casements. The drowsy footman rose from the low marble bench at the bottom of the stairway.

"Please have the groom bring around an easy stepper for me," Bonny instructed.

He bowed. "Yes, your grace."

The smell of baking bread wafted up from the basement as Bonny looked in on a sleeping Twigs, assuring herself of his well-being.

The lad Rusty brought her horse around. "Ye plannin' to go off by yerself, yer grace?"

"Just for a ride around the park," Bonny said, favoring the freckle-faced youth with a smile.

"I dunno if his grace would be 'appy about that."

"You may be right, Rusty. That is why I do not intend to tell him." She swung around to mount her horse.

He gave her a leg up and she rode off without looking back.

Not far inside Hyde Park, Bonny observed the waiting barouche bearing Dunsford's crest and pulled her mount beside it. Dunsford instructed his groom to help the lady dismount and watch after her horse.

Before she got in the carriage, Bonny gave Dunsford the address on Kepple Street, which he conveyed to the driver. Then, Bonny looked around to satisfy herself that no one was watching.

"I am so very nervous," Bonny told him as she settled back on the soft squabs. "Pray, how would I ever explain this to my husband?"

The lanky blond man across from Bonny shrugged and shook his head sympathetically. "I would not wish to jeopardize your marriage."

Bonny only looked away distractedly.

When the barouche pulled up in front of the house on Kepple Street, Lord Dunsford got out first and looked up and down the street before he allowed Bonny to disembark. Then the two hurried up the steps of Number 17 Kepple Street.

As Mrs. Davies opened the door, a healthy baby wail greeted them. The round old woman with capped head shot Bonny a warm smile. "Lord love a duck, but the babe's as spoiled as last week's milk." Mrs. Davies reached to hug Bonny. "She takes to squallin' the minute I set her down." She glanced at Dunsford. "Is this yer husband?"

Bonny kissed the old nurse's kindly face. "No, this is

Harriet's uncle. Harriet was named for his brother, Harold.''

Mrs. Davies started walking toward the source of the wailing. ''Here we comes, little Miss Harriet. Don't ye be frettin'. Ye've got company.''

The minute Bonny saw Harriet's little blond head poking up from the side of the cradle, she flew to the baby and picked her up. ''Good morning, pretty little girl.''

The baby's tears shut off as if a faucet handle had been turned. She met Bonny's babbling with some good-natured babbling of her own, and soon Bonny had her giggling.

''Uncle Henry has come to see you, pretty girl. You must behave yourself and show him how very sweet you are.''

Bonny turned to him. ''Would you like to hold her?''

He quickly shook his head. ''Oh, not now. I might…I might break her or something.''

''Such a silly man,'' Bonny said to the baby. ''Let's go sit on the divan and invite Uncle Henry to sit beside us.''

''Sometimes she'll take to squallin' if you go and sit down,'' Mrs. Davies said. ''That one likes to walk the floor, she does. Or rock. She don't like to sit still.''

''It was the same with Harry!'' Dunsford said, smiling.

Bonny and Dunsford sat beside each other, with Harriet in Bonny's lap. ''Mrs. Davies, we'll watch if you have things you'd like to do.''

''That I do,'' the old woman said, striding to the door. ''I'll be in the kitchen.''

Bonny set the baby on her lap, facing Dunsford. ''Talk to her, Uncle Henry.''

''By God, she's got Harry's mouth!''

Bonny sat quietly and took pleasure in Dunsford's happy discoveries while her hands absently stroked the baby's soft blond hair.

''Look at that!'' Dunsford exclaimed. ''She smiled at me!'' Then he began to talk to the baby, not quite in baby talk but in a voice very different from his own. Softer. Shriller. "Would you like your uncle to bring you a pretty doll?" He wrinkled his nose as he spoke. "When you're a big girl, Uncle Henry will get you a pony." Now he glanced at Bonny and spoke in a shaky voice. "She's really beautiful. I'm glad she was born."

"Her mother is, too."

"From a good family, eh?"

Bonny nodded.

"Of course, she would be. Harry said she was all that was perfect." His moist eyes returned to the babe. "And just look at Harriet. So beautiful!"

Harriet reached out a chubby hand to pull at Dunsford's mustache. "Ouch!" he shrieked.

The baby giggled at his reaction and reached for his mustache again. At this, he put out his arms and took the baby from Bonny. "Don't guess I can drop her if I'm sitting down."

He played with her, kept her giggling. Eventually he got up enough courage to stand up with her. Dunsford seemed fascinated by everything about the baby and was genuinely disappointed when an hour was up and Mrs. Davies returned.

"So how did the little flirt like her uncle?" Mrs. Davies asked.

"She likes him very well," Bonny said.

"I wasn't sure how she'd take to a man. She's never been around one that I know of."

"I plan to remedy that," he said, hugging the soft little body, a winsome look on his face.

It quite brought a tear to Bonny's eyes and she hurried to wipe it away before he saw her. This was too happy a day for tears.

On the ride back to Hyde Park, Dunsford was far more animated than he had been earlier. "By Jove! That was fun. She's quite the cutest thing I've ever seen. When can we come back?''

''When her mother—who comes often—is *not* going to be here. There is also my husband to consider. He doesn't know about the babe, and I hate being deceitful.''

''To be sure,'' he said thoughtfully.

Through the years, Radcliff and Twigs had shared many a raucous adventure, but seldom had they shared such a domestic scene as they did this morning. The two gentlemen silently took breakfast in the sickroom, sipping their coffee while reading their newspapers. Twigs perused the *Morning Post* while Radcliff tried to read the *Gazette*, attempting to get his mind off his wayward wife. Where had she gone so early this morning? Why wasn't she back yet? His eyes scanned the news from the Peninsula. Did Wellington never make a false move? The man must be a bloody military genius.

Action in the Peninsula likewise held Twigs's interest. ''I say, Richard, those bloods in the army are having a devilishly good time. I've a mind to purchase colors as soon as I can stand on this blasted leg.''

Radcliff lifted his eyes from the newspaper. ''Your life has always been the pursuit of adventure. How old are you now?''

Twigs put down his *Post*. ''Same as you, and well you know it. Four and thirty.''

''We're both too old to live life from one escapade to another. It's time you were settling down.''

''You know I'm not in the petticoat line.''

''That's not exactly accurate. Beginning with the fair Denise at Oxford, I believe you've had your share of encounters with women.''

''Not with women of quality. Wouldn't know how to talk to a proper lady.''

"It's time you learned."

"Too old."

"Nonsense."

"Can't talk of anything but horses and boxing. Women don't want to hear such."

"Some women will feign an interest in anything to catch a gentleman like yourself."

Twigs shook his head. "Maybe for a handsome, titled bloke like you but not for a scrawny, tongue-tied man such as myself."

"You do yourself a disservice. Any number of women are attracted to men who are tall and lean, like you." Radcliff thought bitterly of Dunsford, who was tall and rather thin.

Twigs held out his cup while Radcliff poured more coffee and measured a heaping spoon of sugar into it. "That so?"

Radcliff returned the coffeepot to the silver tray. "To be sure. Brings me to mind of the Earl of Dunsford. He's built very much like you. You know him?"

"Don't I, though. Just before my…my unfortunate accident, I had the pleasure of winning a hefty sum from him at hazard. Fellow's taken to drink and gaming in a big way of late. Mourning his brother."

Say what they will, Radcliff knew it was his loss of Bonny, not his brother, that pushed the earl into the depths of the hells. He folded up his paper. "How about a game of backgammon?"

Twigs's eyes brightened and he straightened, wincing.

"Leg bothering you?" Radcliff did not remove his gaze from his friend.

"No. Just need to be careful how I move."

"Today we are going to force you to walk about a bit. Doctor insists."

Frowning, the patient folded up his newspaper and

placed it on the bedside table as his host readied the backgammon board. "Be back to my old self in no time."

His optimism pleased his friend very much. "Guinea a game again?"

Twigs nodded. "And I know you will pay up—not like that Dunsford. Still owes me twenty quid."

His friend's remarks hit Radcliff like a blow to the chest. Dunsford needed money. Could it be Barbara had given money from her grandmother to him?

The door opened. "There you are!" Bonny said happily, flowing gracefully into the room. She had changed into a day dress from the riding habit. Her laughing eyes met Twigs's. "How's the patient today?"

Discoursing with women of quality did not come easily to Twigs, who shot a worried glance at Radcliff.

"I believe he is much improved. We shall force him to walk today."

A deep frown wrinkled her ivory brow. "Won't it hurt?"

"At first, but the doctor assures me he needs to begin using the leg."

Bonny walked to the bed and laid a gentle hand on Twigs's forehead. "Poor lamb." Assured that he had no fever, she turned to her husband and saw him readying the backgammon board. "So you will amuse one another with backgammon?"

Radcliff did not lift his eyes from his task. "Yes. Tell me, my dear, where have you been this morning?"

"I woke very early and could not go back to sleep, so I decided to go riding in Hyde Park."

"Alone?" Now her husband met her gaze.

"Yes."

"I don't like that at all. You should at least have had a groom with you."

"Don't be angry. Rusty said you wouldn't be happy. He wanted to accompany me, but I particularly wanted to go alone. It would embarrass me exceedingly for anyone to see what an unskilled rider I am—especially you. I'm determined to learn not to embarrass you with my lack of skill."

Radcliff's voice, like his eyes, went soft. "You could never embarrass me, Barbara."

She stepped toward him and leaned to place a kiss on his cheek. "Thank you." Her lips softly brushed his weathered face. Then she swept from the room. "Do call me when you begin to force poor Twigs to walk. I want one of us on each side of him."

After she left the room, Twigs said, "Capital wife you've got there, Richard."

Radcliff still looked at the door where his wife had left. How he loved to fill his eyes with her beauty. And how his heart ached at the thought she might have given her money and her heart to Dunsford.

After dinner that night, Bonny and Radcliff played three-handed loo with Twigs. Bonny had been surprised at Twigs's card-playing skill. Nothing in his personality suggested a glimmer of intelligence. He did not quite have the skill her husband had, but Twigs's skill surpassed her own, and she had been considered an uncommonly good player of all manner of games.

Radcliff broke the seal on a bottle of Malmsey, the three of them enjoying the best Madeira money could buy. Town life wasn't so bad after all, Bonny reflected, if it could stay as it was now. As at Hedley Hall, she enjoyed her little cocoon with her husband and had not objected to bringing Twigs, the dear fellow, into their circle.

Warmed by the blazing fire and the contentment of good friends, she felt quite happy, despite the pain low in her stomach.

But suddenly her face went pale and she set down her

cards. "Gentlemen, I was enjoying the game so much, but I've got a dreadful headache."

Her husband's worried eyes locked with hers. "Should I have Mandley bring you up tisane?"

"Don't bother him. I'll be as good as new in the morning."

Radcliff put down his cards. "Perhaps I should come with you."

"No. I beg you to continue your game. I don't want to be the cause of ending so pleasant an evening."

"It has been great fun," Twigs said.

Radcliff looked from his wife to his friend, then back to his wife again. "If you're sure you're all right."

"I'll be fine."

But she was not fine at all. She hurried to her room to see if her suspicions were accurate. Slamming her chamber door behind her, Bonny removed her gown, then her chemise. As she suspected, it was covered in blood. She had started her monthly flow.

With anger, she flung the chemise atop the dress heaped on the floor. She began to clean herself and prepare for bed. She did not want Marie's help. All she wanted was the comfort of her bed. Her body ached so. As did her heart. She had not had a flow since she had married. She had hoped she was already with child. With Richard's child. And now she felt bereft. They had had so many opportunities to conceive a babe. And yet she had failed. What if she were barren? In every way, she was not worthy to be Richard's wife. Now she could not even give him an heir.

She fell into her bed and began to weep.

Something in his wife's manner worried Radcliff. Or was it in her face? As lightning whitens the dark sky, his wife's lovely face had suddenly paled. He could not continue his levity after she departed, and he ended the game early.

"Worried about the duchess, aren't you?" Twigs said.

"You always could read me like a book." Radcliff placed a steady hand on his friend's shoulder and left the sickroom.

He knocked on his wife's chamber and entered. The golden light from the hearth and her bedside candle bathed the room. Radcliff's eyes shot to the bed where Bonny lay, dressed in a woolen nightgown buttoned to the neck. His wife always wore lovely gowns of lace and satin for him. Then he saw her reddened eyes and heard her sniff.

He hurried to her bedside. "You're not well."

"Truly I am. Don't worry." Then, as a cloud burst, her tears erupted and she began to sob.

He sat at her bedside and scooped her into his embrace, burying her wet face in his shirt. "I shall call the doctor."

"Pray, don't. It's just…it's just that I have my monthly flow." Her sobs nearly prevented her from completing her declaration.

His arms tightened around her. "Is that all? I was so worried about you."

"I'm so dreadfully unhappy, Richard. I had h-h-hoped…" she sobbed. "I had hoped I was with child."

"We've been married less than two months. Sometimes these things take time."

"You're not terribly disappointed?" She lifted her gaze to his.

He smoothed her hair with gently caressing hands. "Not at all. I'm only relieved you're all right."

"But what if I'm barren?" She began to cry softly.

"It's much too early to worry about that, my dear."

"I knew I'd be a terrible wife for you."

He kissed her head. "You're no such thing, and it displeases me when you talk like that. I'm quite happy with my bride—even if you cannot make love to me tonight."

He stayed there holding her, stroking her, whispering endearments until she fell asleep in his arms. He gently eased her down, his heart swelling with pride as he gazed upon her and thought of her great disappointment over not bearing his babe.

Maybe she *had* begun to care for him, this woman who owned part of his soul.

Chapter Fourteen

Nothing had ever fit her so well or looked more becoming than this gown, Bonny thought as she stood back, admiring Madame Deveraux's creation in the looking glass, softly rubbing the rich fabric between her finger and thumb. How nicely this fine-quality silk draped.

She glanced at Emily and Madame Deveraux.

"Oh, Bonny, you look the perfect duchess now," Emily said.

No words could have pleased Bonny more. Even if her new clothes were black, Richard would have to be proud of her appearance. He would have to find her dress worthy of his wife.

"I do hope your grace is pleased, for the fit is most excellent, no?" Madame Deveraux queried as she handed Bonny the fur-trimmed muff that matched her dress.

"The fit is indeed most excellent, and I shall be happy for you to design my entire wardrobe when I am out of mourning."

With a beaming Madame Deveraux nodding agreeably, Bonny wore the modiste's creation out of the shop while one of the footmen in the crimson Radcliff livery trailed behind her, shuffling an armload of parcels.

Settling into the soft squabs of the barouche, Bonny studied her quiet cousin. To someone who knew her less well, Emily would appear the perfect lady with her simple beauty and elegant clothes. But Bonny saw beyond the outward signs of prosperity. She noted the dark circles under her eyes and her cousin's wan countenance. "I thought this morning when we visited with Harriet, the color was coming back to your face," Bonny said, "but now you're sallow as a dove. How can you continue to live like this?"

"I don't know what to do." Emily's voice was strained. "I cried off the Gilberts' rout last night, telling Mama I was out of sorts with a ghastly headache, but I can't do that forever."

"Though I daresay it's not far removed from the truth. The only time you are your old self is when you are with Harriet."

"Just so, but I could never tell my parents about her."

From her carriage window, Bonny watched the warmly bundled equestrians threading through Hyde Park. "Em, perhaps you could go with Harriet to live in Milford. Don't make a decision today. Just think on it. We've kept everything at the old rectory just as it was. Mrs. Green is there, courtesy of Richard's purse."

The corners of Emily's mouth lifted into a smile, and a winsome look crossed her features. "That sounds so wonderful. Just Harriet and I in a little cottage. How happy I would be."

The carriage drew up before Emily's magnificent house in Cavendish Square. Bonny watched Emily mount the steps, holding her bonnet to her head to keep the strong wind from snatching it. Once Emily disappeared into Wickham House, Bonny withdrew from her reticule the note to the Earl of Dunsford she had penned that morning. Having one of her own servants deliver it was out of the question. They all loved Richard too thoroughly, and she could not have them thinking her a disloyal wife. Therefore, she determined to hire a street urchin to carry the dispatch to Harriet's uncle.

Bonny instructed her footman to summon a young hostler hovering about Cavendish Square. A lad whose face was red from the stinging wind approached her window, and Bonny asked him to take the letter to Dunsford House on Half Moon Street. She gave the happy youth a shilling. "Please tell the person who answers the door that Lord Dunsford is to be delivered this note at once."

"Yes, me lady," the boy said, skipping off behind a gig clopping in the direction of Mayfair.

Next, Bonny had her barouche taken to the square near Kepple Street, where she asked her coachman to wait while she took a stroll through the park in the center of the square. Tying her bonnet under her chin, she stepped from the carriage and enclosed both hands in the muff's warmth.

Her stroll, once again, ended up at the house on Kepple Street, and for the second time that day, Bonny paid a visit to Mrs. Davies and Harriet.

Bonny wasn't there five minutes when she heard the Earl of Dunsford's strident voice, followed by heavy steps on the wood floors of the narrow entry hall.

"Excuse my appearance," he told Bonny, straightening his cravat as he entered the parlor. "I came as soon as I received your note. Blasted early in the morning."

Bonny handed over a babbling Harriet to her uncle. "It wouldn't seem so if you went to bed at a tolerable hour, my lord."

"I would not have stayed out so late if my luck had been better. Fact is, I failed to win back my losses in spite of playing till dawn. Just dug myself further into debtor's prison."

Bonny frowned. "I am sorry your luck is so poor and your sleep so short, but it now is the most appropriate time for your visit here, since Harriet's mother left just an hour ago.''

Balancing the blond baby on his left arm, Dunsford poked Harriet's chubby stomach with his right hand. The baby grabbed his index finger, wrapping her pudgy fingers around it.

"Look how strong she is!" the earl exclaimed. "It was the same with Harry. Always smaller than me, but he could outfight me any day. Very strong he was." He turned loving eyes on the baby and attempted to speak in a falsetto voice. "She is such a strong little miss. And so precious." His lips brushed the fine, soft hair on top of her nearly bald head.

They passed barely a half hour in the presence of the happy baby when Bonny said, "You are free to stay, my lord, but I must go."

His lips thinned with disappointment. "I have an appointment myself." He handed the baby over to Mrs. Davies.

Harriet clung to Lord Dunsford and commenced the worst crying spell Bonny had seen, worse even than when Emily left. "It seems Harriet has become very attached to you, my lord."

"You may be sure her love is returned tenfold," he said in a sad tone. "Deuced hard to leave her."

It had been a good session sparring with Jackson, Radcliff reflected as he cracked his whip over the high-stepping bay that drove his phaeton through the narrow streets of London. Too bad Twigs hadn't been there. Capital fun.

From the corner of his eye, Radcliff caught sight of something that struck his subconscious as being incongruous. Within a few seconds he realized what it was. The Earl of Dunsford's barouche was parked in front of a house on this unfashionable street.

Radcliff slowed down to examine the crest on the barouche door. Indeed, it belonged to that no-good blackguard. As he passed on, Radcliff heard a door open and turned to see Dunsford's tall frame coming through the door to a narrow little row house.

Radcliff stared hard at the earl.

What he saw caused his heart to nearly stop beating. Beside Dunsford at the top of the stairs stood his own beautiful wife.

Busy talking to each other, the pair did not see him, and by the time they looked up, he was gone from view.

Though Radcliff could no longer see Dunsford and Barbara, the picture of them standing atop the steps, looking into each other's eyes, was etched into his memory like letters on a gravestone. His hold on the bay slackened, allowing the horse to take him wherever it desired. He did not care.

What did he care about anything? The wind pierced through him, but he did not even button his coat. He'd felt on top of the world since the night Barbara had cried so pitifully with disappointment that she was not with their child. He'd thought she wanted to be his wife in every way. But now his world crumbled beneath him.

Bonny sat staring at the leather backgammon board.

"Your turn to roll," Twigs said.

She picked up the dice, then met Twigs's gaze. "You knew the duchess, Richard's mother, did you not?"

He looked puzzled. "Never played backgammon with her, if that's what you mean."

"No, no. I don't mean that. I would just like to know how a duchess acts." Bonny threw the dice and moved her men along the points accordingly.

"Same as anyone else, I expect." He grabbed the dice and shook them vigorously, watching with delight and then triumphantly moving one man past Bonny's and knocking off another. "By Jove, this is capital fun."

"What I mean is, can you remember anything about her that may have set her apart?"

He pondered her question. "Sat at one end of the dining table. That set her apart."

"You mean while the duke sat at the other end?"

"Right you are."

"I believe that's the customary procedure for the host and hostess, but I mean, did she act any particular way that made one think she was...like royalty?"

He sniffed his perpetually runny nose, then stroked his chin. "Never took breakfast. Leastwise, not downstairs. Took a tray in her room and never came down till afternoon."

The fourth duchess sounded to Bonny like any woman of quality. Bonny threw the dice and moved her men.

"Old duchess was very nice—like the new duchess."

Bonny looked into Twigs's watery eyes. "That's so kind of you. I want to act like a proper duchess. I should die if I embarrassed Richard."

"What the deuce kind of talk is this? 'Pon my word, you could never embarrass him. If you ask me, he's deuced glad to have you."

At this, Bonny got up from her chair and came to hug a red-faced Twigs. "You are so very dear, Twigs."

As she spoke, Bonny heard her husband's voice.

"I'll thank you to keep your hands off my wife."

Bonny turned smiling eyes to her husband. "Oh, but it was me hugging Twigs. He is the dearest man."

Radcliff scowled and moved toward them. "What diversion is it for you, today?" He looked at the backgammon board and frowned. "A game of sheer luck."

"Perhaps that explains why I'm losing so dreadfully," Bonny said, trying to sound flippant to soothe her husband's anger. Surely he couldn't be jealous of poor Twigs. "I would hate to think it was because I have no skill."

Still embarrassed over being kissed by the duchess, Twigs said, "Now that you are here, shall we play something else? Loo?" He knocked his men down and went to fold up the board.

Bonny squeezed her husband's hand and gave him an imploring look. "Do play with us, Richard."

Radcliff threw himself into a nearby chair. "I don't wish to play anything."

Startled by his harsh tone, Bonny sat down beside him, folded her hands in her lap, forced a smile and said, "Very well, Richard. We'll just chat. Have you been boxing today?"

He nodded solemnly.

Twigs's gaze shifted from Radcliff to Bonny. "Capital boxer, Richard. He's the only one I've ever seen who could plant a facer on Jackson."

"What's a facer?" Bonny asked.

"Nothing you need concern your pretty head with, Barbara."

She still did not like her husband's tone, or his dismissal of her.

"Very competitive, Richard. Doesn't like to lose," Twigs said.

"I never lose," Radcliff stated flatly, glaring at his wife. He rose and addressed Twigs. "It's time for you to walk." He bent over the bed and assisted his friend to his feet. Twigs's man had helped him into long pantaloons earlier in the day.

Bonny got on the other side of Twigs to hold him. Twigs put one foot in front of the other while grimacing in pain.

"He's moving much better than last time, don't you think, Richard?"

The duke agreed. "You'll be back in the ring with Jackson before you know it."

"By Jove, need to get my movement back," Twigs said haltingly. "Got a mind to buy colors."

Radcliff cocked an eyebrow and glanced at his wife.

She shrugged. "I fear Twigs has a notion he'd look good in a red coat."

"Fancy that the duchess is right," Twigs said, panting.

"You are most determined to deprive us—permanently—of your company," Radcliff said, one of his arms circling his friend.

"Like a cat, I am. Got a few more lives to use up yet."

They reached the door and turned to go back to the bed. Beads of perspiration bubbled on Twigs's forehead.

Bonny wanted to take his mind off his suffering. "Tell me, Twigs, what is your favorite thing to eat? I must have Cook make it up for you."

He took a breath, then spoke. "Most anything suits me. Put it in front of me, and I'll eat it."

Her eyes scanned his thin body. "But surely there's something you've been craving."

"To tell the truth, been fancying plum cake."

"You shall have it tonight," Bonny said as the three of them reached the bed.

After Bonny dressed for dinner in one of her new gowns, she gently rubbed perfume behind her ears. She kept expecting her husband to come into her room as he often did while she dressed, kissing a trail along her shoulders as he clasped on her necklace. But this night he did not make an appearance. Was he really angry because she had kissed Twigs? Surely her handsome husband could never be jealous of his bumbling friend, but that was the only explanation she could think of that would explain Richard's aloofness that afternoon.

She met her husband in Twigs's room, where they had decided to take dinner, and was disappointed Richard still had not noticed her new gowns. Refusing to accept his inattention, Bonny twirled in front of him. Though black, the elegant gown swooped down in front to the lowest-cut neckline Bonny had ever worn. She knew her full breasts, like her creamy skin, were an asset, and tonight, especially, she wanted to look beautiful for Richard. A train of black illusion fell from the back of the gown. A pair of black satin slippers barely showed below the front hem. Bonny felt confident she looked good. Marie had used curl papers to achieve the Grecian goddess effect with her hair.

"Does your grace, by chance, notice anything different?" Bonny smiled into her husband's stern face.

His pensive eyes studied her almost gravely. "I must say, Madame Deveraux has never had so lovely a lady on which to display her artistry."

Her hands cocked on her hips, Bonny gave her husband an insolent gaze. "And how, may I ask, are you such an authority on women whom *Madame* has clothed? I believe I may get very jealous."

The corners of his mouth turned up ever so slightly. "I'm sure I have no firsthand knowledge of the women, Barbara."

If only he had called her "my dear" or "my love," as he often did. Those words, though he had said them without passion, were so much more intimate than the formal-sounding Barbara.

Bonny sat in a Louis XV chair and scooted it up to the table beside Twigs's bed. "I do wish you wouldn't act so grim, Richard." She inhaled the hardy beef au jus. The table was set with all manner of dishes, and two footmen served. "After all, you should be in good humor, since you beat Twigs and me so soundly at loo this afternoon."

Sitting opposite her, Radcliff did not lift his eyes from his plate. "You went to Madame Deveraux's today?"

"Yes."

One of the footmen uncovered the salvers and the other served from the steaming dishes. What a waste to have so magnificent a round of beef for just the three of them, Bonny thought, but she took consolation knowing the servants would feast, as well as the inhabitants of Carlton House.

"You left rather early," Radcliff continued. "Did you go elsewhere?"

"To Cavendish Square. Emily accompanied me to Madame Deveraux's."

Radcliff spread a napkin on his lap. "You went nowhere else?"

Her heart raced. Had one of the footmen or the coachman told him about her using the messenger boy? Had any of them followed her to the house on Kepple Street? She hated to lie, but she had given Emily her word she would never tell anyone about the baby. She swallowed. "No."

She felt Richard's eyes on her and avoided them, turning to Twigs. "You may be sure, Twigs, Cook has prepared plum cake for dessert."

"Much obliged, your grace."

"Now that the duchess has kissed you, you may call her Barbara, or Bonny Barbara—as she's always urged you to do. You're practically one of the family. You don't call me "your grace," man."

Bonny watched her husband's face as the candlelight flickered in his bright eyes. He didn't really seem jealous. "Yes, Twigs, you must talk to me like I'm your sister."

"Quite stout, my sister, not at all like you."

"How a man can be so skilled at gaming and horseflesh and so lacking in all other sensibilities," the duke said to Twigs, "is beyond me, my dear friend."

"You know, Twigs," Bonny said, "I used to think you and Richard an unlikely pair to be such great friends—for I am sure you know how dissimilar you are—but Richard tells me you are extremely amusing and given to setting the bloods into hysterics with your entertaining ways. I long to see that side of you."

Twigs sniffed. "Not fit for a lady's ears or eyes, I regret to say."

Radcliff scooped peas into his spoon and gave his wife a playful glance. "He's right, my dear."

At least he had called her "my dear," she mused.

Her hopes for additional intimacy from her husband went unrealized, though. At bedtime, she climbed into her featherbed and listened to her husband's indistinguishable words to Evans in the ducal chamber. When the conversation ceased, she propped herself on a mound of lace-edged pillows and waited for Radcliff, reading until her candle melted down. Her eyes stung and she told herself that it was from the new wood burning in her hearth, not from her husband's absence.

Chapter Fifteen

Marie curled one of her mistress's black ringlets around her finger. "I've come to a good station 'ere, except for Mr. Nose-in-the-Air. You'd think 'e was the duke 'imself. Too good to eat with us other servants, 'e is. I'd say the man 'ated women."

"Men have a hard time accepting change," Bonny said to her abigail's reflection in the looking glass. "It's just been Mr. Evans and the duke for many years. Evans may resent that women have entered into their all-male domain, but he'll come around."

"Ye are much too kind, yer grace." Marie stood back, head to the side, studying Bonny's hair. "The hair, even if I says so meself, looks quite good, but I can't do nothing for them dark circles under yer eyes. 'Is grace won't like 'em."

Then his grace shouldn't neglect his wife, Bonny thought. She had lain in her bed hours last night, hoping her husband would join her, speculating on possible sources for his anger. Was he upset because she kissed Twigs? Had she behaved totally unlike a duchess? Was he sorry he had impulsively married her? Had he renewed old liaisons with other women? At the last thought, her stomach plummeted.

While Bonny renewed her troubling thoughts, Mrs. Henson brought coffee and the morning's post. Bonny thumbed through a stack of communications from various tradesmen. Half the tradesmen in London courted the patronage of the new Duchess of Radcliff. Near the bottom of the stack, she found a letter penned to her in a feminine hand on scented stationery.

Bonny eagerly tore it open and read the letter written in elegant, flourishing penmanship from the hand of Cressida Carlisle. She informed Bonny she was staying in London with her eldest sister, Mrs. Athena Miller, and would be calling on the duke and duchess. *Athena? Cressida?* The Carlisles must have been enamored of Greek mythology, Bonny thought with surprise. None of the Carlisles had struck her as particularly literary, save for the novels Cressida read about waifs marrying counts and living happily ever after. Of course, the waifs turned out to be noble-born and switched at birth.

That very afternoon, Cressida and her sister paid a call. The duke was not at home, but Bonny presided over tea and cakes in the green salon. She was genuinely glad to see Cressida.

Like the first time Bonny had met her, Cressida wore pink, a color that very much suited her delicate beauty. Squire Carlisle spared no expense in dressing his only offspring remaining at home.

Mrs. Athena Miller, unlike her much younger sister, presented a matronly appearance in her cap and somber brown gown of good quality. Frizzled locks of gray curls poked from the cap, and the woman's figure resembled a bulging sack of flour. She did resemble Cressida when she related her animated accounts of the ton, many of whom she did not know personally.

"I used to see your husband at many functions," Mrs. Miller said, stuffing a piece of cake into her mouth. "He was always in the company of beautiful women, but now I see he waited to marry the most beautiful of all.''

Bonny hated to acknowledge the woman's compliment. She hated to be reminded that Richard may have married her for no other reason than that she was a beauty. A trophy for his collection, she thought bitterly. She inhaled the herbal aroma of the specially blended Radcliff tea and mumbled her thanks.

''I suppose since you're in mourning, you haven't made the acquaintance of the duke's crowd,'' Mrs. Miller said.

''The only one I've met,'' Bonny admitted, ''is Tw—James Twickingham, who recuperates here from a serious injury.''

Mrs. Miller threw her head back and laughed. ''Twigs Twickingham is said to be one of the most entertaining men in London. Quite a character, I'm told. Of course, I've never met him, nor the others in the duke's set. Most of them are still unwed, except for William Clyde. Pretty little wife he's got. She's confined, awaiting their third child. Not that that's settled him down any, I hear. The second child was his heir, and the boy being born, Mr. Clyde, who's enormously wealthy, is free to resume his alliances with lightskirts.''

''Surely he wouldn't do anything of the kind while his wife is confined having his babe,'' Bonny protested.

The matronly Athena waved her pudgy, bejeweled hands in the air. ''My dear, you have a lot to learn about the ways of the ton. Their marriages aren't like my parents' or yours. Those in the ton marry to beget an heir, and their lives are chiefly a pursuit of pleasure.''

Bonny watched as Mrs. Miller's eyes lifted to the soaring, gilded ceiling, taking in the opulent surroundings.

Cressida, who had been silent heretofore, leaned forward and whispered, ''Pleasures of the flesh, if you know what I mean.''

That a maiden like Cressida Carlisle knew of pleasures of the flesh surprised Bonny considerably. What was in those Minerva Press novels? "Yes," Bonny lamented, "I've heard that men can be very immoral."

Mrs. Miller set down her teacup. "Not just men, your grace. Many married women are unfaithful wives, though I fail to understand how a well-brought-up lady could welcome such intimacy with a man she's not wed to. I vow I'd be most happy myself to never have any man climb in my bed." She lifted her eyes heavenward, and Bonny felt herself most uncharitable for thinking no man would *wish* to climb into Athena Miller's bed.

Cressida leaned forward again and whispered, "They say Lady Jersey herself had an affair with the Regent."

Bonny put down the cake she had not touched. She had lost her appetite, sickened by the people who comprised her husband's crowd. Sickened by those who broke sacred vows. But most of all she was sickened that her husband could be of like mind with the others. Did marriage mean nothing to him? Did he hunger after other women? Is that why he did not sleep with her?

"It's very glad I am that my only daughter is wed and living quietly in Hampshire," Mrs. Miller said.

Bonny nodded. "After what you've told me, I strongly wish to return to Hedley Hall."

"Pooh!" Cressida said. "Richard's not like those others, I'll vow. I've known him all my life, and I'd say he'll make a wonderful husband—and father."

Going into the marriage, Bonny believed Richard to be sensitive to the ties of family. She and Radcliff had been drawn together by their loneliness. Their shared loss of loved ones was one of the foundations upon which they were building their lives together. And he had shared with her his desire to have a child. If only she could make Richard a father, Bonny thought, her heart heavy. God help her if she were barren.

She watched her guests, who by now had finished their tea. "I've had a sudden idea. With Mr. Twickingham, there would be four of us—enough for a rubber of whist. I would be ever so obliged if I could persuade you to play one game. The poor man is quite bored to death in his sickbed."

Mrs. Miller's face brightened. "A most agreeable idea, to be sure." She hoisted her round body off the satin settee.

"But, Athena," Cressida protested to her sister's back, "I am very poor at whist. I'm always getting admonished for not following suit."

The woman patted her sister, threw a glance across the broad hallway toward Twigs's room, and whispered, "You'll do fine, Cressy. Men don't want women to be too clever."

Twigs's pallid face brightened when the ladies entered his room. One would never know he was mending, since he was fully dressed in the latest fashion, including the rather loose-fitting pantaloons.

After she made the introductions, Bonny proposed that Cressida be partners with the skillful Twigs, and she would take Mrs. Miller for her partner.

If Mrs. Miller had expected to be entertained by Twigs, she must be sadly disappointed, Bonny thought, noting the young man's stiff demeanor and formal address. He scarcely said two words to the three women seated around his bed.

True to her word, Cressida was an extremely poor player. Her sister, while not outstanding, made up for skill with a fierce competitiveness. She was quick to notice that Cressida did not play her trump. "I declare, Cressy, if I didn't know you better, I'd say you were cheating. Just put that three of diamonds back in your hand and throw out your jack of clubs."

Cressida gave her sister an incredulous stare. "You must be positively clairvoyant. It quite reminds me of Rosemary in *The Lost Bridegroom of Ravensport.*"

"More likely she drew out everybody else's clubs when she led with the ace," Twigs said.

Cressida turned her delicate face to Twigs and fluttered her eyelashes. "If only I had your skill, Mr. Twickingham. Do you think if I played often with you, it would rub off on me? I do so want to be good at whist."

"Daresay you'd be good as gold in no—no time," Twigs said, stammering. "Not that you play badly now, Miss Carlisle. Don't see why women need to be skillful at whist."

"My sister wants only to be well rounded, Mr. Twickingham," Mrs. Miller said sweetly. "She's quite accomplished on the piano, and you should see her watercolors."

"Regret to say I wouldn't know good from bad," Twigs mumbled.

Cressida sent a pert smile toward Twigs. "I don't for a minute believe that, Mr. Twickingham. I am sure you're a fine judge of talent."

"Well, when it comes to pugilism or riding..."

"I imagine you're a whip of the first order," Cressida said, tossing out a card and smiling sweetly into Twigs's face.

Bonny was only too happy to get the hand going again, but the remainder of the game continued with Cressida praising Twigs's playing, admiring his pearl-encrusted snuffbox, complimenting him on the fabric of his coat and the tie of his cravat, all of which left Twigs quieter than normal. Bonny remembered Twigs telling the duke he didn't know how to act around females, and now she realized it was time he learned.

Simple little Cressida Carlisle had completely flustered this buffoon who so entertained the bloods of the ton.

* * *

That night Bonny was to meet the young bucks when they came to call on Twigs. She even met William Clyde. She had not known they would be coming because she had neither seen nor spoken to her husband all day. She had taken dinner with Twigs at his bedside. Just the two of them. She had been silent, only picking at the veal cutlet and French beans. Her husband's absence made her morose.

Twigs tried heartily to cheer her. "Mark my words, Richard's just been delayed at White's."

"Were he that close, I'm sure he would have sent a note round to tell us not to wait dinner," Bonny said, her potatoes sticking in her throat.

"Believe you're worried about the man."

She worried far more that her husband was with another woman.

"Why don't you send a man round to see if his phaeton's at White's?"

"I could never do that. It would appear I was spying on him, that I didn't trust him."

After dinner, she did not feel like playing games with Twigs and retired to her room, where she paced its cream-colored carpet. She was still wearing the gown she had on for dinner, its train skimming over the gold fleur-de-lis pattern of the carpet. Her activity and the blazing fire in her hearth spread a heated flush over her body.

Her worry mounted. Had her husband already grown tired of her? Had he found a woman of greater beauty?

While in the midst of her gloomy thoughts, she heard noises from the first floor. She ran to inspect her face in the mirror and was displeased with her hot cheeks. A little powder should cover them, she decided. Before she went downstairs she dabbed perfume behind her ears and inside her wrists.

As one servant came out of Twigs's room bearing a tray

with two empty bottles of Madeira, another walked into the room carrying a tray with three unopened bottles.

Bonny followed the fellow into the room in time to see her husband lift his glass in a toast. "To Twigs's total recovery."

Twigs, his face alight, lifted his glass in agreement, while three other fashionably dressed young men also toasted the return of Twigs's good health.

Radcliff briefly met his wife's gaze before he brought the glass to his lips and drank the whole at once.

Something about his eyes disturbed her. A certain glassiness. And his speech, too. His pronunciation was not as crisp or as thoughtful as normal.

"Ah," he said, looking back at Bonny, "my beautiful wife. I must introduce you to my friends, my dear."

Smiling shakily, Bonny crossed the room to her husband's side and stood gracefully rigid as he leaned to kiss her cheek. And then she knew why his eyes and voice disturbed her. He smelled strongly of liquor.

Radcliff introduced Bonny to William Clyde, who was taller than her husband and rather handsome with dark auburn hair; to Huntley Harrington, who was short and jolly, with a red nose and red eyes; and Stephen Langford, a nice-looking young man who couldn't seem to remove his eyes from Bonny.

What was William Clyde doing here drinking with her husband if his poor wife was being confined? "Do I understand, Mr. Clyde," Bonny said, "that you are to be congratulated on the impending birth of a third child?" *Make him feel guilty,* she thought.

He coughed. "Thank you, your grace."

"Your wife stays in London?" Bonny asked.

"No. In Fairfield with her mother."

Bonny stiffened, then held out her hand to the other two young men, who assured her they were single.

"I had heard the duchess was beautiful," Langford told her, "but you are beyond anything I expected."

She saw a smug look pass over Richard's face at this comment and she thanked Langford, then turned to her husband. "We missed you at dinner."

"Our first dinner apart," he said snidely.

By his tone, she feared it would be the first of many dinners apart.

"If you ask me," Twigs said, "she was damned—" He cast an apologetic glance toward Bonny. "Pray, forgive my language, but, Richard, the duchess was deuced worried about you. Couldn't you have sent a note around?"

Radcliff's eyes met hers. "Were you worried that highwaymen slit my throat for my purse, my dear?"

His cool manner sent a chill along her spine. "I filled my head with all manner of worries about you, sir."

A flicker of warmth lit his eyes as he trailed a finger over his wife's smooth cheekbone. Then he stiffened and spoke casually. "Pray, don't worry about me tonight, for I intend to spend the evening in the company of my friends."

When the three bottles of Madeira were dry, Radcliff and the blades took their leave of Twigs and Bonny.

Although she was downcast over her husband's behavior, Bonny determined to play cribbage with Twigs, who was quite low himself.

Like Bonny, Twigs's thoughts were not on the game. "I say, would you mind dreadfully if I don't finish the game?" he asked Bonny. "That fox of a husband of yours knows how to restore my health."

"Whatever do you mean?"

"Deuced well made me want to walk, he did." Twigs swung his legs round the side of the bed, and holding on to the table, he removed himself from the bed.

Bonny jumped to her feet to assist him.

"No, Duchess, I've got to do this on my own," he said,

gritting his teeth. He put his weight on both legs and stood there for a moment as Bonny watched in silence.

After a minute, he took a step on his good leg, then dragged his injured leg behind him. He followed by taking another step, but this time he lifted the mending leg off the carpet and set it back down as if he were walking.

He proceeded to cross the long room slowly.

Bonny felt helpless as she watched. What if he fell and reinjured himself?

He did neither. Slowly and not without a great deal of pain, he came back to the bed and collapsed.

Bonny turned to Twigs, her eyes flashing with excitement. "I can't wait to tell Richard of your progress."

A troubled look swept across his face. "You'd best wait till tomorrow. Don't expect to see Richard tonight."

Hours after her husband left the house with the three rakes, Bonny called for Marie to help her undress. Marie took the pins and plumes from her hair and brushed it out, black ringlets falling over the ivory lace nightgown. Before she left the room, Marie stoked the fire for the night and put a fresh candle beside Bonny's bed.

At first Bonny tried to read, but she could only think of Radcliff. The strong smell of liquor on his breath had repelled her. She wondered if her husband had been foxed. She had little experience with drunkenness save for Mr. Woods back in Milford, who beat his wife when he was in his cups. Many a time her father had been called to assist Mrs. Woods after her husband had imbibed.

Would Richard beat her? That was a stupid question. She knew her husband could never harm anyone. This was the man who took the orphaned Rusty off the streets and gave him a job as groom, the master who was revered by his adoring servants, the duke who gave his title to the penniless daughter of a country cleric.

She remembered a hundred kind gestures from her husband and wanted so much for things to be the way they had been during the first weeks of their marriage. She wished so very much that he was beside her this very minute. How she longed to feel his arms around her, to have his life spring passing into her body, to feel his lips against hers. Even if he did smell of liquor.

If tonight he remained in his room as he had done last night, she decided to let herself into his chamber. She would say she was excited to tell him that Twigs walked on his own. And then, maybe, her husband would see her in the soft nightgown and want to make love to her.

Bonny plumped up her pillows, picked up her book and read. At three in the morning her eyelids became heavy. She blew out her candle and went to sleep.

The next morning, after Marie had done her hair and helped her into a muslin day dress, Bonny went through the dressing room to her husband's chamber.

He was not there, and the smooth silk bedspread indicated his bed had not been slept in.

Evans entered the room, gave a Bonny a stiff greeting and proceeded to the dressing room to gather up his master's boots.

Bonny followed him and sat down in Richard's gilded chair. "How long have you been in service to the duke, Mr. Evans?"

He continued about his task of polishing one boot and did not look up. "Since the fourth duke died. I was valet to the father before the son."

"Then you knew my husband when he was a child."

"Yes, your grace."

"Was he an affectionate child?"

Evans glanced up from the already shiny black boot and gave her a quizzing gaze. "He was much like his father.

The Moncrief men do not speak of emotions except by their actions.''

''The old duke was fond of his son?''

''He never spoke of it. Nor would he boast of the young duke's many accomplishments, though those who knew him could see he was proud of his son. We always knew when the young master was coming home from Eaton or Oxford by his levity.''

How very much Richard must be like his father, Bonny thought. Obviously, something troubled him, but he had been schooled not to allow anyone past the cool barriers he had erected around his heart.

She watched Evans rub more polish onto the boot. ''I know you could not welcome the idea of his grace taking a wife, Mr. Evans, but I do assure you that you and I have the same goal. We both want his grace to be happy.''

''Quite so, your grace,'' he said placidly.

Chapter Sixteen

His blond head towered over everyone on the dance floor, and he was coming straight toward her. Emily's knees began to quiver. She looked away from him and feigned interest in her mother's conversation.

"My poor daughter needs to sit this one out, Lady Sutton, for she's quite fatigued from dancing every dance."

"But, Lady Landis," the other woman said, "it appears Lord Dunsford wishes to dance with your daughter."

Three pairs of eyes turned to examine Dunsford as he stood shyly beside Emily.

"I have waited all night for the opportunity to ask you to stand up with me," Lord Dunsford said to Emily.

At first she merely sat in her armed chair looking at him, stunned that his voice was not Harold's voice at all, though he looked so much like Harold. Then, she cast her gaze at her satisfied mother, got to her feet and moved silently to the dance floor with the earl, her breath ragged and her insides shaky.

"Allow me to introduce myself," he said to her as he clasped her hand. "I am Henry Blackburn, the Earl of Dunsford."

"And I am Emily Wickham," Emily said softly.

"Alfred's sister?" he asked as he held her at arm's distance to begin the waltz.

"Yes, do you know my brother?"

"We were at Oxford together, but he was ahead of me."

Emily found it difficult to converse with the earl. Had he asked her to dance because she had been staring at him all night? She had tried to look away quickly every time he directed his gaze toward her. Now, as it had throughout the night, his presence evoked painful memories of her dead lover.

The earl's tongue was as unskilled as his clumsy dance steps. He spoke no more until the waltz was nearly finished. "How is it that I've not seen you before, Lady Emily?"

"I've been out of London most of the past year."

"Where?"

She started to say Spain, but decided against it. It would do neither of them any good to think of Spain. "I have been to my cousin's wedding in Northumbria. My cousin, Bonny Barbara Allan, has recently married the Duke of Radcliff."

Dunsford's step slowed and she felt a stiffening in his manner.

When the music stopped, he walked her back to her mother. "May I have the pleasure of calling upon you, Lady Emily?" he asked.

She nodded.

And cursed herself for it.

The following day Emily called to coax Bonny into accompanying her to look for ribbons, but Bonny cried off, begging her cousin to stay with her awhile. Bonny would not budge from Radcliff House until her husband returned.

Emily, dressed in a fine mint green worsted dress and matching pelisse, took a seat in Bonny's sunlit study. "I only used the ribbons as an excuse to talk to you. You will never guess whom I danced with at the Teagues' ball last night.''

Bonny laid her embroidery on her lap and cocked a brow.

"Harold's brother," Emily said.

"The earl?"

Emily nodded solemnly.

"And you didn't faint?"

"No, for I had rather been watching him throughout the night. He looks so very much like Harold. That is, until I heard his voice. It sounded so strange for that unfamiliar voice to come from that so-familiar face.''

"Did you tell him you knew Harold?"

"No. I was afraid I might break down and cry."

"Then it's best you remained silent."

Emily stayed silent for a moment before she calmly said, "He asked if he could call on me."

"And what did you say?" Bonny ran her needle into the cloth.

Emily twisted a handkerchief. "I said he could."

"Then why are you here this morning?"

"I can't be with him and not want to confess everything.''

"You wouldn't do that with your mother sitting right there."

"That's just the problem. If an earl came to call, you can be sure she would find a reason to leave me alone in the room with him—anything to compromise my virtue and aspire for a noble offer.''

Bonny knew good manners demanded that she defend her aunt, but good sense told her that Emily spoke the truth. She remained silent.

Emily got up. "I must make an effort to get some ribbons before I go home. Mama will be furious enough if

Lord Dunsford called while I was out.'' She turned from the door of the duchess's study. ''Need ribbon?''

Bonny shook her head. ''Please leave the door open.'' She wanted to hear Richard when he returned. Long after Emily left, Bonny sat quietly sewing, listening for her husband. She saw Evans stealthily creep down the hall toward his master's room. Shortly afterward he walked past her open study door, a valise in one hand and a suit of Richard's clothing in the other.

Seeing Evans with her husband's clothing was nothing new. Fine coats and trousers were frequently draped over his arm as he saw to their needs. But the valise? Was he taking Richard a fresh suit of clothing?

She thought of how extremely neat her husband was about his clothing and appearance. Not that he was vain. Just very clean. The only man she could measure him against was her father, who had a habit of wearing his favorite clothes for days on end.

Could Richard have sent a note to Evans and not to his wife? she wondered, anger welling within her like a steaming cauldron.

Before an hour passed, Radcliff returned home wearing the clothes Evans brought him. ''Is the duchess home?'' he asked Mandley, passing his gloves and riding crop to a nearby footman.

''Yes, your grace. I believe she is in her study.''

''Alone?''

''Yes, your grace. Lady Emily left some time ago.''

Radcliff nodded and went to sit at the rich walnut desk in his own study, hanging his head in his hands. God's teeth, but his head ached unmercifully. He was too old and too unused to the excesses for which his crowd was noted. He had been so ripe for aging at Hedley Hall with Bonny by his side and a nursery full of their children. Why had they ever come back to London? Bonny had seemed happy with him in Kent. He thought perhaps she had been growing to love him.

He pounded the desk at the thought of his rival.

"Are you all right, Richard?"

He looked up to see Bonny, lovely as ever, standing before him, a look of concern on her perfect face. "I have a bad head."

She slid into a velvet chair near his desk, a sly grin on her face. "I feared you would have a bad head today, dear husband. I understand that generally follows a thorough foxing."

"Thank you for such sympathetic words, my dear."

She got up and came to feel his forehead. "I'm sorry to be so callous. Would you like Mandley to bring you tisane?"

"Pray, no. It won't help." His eyes raked over her as she sat back down. "You've been here all day?"

"How could I leave, not knowing where you were or if you were all right?"

"Keep it up and I will believe you worried about me."

She squared her shoulders and shot a cold glance at him. Why hadn't she asked where he had been? Didn't other wives pry? But, then, Bonny was not like all wives, he thought with a tightening in his chest.

"Have you see Twigs today?" she asked.

He shook his head. "I'm too bloody miserable."

"Then you need to be in bed."

"I would feel no better there." He shuffled through papers on his desk, feeling his wife's eyes on him.

"Twigs walked on his own last night," she announced quietly.

He turned smiling eyes on her. "This calls for a celebration."

"Please, no more toasts, sir."

"I was thinking you could have a small dinner party for him. Have your aunt and uncle and Emily, and any others you may wish."

"Like your cousin, Stanley?"

He nodded. "You have complete liberty with the guest list."

All signs of old Lord Heffington were now gone from the late baron's morning room, Stanley Moncrief reflected as he waited for the baron's merry widow to come down. Lady Lynda Heffington's touch shone everywhere in the room, from its brocaded sofas the color of saffron to the Sevres urns on the marble mantel. Color and light and delicate objects had replaced the heavy wood, suits of armor and deep claret-colored trappings of the morning room.

Lady Heffington floated into the room, her heavy floral scent announcing her arrival before she greeted Stanley in her deep, rich voice.

He rose and took her outstretched hand, his eyes skimming past her loveliness to observe her deaf companion, Mrs. Breedlove, as that old woman sat in a French chair near the window and took up her embroidery. "Surely a lady of your prestige no longer needs the appearances of a watchdog," Stanley said mockingly.

Lady Heffington stiffened and withdrew her hand. "A woman alone in the world always needs a protector." She sat on a sofa behind the tea table recently set by her butler. "Your cousin's ill use of me did nothing to improve my reputation."

Stanley came to sit beside her. "Ah, my cousin. He is the reason I am here today."

She shot him a questioning glance.

"I regret to say his marriage does not go well. I am sure you know he stays away from his young bride for days at a time."

"Such talk has come to my ears. I am given to understand he prefers the company of other bloods over that of his wife."

"You of all people must know a man like Richard cannot be content with only a pretty face. He needs a mature woman of experience and intelligence."

"You and I are in complete agreement on that, Stanley. However, if dark clouds threaten Richard's marriage, I cannot but believe you would rejoice. I know you dislike the prospect of Richard begetting an heir that would displace your hopes."

"It seems you and I understand each other well, Lynda." She handed him his tea. "Why are you here?"

"To enlist your help in my plan to sabotage Richard's...I hate to call it a marriage...his misalliance."

Her brows lifted, then she leaned toward him, a smile spreading across her pretty face. "Pray, how can I be of service?"

Bonny knew a dinner party for a dozen was child's play for her experienced servants, who had to remove several leaves from the great dining table to accommodate so small a gathering. Nevertheless, this was her first dinner party, and she wanted to be certain everything went smoothly. Above all, she wanted Richard to be proud of her.

She stood back to study the table. She had arranged the flowers herself and had to admit no one could have done better. She examined each of the twelve place cards. Assured the table was in perfect order, Bonny scurried up the stairs to her chamber, where Marie skillfully arranged her hair and helped her into the low-cut black sarcenet gown with train. She thought of how lovely the Radcliff Jewels would look but knew they were too showy for one in mourning. Instead, she pulled from her jewel case a simple strand of pearls. Marie fastened them on before she left the room.

It had been weeks since Richard had clasped anything around her neck, she thought sadly. In fact, it had been weeks since he had touched her.

She heard the sound of a door opening into the dressing room and looked up hopefully.

Her husband strolled into her room. "It's too bad, my dear, the Radcliff Jewels are so gaudy for one in mourning, for I would love to see them on you tonight."

She rose and met him halfway across the room.

He stopped to look at her. "You will do very well. Very well indeed."

"Do the pearls look all right?" She felt his eyes on her bodice.

"No. You don't need them, Barbara." He moved closer, his hands finding the clasp and removing the pearls, his palms sliding down her soft shoulders. "A beauty such as yours needs nothing else."

She spun around to face him, wanting to fling herself into his arms, but he stiffened and offered his arm. "Shall we go downstairs, your grace? Our guests await."

Her heart heavy, she took his arm.

In the drawing room Bonny felt more insignificant than ever. The guests who had already arrived—with the exception of Emily—completely ignored Bonny in their enthusiastic reception of her husband. Would Richard take their slight of his wife as confirmation that he had married beneath his station?

If only she could distinguish herself in his eyes. Perhaps tonight's dinner party would be such a success he would be very proud of her. She stood at her husband's side and looked at the gathering. Twigs, nattily dressed in a rather loud satin coat, leaned on a cane between Richard and Bonny's Uncle David. Emily and her mother, along with her brother, Alfred, had arrived, as had Cressida Carlisle with her sister and brother-in-law.

"Athena Carlisle," the duke said, taking the matron's hand, "it's been an age since I've seen you. But, of course, your name's no longer Carlisle."

The woman's whole air changed from subservient to glowing. "Miller's the last name now, your grace, and this is my husband, Gregory."

Radcliff politely greeted the bald-headed man, then said, "Do me the goodness to welcome my lovely wife, the Duchess of Radcliff." His arm tucked around Bonny as his eyes met hers.

Once the duke alluded to his wife, the others could not praise her highly enough.

Bonny's Aunt Lucille listened to all the charming compliments before adding her own. "I am so very glad the duke insisted Bonny get Madame Deveraux to clothe her, for the poor thing had no sense of fashion at all, and look how well she looks now! Of course, she will look better when she can wear color again. Those with black hair don't look good in mourning, not like blondes, don't you think, Mrs. Miller?"

Mrs. Miller, whose pretty, unwed sister was blond, agreed most heartily.

"I beg to disagree," the duke said. "I've never seen anyone wear mourning better than my wife." He turned to Lady Landis. "And I find my wife has excellent taste—with or without the services of an expensive modiste."

"Quite so," said Bonny's uncle, who had acted especially proud of Bonny since her marriage.

Mandley entered the drawing room and announced the newest guest, "Henry Blackburn, the third Earl of Dunsford."

Knowing that he was not acquainted with most of those in the room, Bonny went to greet him. "How nice of you to come, my lord." She took his arm and led him toward the other guests.

"Do you know my husband?" Bonny asked Dunsford.

Radcliff's cold eyes met Dunsford's. "We were at school together," the duke said stonily.

Dunsford threw a nervous smile at Radcliff. "That was a very long time ago, to be sure." He bowed. "Please accept my felicitations on your marriage."

Radcliff merely nodded, prompting an awkward silence.

"I believe you know my cousins, Lord Alfred and Lady Emily Wickham," Bonny said to Dunsford.

As Alfred began to speak to Dunsford, and Mrs. Miller chatted with Lady Landis, Radcliff drew Bonny toward the window.

"Why didn't you tell me Dunsford was coming?"

"Why didn't you ask?" she snapped. "You've hardly spoken to me since the day you said I could have the party. You're never home anymore."

Mandley cleared his throat to announce the last guest. "Mr. Stanley Moncrief with Lady Lynda Heffington."

Chapter Seventeen

Lady Heffington did not walk into the room, she glided into it quietly like a cat on soft paws, a smile fixed on her face, her eyes riveted on the duke's. Completely ignoring Bonny's presence, the redhead laid a bejeweled hand on Radcliff's arm. "Pray, it was so good of you to ask me," she said loud enough for everyone in the room to hear.

Radcliff's eyes darted from Lady Heffington to Stanley Moncrief. "You came with Stanley?" he asked, his face stern.

"Yes, he's so very obliging." Lady Heffington turned then to Bonny. "I do hope I don't make an odd number for your table."

"Well—"

"Do me the goodness of placing Lynda near me, your grace," Stanley said to Bonny.

Before Bonny could respond, Mandley announced dinner. Bonny took the butler aside and told him to set a place for Lady Heffington beside Stanley.

It wasn't until Bonny pulled her skirts beneath her and sat down that she remembered Stanley was to sit next to her husband. Her heart stilled when she looked down the length of the table and saw Lady Heffington at Radcliff's left.

Oblivious to the three footmen serving wine and buttered crab, a dazed Bonny poked at the food for which she no longer had an appetite. Putting aside her humiliation that her husband had invited his former mistress to his wife's table, Bonny still stung from her husband's utter rejection of her.

She tried to swallow a bite of parsnips, but they caught in her throat. She felt tears welling up and prayed she would be able to hold them back. The only thing more humiliating than having to entertain your husband's mistress was crying at your own dinner party.

"Your flowers look beautiful, Bonny," said Emily, who sat beside her.

"Yes, I must find out who did them for you," said Lady Landis.

"I did them myself, Aunt Lucille."

Bonny's aunt's eyes narrowed. "Well, of course, the duke does have the finest garden in London. How stupid of me not to have realized how easy it would be for you to have gorgeous bouquets."

Lady Landis's words made Bonny realize the garden wasn't hers, though Richard had urged her to consider everything he owned as hers, too. Even her first dinner party was not hers. Her party for a dozen now served an unlucky thirteen.

As if through a fog, Bonny watched those at her table. She observed every gesture or word that passed between her husband and the woman who had been his mistress. She noticed the easy intimacy between them and wondered if it was Lady Heffington who kept Richard from her each night.

Though those thoughts tore at her heart, that her husband would humiliate her like this hurt even worse. A man who could wound so had no heart. The man she had married possessed a heart that knew no bounds. What had become of that man? she wondered morosely.

Lady Heffington lowered her voice, but her words could be heard at the other end of the table. "I am given to understand you have been neglecting your poor little wife, Radcliff."

"I beg you not to repeat such groundless gossip, my lady," Radcliff said sternly.

While her husband's reply lifted Bonny's spirits, they fell again a few minutes later when she saw Lady Heffington stroke her husband's hand, and he placed his over hers and said something Bonny could not hear.

As if to deny her own eyes, Bonny spun to face Dunsford, who sat at her left. Sitting at the end of the table herself, she had put the shy Emily beside her and intentionally placed Dunsford opposite Emily in hopes of furthering their acquaintance. "What was that you said?"

"I was merely telling Alfred here," Dunsford responded, "that it's not proper to talk about gaming houses in front of ladies."

"Pooh," Bonny said. "I am a married lady."

Bonny saw Dunsford's pale eyes indicate Emily across the table from him and knew to whom he referred.

"She doesn't count, old boy," Alfred said. "She's my sister. Knows all about the hells."

Emily's gaze met her brother's. "Yes, and I know you should stay away from them."

"Daresay your sister's right," Dunsford said.

Bonny attempted a smile. "We women are always right, my lord."

Determined to present a placid countenance, Bonny drew out the bashful earl by asking him about his school days and to kindly repeat any stories he knew of Twigs that were fit for mixed company.

* * *

While Bonny appeared to listen with lively amusement to Dunsford's narrative, Radcliff watched from hooded eyes. How could his Barbara bring Dunsford into this house? He could not believe the sensitive woman he had married could be guilty of so cruel an action.

He ached to watch her lovely face smile at the arrogant Dunsford. But he ached far more to think of her twisting and writhing with pleasure beneath Dunsford. God's eyes, but nothing had ever hurt so much. Not even when his parents died.

Although Bonny had captured his heart, he could at least salvage his dignity. His pride. He couldn't let her know how utterly devastated he was. Far better to let her think he was having a jolly time with Lynda.

He feigned interest in what Lady Heffington said and even took her hand in his a time or two. He displayed excellent thespian skills when he could gladly throttle the lying redheaded baggage for telling his guests he had invited her. Had he not been a gentleman, he would have shown her the door.

Before she left tonight, he vowed, Lynda would know better than to set foot in his wife's home again.

"I say, Richard," Twigs said from the duke's right, "when did that bloody doctor say I could ride again?"

"Why do you want to know?"

"Miss Carlisle wants to know when I can trot in the park."

Radcliff's gaze flickered to Cressida. "I daresay you could manage a phaeton by next week. Riding a horse will be quite a bit longer."

"I did so want to see Mr. Twickingham at the ribbons," Cressida said. "For I am sure he is very skillful."

The duke lifted his wineglass and gave Cressida a knowing glance. "To be sure."

* * *

After dinner the men took their port and smoked cigars in the salon, where Radcliff made himself a very agreeable host, inquiring into Mr. Miller's job as a barrister, speaking of Northumbria to Barbara's uncle David—Lord Landis— and talking about mutual friends with Alfred.

"Believe I remember where the facilities are," Stanley said, slipping from the baroque room.

Indeed, he remembered everything about Radcliff House, where he had spent so much time when he came up from Oxford. He mounted the marble staircase, running his hand over the bronze banister, his discerning eye taking in all the treasures within his view. When his grandfather had built the house, it was said to be the finest mansion in London.

Stanley crept past the unused ballroom. If only he could have seen the room when its huge crystal chandeliers cast bright lights over the most select members of the ton.

Well, when he was master here, it would once again be the grandest address in all of London. And the balls he would give! The undeserving Richard did not appreciate what he had.

Without having to think about where he was going, Stanley let his legs carry him to the duchess's room. He wondered if the new duchess had changed the decor. He could almost see his aunt sitting there at her gilded dressing table in the ivory-and-gold room.

Before he opened the door, he turned to make sure no one was watching him, then he entered. He was pleased to find the room well lit from twin torchères flanking the dressing-table mirror, a candelabra on the mantel and another candlestick beside the bed. The room remained exactly as he remembered it.

The jewels must be in here, he thought, walking to the dressing table and opening its small drawers. In the very

top drawer he found a velvet case and took it out. His
breath grew ragged as he held the box in his hand and
slowly opened it. Brilliant emeralds caught the light of his
candle. The Radcliff Jewels. Now they would be his. He
fingered them lovingly, then placed them in the deep pocket
of his coat, replacing the velvet box in the drawer.

His hands sweat and his throat grew parched. Damn, but
he needed a drink. He crept from the room and down the
stairs.

Evans always liked to wait up for his master. A gentleman needed the assistance of a good man, he thought
smugly. While he waited for Radcliff, he took inventory of
the duke's dressing room. Surely it was time to replace
some of the breeches that had straddled one horse too
many.

As he busied himself in the dressing room, he thought
he heard the duchess's door open. He tiptoed to the adjoining door and ever so slowly eased the opening wide enough
to peek into her grace's chamber.

At first he did not recognize who was snooping into the
duchess's things, but as the man turned his face toward the
candlelight, Evans remembered Stanley Moncrief. Never
cared for the boy, he thought. Stanley did not admire his
master, and if there was anything Evans did not like, it was
someone who did not like Radcliff. No woman could ever
have had a better son than his grace. No bride ever had a
better husband. And no valet ever had a better master.

But that sly Stanley Moncrief had always been jealous
of the duke.

With anger, Evans watched Stanley pocket the Radcliff
Jewels. *I knew it! He's not only coveting his cousin's
goods, he's stealing them.* Evans almost burst into the room
to apprehend this reprobate thief when he stopped himself.

If the jewels turned up missing, who would be blamed? Whose room were they in?

A slow smile spread over his sagging face. He did not care for that chit the master had wed. God, but things had been so much better before she came. She and that prattling maid of hers. This house had been so lively when it had been filled just with bachelors and their never-ending escapades. Oh, the times those young men had!

While the men took their port after dinner, the women retired to the drawing room. To avoid having to speak to the odious Lady Heffington, Bonny asked Emily to sing, and when Emily finished performing, Bonny invited Cressida to entertain with her sweet voice. By the time she finished singing, the men had joined them.

With Cressida on one side of her, Mrs. Miller sat on one of the satin settees, locked in conversation with Lady Landis over mutual friends. Twigs had asked Bonny to be his partner in a game of whist with Stanley and Alfred. Lord Dunsford shyly looked up from his highly polished boots to ask Emily if she would play cribbage with him, while Lord Landis and Mr. Miller went on the balcony to smoke.

At this time Radcliff said, "Lady Heffington, there is a book I would like you to see." He took her across the room, where he opened a picture book and spoke to her in soft tones.

"Oblige me by listening very carefully, Lynda," he said through gritted teeth. "I don't know what game it is you and Stanley play, but I vow I will have you physically removed from Radcliff House if you ever have the gall to show your face here again. Is that clear?"

"Pray, don't be mad at me, Richard dear. It is only that I love you too dearly, *mon chéri.*"

He gazed at her with eyes like hot coals, slammed the

book shut and said, "I am a married man." Then he stalked across the room.

Her face red, Lady Heffington pretended to be interested in the book for a long time after he left.

Radcliff walked to the game table where his wife played and looked over Twigs's shoulder.

"Would you care to take my place, Richard?" Bonny asked.

"No, my dear, I fear Twigs would box my ears if I deprived him of your most excellent partnership. I am happy to watch."

"I fear my play has been most poor tonight," Bonny said. Indeed, twice Twigs had kindly rebuked her for not following suit.

As the game continued, Cressida, too, came to watch. "How I should love to be a skillful player."

"Perhaps you can come more often to Mr. Twickingham's sickroom, and he could teach you," Bonny offered, wondering how she had the presence of mind to have heard any of the conversation around her.

Since seeing her husband escort Lady Heffington across the room, Bonny had felt as if she were bleeding inside. If she hadn't been to the heavens in Radcliff's arms, this hell wouldn't hurt so deeply.

Now her hand balled into a fist as she saw Lady Heffington approaching the table.

"That's a capital idea," Cressida said. "Would I be a wretched bother to you, Mr. Twickingham?"

"Not at all," Twigs mumbled, more intent on his game than on her. "Deuced rotten luck that you pulled that king from my hand, Landis."

"Stanley," Lady Heffington snapped, "I fear I have a dreadful head and need you to see me home."

Stanley looked at Richard. "Take my place, old boy."

Radcliff shrugged, then exchanged places with his

cousin, after which Stanley and Lady Heffington bade farewell.

Bonny joined the others in saying goodbye to Stanley but refused to speak to that contemptible widow.

Radcliff was so absorbed in the cards, he neglected his hostly duties and completely ignored his departing guests, much to Bonny's satisfaction.

When their guests left, Bonny glared icily at her husband, then mounted the stairs to her chamber, where Marie awaited. The abigail deftly removed the pins from Bonny's hair and brushed it out, then assisted Bonny into a simple muslin nightgown.

With Marie gone and her head clear, Bonny thought back over the night's events. She could stand the humiliation. Where Richard was concerned, she had little pride. But worse than his bringing that woman here was the picture burned in Bonny's mind like a recurring nightmare of Richard's broad hand gently lying over Lady Heffington's as they strolled across the drawing room to have a private tête-à-tête.

The more Bonny remembered, the madder she got. No matter if she hadn't been raised to be a duchess. No matter that her husband might not be in love with her. She was Richard's wife, and he had absolutely no right to bring his mistress into her house.

Bolstered by her mounting anger, Bonny stormed from her room and down the stairs to her husband's study, throwing open the door. The sight of her manly husband looking so wretched completely disarmed her. His cravat had been thrown off, along with his coat. His eyes were red and glassy, the look on his face forlorn. Was he so terribly unhappy with her?

Perhaps, then, she should free him. After all, their marriage could not continue like this. "Richard, I came to tell you that I think it a contemptible practice to invite your former mistress to dine with your wife, and I won't have it."

His eyes caught the light from the fireplace as he lifted his gaze to her. "And who is supposed to be my former mistress?"

"That odious Lady Heffington."

The corner of his mouth lifted, deepening the dimple in his craggy cheek. "When you quit inviting unmarried *gentlemen,* I will quit inviting unmarried ladies."

"What are you talking about?"

Radcliff glared at her. "Lord Dunsford."

"I invited an unmarried man, hoping to make a match for Em. I did not know you disliked him."

Radcliff lifted the decanter and poured a bumper of straight scotch. "Go to bed," he commanded. "I wish to drink alone."

Bonny stomped her foot and left the room.

Chapter Eighteen

His clothes were much too fine to expose to the elements, Stanley told himself as he rode his mare through Bloomsbury. One day he would have his own four-horse carriage. Too damned expensive to keep stables and a driver now. If only he could come into money while he was young enough to enjoy it. Because of his cousin's intercedence, Stanley held a thousand-a-year post that offered a comfortable living. And he could always hope for an heiress. Trouble was, all the heiresses out this season were bloody ugly, and not one of noble birth.

He thought again of how he would have thrown away his hopes for an heiress if Bonny Barbara Allan had so much as given him a kind word. Despite her lack of fortune, she was, after all, the granddaughter of a viscount. With him being the grandson of a duke, their marriage would have been looked upon quite favorably by the ton.

But it was Richard who had won Bonny Barbara's heart. Always it was Richard. Richard who got the title and the properties. Richard whom the cursed servants revered. Richard who distinguished himself at Oxford. Richard who was damned near worshiped by his parents while Stanley was left in the constant care of his nurse, then later his bloody governess.

While his thoughts were thus engaged, Stanley caught sight of Richard's fine barouche parked in an unfashionable square in Bloomsbury. He reined into the square and drove alongside the barouche, where the driver and tiger prattled.

"I say," Stanley interrupted, "I believe this is my cousin's carriage. Is the duke within?" His glance indicated the house the carriage was in front of.

"No, sir," the driver replied. "And it's her grace, the duchess, we're driving. She likes to walk in the square by herself."

Stanley looked past the iron gate to the square, which was hedged in chest-high yews. "But I don't see her grace. Do you know where she is?"

The driver shook his head. "I couldn't say. I'm not paid to snoop into her grace's activities."

"She went out the opposite gate and turned left, like she always does," the tiger said.

Stanley tossed a shilling to the tiger. "Thank you."

Turning his bay around, Stanley went to the other end of the square and turned left. One block down, he beheld a curious sight. Parked in front of a slender little row house was another crested barouche. For the life of him he could not remember whose crest it was, although he knew he had seen it recently.

He rode a short distance past the house and dismounted, positioning himself behind his horse so that he could peek over the saddle to see who came out the door of Number 17 Kepple Street.

He didn't have to wait long. Very soon he saw Bonny come through the doorway alone and scurry down the stairs. At the end of the block, she turned toward the square where her barouche was parked.

Stanley did not have to follow her; he knew where she was bound. He would have to be patient.

Presently, he heard the door to Number 17 open again, and he recognized the tall, thin body of Lord Henry Dunsford. No wonder Richard had been in such deuced low spirits last night. He must know about his wife's infidelities, Stanley thought with satisfaction. By God, it was time Richard lost at something!

And Stanley knew just the person to share his good news with. How fortunate he was to have been traveling through Bloomsbury today.

Bonny settled back in her barouche, pleased with herself. She had bought every single hat she liked at the most expensive milliner's on Conduit Street. Still angry with him, she couldn't wait for Richard to get the bill.

Across from Bonny, Emily settled in the carriage seat. "Em, I believe Richard does not at all like Lord Dunsford."

"Upon my word, I cannot imagine why. Lord Dunsford is uncommonly nice. You know, he called upon me this morning."

"How very agreeable. Did your mother behave tolerably well?"

"I am happy to say my meddlesome mother was away when he called," Emily said with a mischievous smile.

"You didn't see him alone?"

"Oh, no, to be sure. I had Martha come sit with her sewing."

"Did anything interesting occur during his visit?"

Emily gazed into her lap. "He asked me to ride with him in the park this evening."

"Did you agree?"

"I did, though I can't think why. I don't know what I'll say to him."

"There's always the weather," Bonny suggested.

"That's what we talked of this morning."

"I don't suppose you'll want to tell him you knew Harold."

"I'm afraid to."

As they rode, Bonny wondered if Dunsford had guessed about Emily. He had to have, given the fact he knew her first name and knew she was close to Bonny. The man was not an idiot. "I really cannot imagine why my husband has taken such a dislike to him." If she wanted to prevent that horrid widow from returning to her house, she could never again invite Dunsford.

Stanley sat in the elegant drawing room at Wickham House awaiting Lady Landis. He had a particular interest in talking with her. The flamboyant peeress was noted for her wicked tongue and even more noted for her propensity to gossip. She would serve his purposes very well.

"My lady," he said, getting to his feet as she entered the room. He took her hand. "How lovely you look. Much too young to be Alfred's mother."

She gave him a coy look. "I must say, my Lord Landis took me practically from the cradle." She settled on her plum-colored damask sofa and begged Mr. Moncrief to sit in an armchair near her. "What a pleasure it is to have you call," she said in a questioning tone.

"Now that we are related through the duchess, I thought I should strengthen our family bonds. Where is your lovely daughter today?"

"She has taken the poor duchess under her wing and is escorting her to Madame Herbert's millinery shop."

"How very obliging of your daughter to share her excellent taste."

Lady Landis shot a questioning look at Stanley. "Did you desire to see Emily today?"

He scooted closer. "Actually, you are the one I particularly wanted to see, for what I have to discuss is of a private nature."

He could almost see the woman's ears perk up as she leaned closer. "It is because we are family and because I am so concerned about your niece that I am here."

"Why are you concerned about Barbara?"

"I don't wish to see her hurt my cousin. Richard's very taken with her."

"Whatever are you talking about, sir?"

Stanley leaned closer and spoke in a hoarse whisper. "What I say dies in this room."

"To be sure."

"I came straight here because I was so distressed at what I observed with my own eyes."

"Pray tell," said Lady Landis, mock concern across her face.

"I saw the duchess leave an unfashionable house in Bloomsbury in the presence of Lord Dunsford, which in itself might be explained, but for the fact her coachman told me that going to that house is a regular practice of the duchess's." Stanley complimented himself on how well he embellished the story in his telling.

Lady Landis began to fan herself rapidly. "Poor Radcliff! I hope I don't faint at such ghastly news. He's done nothing to deserve such shameful treatment from that...from my niece."

"Indeed."

"I do hope you can take tea with me, Mr. Moncrief."

He tugged at his fob and noted the time on his watch. "Alas, I have an appointment and must be on my way." He got to his feet. "If your man could only retrieve my riding crop, I'll be on my way now. I am heartily sorry to be the bearer of such disturbing news."

Lady Landis shook her head somberly, though the glint

in her green eyes belied her concern. "How very obliging of you to come to me with this…situation."

Bonny scooped up Twigs's markers from the table. "Pray, sir, you will owe me your next quarter's portion if you keep this up." That she had no intention of collecting, she was not telling him.

"Can't fathom it. Beat by a lady. Not supposed to be that way."

"Ladies, in many ways, sir, can be quite as smart as men."

"Don't mean nothing against you, Duchess."

Bonny looked at the mantel clock. "You had best hurry if you want to ride in the park with Miss Carlisle while it is still light outside."

"Oh, quite so," he said, rising from his overstuffed chair and limping from the room.

With mixed emotion, Bonny listened to his uneven steps along the marble hall. She was glad he was mending so well, but she would miss him dreadfully. He had been her only companion during the weeks of her husband's sporadic appearances at Radcliff House.

She mounted the stairs to dress for dinner. How ridiculous it was to continue with these customs. Night after night she wore lovely gowns to sit and dine alone or to share the gloomy table with Twigs. He did his best to make excuses for her husband and tried mightily to cheer her.

Marie fixed Bonny's hair in an elegant enough style to go to court. Bonny donned one of the evening dresses Madame Deveraux had created for her and allowed Marie to stick a black ostrich plume in her hair. How silly she would look, all dressed up, to sit alone at that huge dining table.

But always she hoped Richard would come. She dismissed Marie and sat before her dressing table, listening, as she often did, for noises from her husband's chamber.

She began to open the drawers in her dresser out of sheer boredom.

She took out the velvet box containing the Radcliff Jewels. Just to look at them. To try to feel as if she were a Radcliff. If only she could have conceived a child. But now there was no opportunity. Would she go to her grave barren? she wondered as she opened the box.

Her heartbeat stilled. The jewels were gone!

With trembling hands, she quickly opened the rest of the drawers, searching for the jewels, but they had vanished like her husband's warmth.

Who could have taken them? Could it have been one of her servants? A fleeting, sickening thought crossed her mind. Could Richard have taken them to give to Lady Heffington? No. *No.* Whatever his feelings were toward his wife, he could never be so dishonorable.

Why hadn't she made Richard put them back for safekeeping? She thought of how many servants had access to her room. There was no way she could learn which servant might have removed the jewels. Should she tell Richard right away so he could take steps to apprehend the thief? She deplored the idea of telling him about the theft. The jewels had been in his family for two hundred years, and now that she had entered the family, the jewels were gone.

She couldn't tell him. Not while he was so distant from her. It would be another wedge driving them further apart.

Her door creaked open and she turned, thinking it might be the upstairs girl with wood for her fire. But it was her husband.

She shoved the jewel case back into the drawer.

Without speaking, Radcliff crossed the floor and stood behind his beautiful wife, studying her reflection in the looking glass. He wanted to hold her so badly he physically ached. "How lovely you look, my dear. Expecting company?'' He forced his voice to sound casual to mask the rapid beating of his heart, invariably caused by her presence.

"No, Richard," she said evenly. "I only hoped my husband would be here to share my table. Why do you stay away so much?"

He had planned to dine with her tonight, but perhaps he should withhold his company a bit longer. His plan appeared to be working, judging from Barbara's words. It actually sounded as if she cared. Could it be that absence was the path to her heart? Absence and carefully orchestrated disinterest. "We are in town now, my dear. My town habits are different than my country habits."

"If town habits mean getting foxed every night, neglecting your wife, spending all your time with your bachelor friends and bringing your mistress to dine at our table, then I must say I prefer country habits."

By Jove, but she acted as if she did care. His plan was working. If only he could be strong enough to leave her once again tonight. "My, but my little wife is getting some spunk in her married life. By the way, you forgot. Lynda is my *former* mistress."

Bonny turned around to face her husband. "You expect me to believe that in light of your present behavior?"

God give me the strength not to take her in my arms and dissolve in her embrace. He met her stern gaze and could not resist trailing his finger over her smooth cheek, down to her chin. "It's the truth, Barbara."

"Will you dine with me tonight?" she asked somberly.

He lifted her hand and brushed his lips over it. "I regret I have made other plans."

Chapter Nineteen

Company at White's was thin. The night had yet to get started, but that did not prevent Radcliff and his closest friends from meeting there.

"Remember the time Huntley dressed up as a Covent Garden flower woman?" William Clyde recalled as his chums fondly laughed.

Of the four well-dressed pinks of the ton, William most exemplified a man of style. His Hessians shone so sharply he could have shaved his reflection in them, and his coat of blue superfine with diamond buttons fit to perfection.

"'Course, that was a much thinner Huntley," Stephen Langford reminded.

Huntley Harrington brought a bumper of port to his lips. "Made half a crown, I did!"

His friends laughed heartily.

"But you paid the old woman two guineas for her clothes and flowers," Radcliff said.

"Oh, the times we've had," William said. "Not many pranks we haven't pulled. Except for Richard, who always stands back watching, arms folded, with that merry gleam in his eyes."

"He don't have to do the funny things. Always got Twigs to amuse him," Huntley said.

"I say, I'll be bloody glad when Twigs is back to his old form," William added.

Radcliff frowned. "I fear he may never get back to his old form."

The other three men lowered their brows and shot Radcliff worried glances.

"But I thought he was showing excellent improvement," Stephen said.

"Oh, he is," the duke answered. "I didn't mean he would not mend tolerably well. I said he may never get back to his old self."

"Why? Pray tell," Stephen said.

Radcliff's lips thinned. "I fear he may be settling down."

"A woman?" Huntley asked.

Radcliff nodded.

"But that, sir, doesn't mean anything," William said, smiling. "Look at Radcliff and me."

Radcliff gave his friend a cold stare. "Yes, look at the two of us. Acting as we did when we were one and twenty, when we should be settling down."

The foursome grew quiet, then Twigs limped into the club room, putting much of his weight on a walking stick. Because this was his first visit to White's since his injury, his friends gathered around him, enthusiastically patting him on the back and extending him hardy greetings.

Within a few minutes, Twigs carefully lowered himself into a chair next to Radcliff and whispered, "I came especially to see you, Richard. It ain't right that you never eat with the poor duchess, and I jolly well won't leave here without you."

The duke's eyes flickered with pleasure. "Did she send you?"

"No. Be mad if she knew." Twigs rubbed his reddened nose with the back of his hand. "Poor thing in mourning. It's not like she can go out into society. Just sits there every night waiting for her bridegroom. I thought you cared for her."

Radcliff swallowed. "Of course I care for her. She's my wife. She'll bring me an heir."

"And how's she to do that? You plan to send your seed by post?"

"What happens between my wife and me is none of your affair," Radcliff said angrily, lifting his Madeira to his lips.

A few minutes later, Radcliff got up from his chair and announced, "I had completely forgotten until Twigs reminded me, I have promised to dine with my wife tonight. I regret that I must leave your excellent company, gentlemen." He turned to Twigs. "Coming?"

Radcliff stole a glance at his wife across the brightly lit dinner table. He had not really allowed himself to gaze upon her face in weeks. Now he felt no rush of possessive happiness when he looked at her. She appeared to be losing weight. No wonder, for she barely touched her food. He did not feel like eating himself, but he knew he needed to after drinking all afternoon.

"Will I have the pleasure of your company tonight?" Bonny asked her husband.

"Yes, I plan to work in my library. I have neglected many things that need my attention."

"Like me, your grace?" Bonny cast an insolent look at her husband.

The duke met her gaze. "I was not aware you required my attention, my dear."

Her cheeks hot, Bonny put the cover back over the steaming plate of French beans and turned to Twigs. "And do you have plans tonight?"

Twigs took a big sniff and sighed. "I regret to say I am to go to Almack's."

Radcliff laughed. "Whatever possessed you to go there? They serve nothing stiffer to drink than lemonade."

Twigs gulped his wine. "Bloody dull it'll be, but Miss Carlisle particularly requested that I go."

Making a steeple of his fingers, Radcliff nodded and said, "I see."

His wife met his gaze with mirth. "We are so very happy to see you getting about so well, Twigs," she said.

A footman poured more wine into Twigs's glass.

"Storing up now for the temperance of Almack's?" Radcliff asked with a smile.

"Bloody well better," Twigs said, taking a drink. "Good care I've got here. Suppose I'm well enough to go back to my own lodgings."

"I cannot abide such talk," Bonny said, "for I should be so dreadfully lonely if you left."

Radcliff studied his wife's thin face. It pained him to see her look so forlorn. She had been left alone too much, but what else could he do? If he hadn't seen her in Dunsford's company with his own eyes, he would never have believed it of his sweet Barbara, but she must have given her love to another. A thousand times he told himself there must be some other explanation. He had considered posting a servant to watch the house at Number 17 Kepple Street, but he did not want to hear of his wife meeting Dunsford.

The thought of her in another man's arms drove him mad. He could no longer trust himself around her. He still wanted her, but the tenderness was gone, and he was afraid what he might do to her.

"Need your privacy. Newlyweds and all that." Twigs's face turned very red.

"I daresay I see more of you than I do of my husband."

Bonny peered over her soupspoon into her husband's inscrutable eyes.

Twigs's attention was drawn to his own clear turtle soup.

After dinner, Bonny removed to the drawing room while her husband and Twigs remained at the table and imbibed their port and smoked cigars.

When Twigs left for Almack's, Radcliff entered the drawing room. "I shall be working in my library, my dear."

She looked up from her needlework, but all she saw was his back as he left the room.

Sometime later, Bonny put up her embroidery and went to Radcliff's library. She opened the door and saw him sitting behind his desk in the dark room. A fire blazed in the hearth and a single taper burned beside him, but there were no other lights. Despite the darkness, Bonny could tell by her husband's eyes he had drunk too much. A snifter of brandy was at his right hand and an open book in front of him.

"I wanted to read," Bonny said, advancing into the room, "and since your study is so much warmer than mine, I thought I would join you. That is, if it does not displease you."

"It does not displease me," he said formally, then resumed his reading.

She closed the door behind her and walked around the library, looking at the volumes. She found one section where the books appeared well-worn, as if they had been purchased used rather than new, like all the other works here. Upon examining the titles, she realized her husband had acquired all of her father's writings.

And she was touched. It was the act of a man pledged to uniting his family with another. He *must* be interested in begetting a child with her, she thought with happiness.

She selected a book and sat down on the sofa before the

fire and tried to read, but instead watched Richard as he drank more and more. The crackle of the fire and his turning of pages were the only noises in the room.

When she could no longer stand his silence, she said, "What are you reading, sir?"

He did not answer right away. "If you must know," he said with irritation, "I am reading your father's work on Corinth." He continued to read.

Determined to outlast him, Bonny sat there several hours, attempting to read a tome on democracy. As the fire reduced to embers, and Radcliff's bottle of brandy stood empty, he glared at her, a strange look in his reddened eyes.

"Come here, Barbara."

She got up and slowly walked to his desk, keeping her eyes fastened on him. She skirted the desk and came to stand beside him.

"You are a clergyman's daughter. How well do you remember your Bible, my dear? Matthew six, verse twenty-four?"

She gave him a puzzled look.

"Did your father ever preach about 'No man can serve two masters'?"

Her brows furrowed. "I don't remember."

His eyes challenged her. "I want you to serve me."

"Of course, I am your wife," she replied shakily.

"Come closer."

She moved so close she could smell the brandy on his breath. Her hand gently swept stray strands of his sandy hair off his forehead.

He grabbed her wrist tightly and spoke in a frightening voice she did not recognize. "Serve me now, dear wife." He pulled her to him with great force and buried his head into her bosom. Freeing one hand, he lifted her skirts and began to stroke upward from her thighs.

"The servants might come in," Bonny cautioned in a whisper.

"Then let us go to bed, dear wife."

She did not like his tone, but she started for the door. As Bonny mounted the stairs, her fear increased with each step. The thought of lying with this gruff man her husband had become sickened her. In the past their lovemaking had been spontaneous, pleasurable. It had felt so right. But what was certain to occur in her bedchamber tonight seemed sinister.

In Bonny's room, they found Marie waiting up for her mistress.

"You are dismissed," the duke snapped at the abigail, who directly removed herself from the room.

Bonny walked to her bedside table to blow out the candle.

"Don't!" Radcliff commanded. "I want to look at you."

Bonny felt herself coloring as she began to unfasten the tiny buttons of her gown. She had dreamed of this night for weeks, but now that she was about to share her bed with him, there was no happiness. The man who stood before her with blazing eyes and rough voice was not her beloved Richard, she thought with empty longing, remembering what a tender lover her Richard had been.

"Here, I will do that," Radcliff said. He patiently unfastened half a dozen buttons before he let out an oath and tore off the rest of the gown.

"Richard! You ruined a brand-new dress."

"You married a very rich man, Barbara. You can buy all the dresses you want."

She stepped out of the gown and her satin slippers, then turned her back to remove her ivory-colored shift.

"I said I want to see you," Radcliff said sternly.

She turned to face him, flushing, and trembled as she

took off the rest of her clothing while her fully dressed husband stood watching.

"Now lie on the bed," he ordered.

She did as he instructed, keeping her eyes on him.

"It grows cold. Get under the counterpane."

Bonny slid between the silken sheets.

His eyes never leaving her, Radcliff shed all his clothes and stood before her.

She saw that he was fully aroused.

He got in the bed and pulled her face toward his for a bruising kiss, sliding his hand between her legs, stroking her. "You are not ready for me, my dear," he said, displeasure in his rough voice.

"Yes I am. I have removed all my clothes."

"Do you not know what I mean, Barbara?"

She gave him a questioning gaze.

"A woman who wants a man gets slick inside. In that special place." His fingers stabbed into her and she cried out.

"What's the matter, dear, don't you want to make love to your own husband?"

"To my old husband, yes, but not to the man you are tonight."

"But you are my wife, Barbara."

"Can't you be gentle as you once were?" she pleaded, her voice shaky.

He cupped one of her breasts as if he were weighing it. "You will accept me no matter how I am, for I am your husband." His harsh voice frightened her. It was as if a strange man lay beside her.

Tears seeped from her moistened eyes.

His face softened, and he drew her rigid body into his embrace and kissed a path of light, butterfly kisses from her neck to her mouth, where he slowly, tenderly kissed her.

Brushing the hair from her face, he whispered, "Forgive me. I daresay it's the brandy that has made me so crude."

"You will be your old self now?"

He reached for the candle and blew it out, then gathered her into his arms. She relaxed, her head resting on his chest. Lifting her face, he dried her tears with gentle hands, then dropped a soft kiss on her nose. Her lips sought his. When her lips parted, the kiss deepened, his hands gliding possessively over her back, her hips, drawing her even closer.

Her body came to vivid life, his warmth filling her soul, driving away all awareness, save for the scent of him, the liquid movement of her body against his, her obliterating need of him.

With a lover's wisdom, he knew she was ready for him now.

And he buried himself within her.

When Bonny awoke later, she felt the moistness of her husband's seed and smiled, reaching for him.

But he was gone.

Chapter Twenty

Another day and night and another day passed before Bonny was to see her husband again, and by then he suffered from the effects of heavy drinking. She had taken another solitary dinner and retired with her needlework to the drawing room, when she heard Mandley talking with Radcliff in the outer hall. By the time she put up her sewing and left the drawing room, Radcliff was no longer there. She walked down the hall, opened the door to his library and was taken aback at the sight of her husband.

He sat before his desk, which bore a single candle and a full bottle of Malmsey. His cravat hung loose, his hair was disheveled, and the heavy growth on his face indicated he had not shaved since she last saw him.

"Are you all right, Richard?" Bonny questioned, worry in her voice.

He glared at her. "Actually, my dear, I am not well. In addition to feeling wretched, I find my life very repetitive."

She strolled into the room and sat in a wing chair near his desk. "I am not surprised you find it so. One would expect as much from the hollow existence you've led these past fifteen years."

"You sound like a cleric's daughter, my dear."

"Not a nagging wife?"

"That, too," he said.

"A wife would be expected to show concern when her husband continues to live as he had before his marriage," Bonny replied.

Radcliff lifted the full bottle to his lips and drank. "It's a worthless existence I've led. If I died tomorrow, there would be nothing to show for my life. Not even an heir."

"I hope you do not fault me for that."

He shook his head. "No, I cannot fault you. You have never refused me, my dear." His cold tone did nothing to assure her.

"Why do you speak so maudlin, Richard?"

"Think on it. What would be left of me if I died? At least my ancestors built grand houses that will stand for centuries. They fought valiant battles for the kingdom. They left heirs." He took another drink. "I have a very strong longing to fight on the Peninsula. Nothing could be more noble than to die for England."

Bonny caught her breath, her insides flinching at the grief caused by his words. "I pray you will say no more."

His glassy eyes met hers. "Would it bother you if I died, Barbara?"

"It does not bear thinking of. It is far too painful."

"But you would be the richest woman in the kingdom."

"You think I care about that?"

He shook his head sadly. "No. I cannot say that I do. I don't think you are interested in wealth and title. I have often wondered, my dear, just why you married me. I suspect it was to please your mother."

Her heart pounded. "Did it never occur to you that I might be in love with you?" She had not wanted to force her love on him, but she'd been unable to hold back the words.

"Only when you are in my arms. Then, I must admit, your ardor is most pronounced."

Bonny colored. "You underestimate your charms outside the bedchamber."

He laughed a mirthless laugh. "Barbara, my love, you must remove yourself from this room. I have papers that demand my attention, and it is much too difficult to look upon your face and not want to seduce you beneath this very desk."

"I grow very tired of your homage to my face. I am a real woman with real feelings, Richard." With a defiant tilt of her chin and a scolding tone, she added, "I think all you wanted in a wife was a beautiful woman to display, and because I am in mourning and you cannot trot me out like one of your prize horses, you have no desire for my company."

"I do greatly look forward to the day I can present you to all of London."

That he did not deny marrying her for her beauty hurt her more than all the lonely nights she had lain in her empty bed and imagined him in the arms of other women, but she could not allow him to know how deeply he wounded her. "Perhaps you could present me at a small dinner party. Twigs wishes to leave Radcliff House, and I believe we should host a farewell dinner for him."

"Whatever you wish, just do not ask Dunsford," he warned in a menacing voice, his eyes scowling.

"Had I known how strongly you dislike him, I should never have asked him, though I do not understand why you detest him so. He seems a most amiable man. I hoped that Emily might look upon him with something more than friendship."

Radcliff gave his wife a puzzled glance, then opened his drawer and took out some papers, which he began to read.

"Pray, leave the room, Barbara. You distract me much too much."

Evans dragged the sharpened razor across the heavy stubble on Radcliff's cheek. "It is to be hoped no one of consequence has seen your grace today in such deplorable condition. Had you only sent for me, I should have been most happy to have brought you around a fresh change of clothes and seen to your appearance."

"I fear I slept too bloody damned late, Evans. It was after dawn before we got to bed."

"I must say I am happy you still see your old friends. A fun-loving lot they are, your grace."

Radcliff thought of his father and how he would have viewed those fun-loving friends and disapproved of his son's rakish behavior. No man had ever been nobler than the fourth duke. Nor had Radcliff ever known a happier man. "Still carrying on as we did when we came from Oxford."

A rather pleasant grin flashed across Evans's normally placid features. "Oh, yes, indeed, your grace." He stood back and surveyed his master's smooth face. "Now you will look proper for your dinner party tonight."

"Has the duchess been worried that I may not show?"

"Not five minutes could go by that she did not scurry from her chamber, inquiring if you had come."

"I do not understand why my wife does not scream and cry or come flying at me with a dagger over my lamentable conduct."

"She knows her place. You are the master."

"Her place?" Radcliff screwed up his face. "By God, man, she's my wife. You are speaking of the Duchess of Radcliff. She has as much right to be here as I do."

With his mouth in a straight line, Evans moved to take up the suit of clothing his master would wear to the dinner party, which was due to begin in half an hour. After he assisted Radcliff in getting dressed, Evans was dismissed.

Radcliff entered his wife's chamber through the adjacent dressing room. His breath caught at the sight of her sitting before her dressing table. She wore a low-cut black crepe gown, a black plume in her hair.

After Marie left, Bonny turned to stare at her husband. "I feared you had forgotten about tonight."

He walked up and kissed her forehead. "You can depend upon me, Barbara."

Her simmering eyes met his. "Can I?"

Radcliff's finger trailed over his wife's ivory shoulders and along the length of her neck. "I should like my friends to see you in the Radcliff Jewels tonight, my love. I want them all to know you are mine."

Bonny's face went white. Averting her gaze from his, she said, "I...I cannot find them, Richard." She burst out crying.

"You cannot find them?" he said angrily.

"I...I opened my drawer to look at them—" she stopped, her voice breaking "—and they were gone." Her hands covered her face as she continued crying.

"What do you mean, 'they were gone'? You believe someone stole them?"

She nodded.

"Where were they?"

"I kept them in the drawer."

Radcliff began to open all the drawers. After finding nothing that resembled the Radcliff Jewels, he gave Bonny a cold stare, his face reddening. "No one will ever get away with stealing from the House of Radcliff." His cold eyes traveled over her. "Get control of yourself," he said sternly. "You cannot greet our guests looking like a watering pot."

"Oh, Richard, I'm so dreadfully sorry. You'd have been better off had you never married me."

He did not respond.

Dinner was a disaster. Bonny's plans to display her husband in a happy domestic setting to his friends blew up in her face. No one could have looked more brooding than Radcliff did throughout dinner. He barely said two words. And every time one of the footmen passed his chair with a bottle of wine, he demanded another glass. By the time the men retired to Radcliff's billiard room, he was well on his way to a thorough foxing.

At least the ladies' assemblage in the salon lacked the awkwardness of her last dinner party with the unwanted Lady Lynda Heffington, Bonny thought, still holding back tears.

Why had Richard been so dreadfully inhospitable? And the way he had looked at her! As if he could wring her neck. His wicked friends were sure to be more desirous than ever of removing him from so wretched a household.

As the finely dressed women sat around on silken sofas discussing delicate topics, Lady Landis directed her gaze at Bonny. "I must say, marriage does not seem to agree with either you or your husband, Barbara."

Bonny, jolted from her reverie, shot a puzzled glance at her aunt.

Lady Landis's eyes danced. "Why, you're getting as thin as a poker."

Her aunt was sharper than Bonny had given her credit for. Not even Marie had noticed how Bonny's gown had begun to hang on her thinning frame. Ever since this estrangement from her husband, Bonny had lost interest in eating, to the degree that she sometimes felt physically ill at the sight of food. "It is probably just your imagination, Aunt."

"Bonny looks perfectly beautiful to me," Emily said.

To which Mrs. Miller and Cressida readily agreed.

Bonny, sitting next to her cousin, placed her hand over Emily's. "You never can see any fault with me."

"I suppose I am very loyal to those I care about," Emily whispered. "Even if you haven't been to see me of late."

"I'm sorry, Em. I have been feeling wretched lately." Her face brightened. "I did come to see you twice, though, and both times you were riding in the park with Lord Dunsford."

"I...I had hoped he might be here tonight. Since you invited him the last time."

Bonny watched her cousin's face carefully. And she knew. Emily had transferred her love for Harold to his brother.

"I do wish William Clyde's little wife could have been here tonight," Mrs. Miller said.

"Did I hear him telling you at dinner that she recently presented him with a second son?" Cressida asked.

"Yes. She has been at her mother's for her confinement."

"I think she should have been at her own house, with her husband," Cressida said. "Instead of him carrying on in London as if he had no family and no responsibility. I told Mr. Twickingham my thoughts on the subject, and he quite agreed."

Poor Twigs, he would probably agree to anything Cressida said, Bonny thought. Cressida fairly well led him around by the nose. There was nary a thought in his head that was not put there by the lovely blonde he had taken off the shelf.

Lady Landis strode across the room, smiling, and reclaimed her seat next to her daughter. "These bloods appear to have little interest in the married state."

At this point, the men entered the salon.

"Radcliff," Lady Landis snapped, "don't you find your wife getting thinner?"

He turned to Bonny. He was still so angry he could have shaken his beautiful wife senseless. She must have sold the Radcliff Jewels—jewels that had been in his family for two hundred years—to pay her lover's gaming debts. Everyone in London knew of Dunsford's heavy losses. Radcliff's eyes swept over Bonny's body. "You are correct, my lady." He turned back to his friends. "Whist anyone?"

"Mr. Twickingham has promised to teach me the finer points of the game," Cressida said, removing herself from the sofa and strolling to Twigs's side.

There was enough interest for two tables. The four young men who took their gaming rather seriously sat at the other table. That group included Bonny's cousin, Alfred, and the duke's three friends.

Not being particularly close to the duke's circle, Stanley Moncrief stayed with the women and attempted to charm them.

"Have you ever seen Richard's hunting lodge in Scotland, your grace?" Stanley asked Bonny.

"I did not even know of its existence," Bonny said.

Stanley got to his feet and held out his hand to Bonny. "Come, I will show you a painting of it."

He led her to Radcliff's library. Over the blazing hearth hung an oil painting of a rather Tudorish two-story house nestled among fir trees, a blue stream running beside it. "Lovely, isn't it?" Stanley said.

Her eyes on the painting, Bonny nodded.

"Like you," Stanley said, encircling her with his arms as he bent to kiss Bonny.

She tried to wriggle from his grasp. "Stop this!"

Angered by her protest, Stanley grasped her slender arms with his bruising hands and pulled her to him, his mouth crushing hers.

Bonny twisted her head frantically, her lips tight, but she could not break from his hold. "I am married!" she shrieked.

Stanley answered with a frightening laugh, his hands still painfully digging into her. "Your husband does not act like a married man. Everyone knows he does not plan to keep you. He has admitted that he made a mistake by not marrying his true love."

Bonny's heart thundered. "His true love?"

"Lady Heffington."

Seized by an overwhelming rage, Bonny found the strength to break from Stanley's hold and slap him across the face.

Just then her husband walked into the room.

Chapter Twenty-One

"Take that away, please!" Bonny demanded as Marie angled her way into the bedroom, balancing her mistress's breakfast tray in one hand and attempting to close the door with the other.

Marie glanced at Bonny sitting up in her bed, her face white as a ghost. Shrugging, she pivoted and turned to exit the room.

"No! Get me something. Quick! I'm going to be sick," Bonny said, tightening her palm over her mouth.

Marie hastily put down the tray, ran to the dresser, removed the pot and brought it to Bonny, who began retching immediately while motioning for Marie to leave the room.

Ill as she was, Bonny desired to spill the meager contents of her stomach in privacy. If there was one good thing about the estrangement with her husband, it was that he wouldn't see her heaving and retching and turning blue.

After giving Bonny a long enough period to be thoroughly sick, Marie came back into the room—minus the hot breakfast—and gave Bonny an appraising glance. "There now, yer grace," Marie said tenderly, taking the pot from Bonny's trembling hands. "Ye'll be good as new in no time. Mrs. 'enson says ye'll be back to yer old self before long.''

"Mrs. Henson knows of my illness?"

Marie set the pot outside the door and came back to stand at Bonny's side. "Mrs. 'enson knows everything that goes on in Radcliff House." The kindly maid wiped a gentle hand over Bonny's damp forehead and smoothed away her mistress's wayward strands of hair.

"And how, pray tell, does she know precisely when I shall get well?"

Marie held up a day dress she had selected from Bonny's wardrobe and spoke matter-of-factly. "She had two babes of her own."

Bonny's mouth gaped open. "Pray, whatever are you talking about?"

"About ye being with child." Marie calmly walked over to Bonny's bed. "Do ye feel up to getting out of the bed, yer grace?"

Bonny leaned back on the mound of pillows, her mind spinning from Marie's casual comment. "You think...you think I'm going to have a baby?"

Marie smiled broadly and nodded. "It's very happy we all are. All except fer poker-faced Mr. Evans."

"But... but..." Bonny began to protest. Then she remembered the night Richard had acted so strange in the library. When he had said, "No man can serve two masters." When she had prepared to serve him as he instructed, but his shell had suddenly melted, revealing the same tender, loving man to whom she had given her heart.

The memory of that night grew even sweeter now that she realized a child, their child, might have been conceived then.

Bonny flung off her covers and stepped from the bed, smiling and throwing her arms wide in a huge stretch.

"Pray, Marie, open the windows. To be sure, it must be a lovely day."

"I say, Radcliff," William Clyde said, "I believe Fanny Tuttle to be the most beautiful of all the opera dancers, and she clearly lusts after you."

"Not in my style," Radcliff said distractedly, eyeing the young man who had just barged into Mrs. Ferndale's gaming establishment. The fellow looked very much like his wife's cousin, Alfred Wickham.

"Pray, tell us what is your style?" said Stephen Langford. "You used not to be so particular before you were ensnared by the lovely Bonny Barbara Allan."

William helped himself to a glass of brandy off the tray of a waiter passing by. "Now you find fault with all the ladies. If she's not too tall, she's too small. Or her breasts are too flat or her arms too fat. I beg you to tell me what is wrong with the lovely Miss Tuttle."

"Miss Tuttle?" Radcliff asked. "Oh, yes, the opera girl." His eyes followed the man. It was Alfred Wickham.

"Will you fellows leave poor Radcliff alone," Twigs said. "Can't you accept he's a happily married man?"

"It's not a happily married bridegroom who leaves his bride alone night after night," Huntley said.

"I beg you will excuse me, gentlemen," Radcliff said, pushing back his chair and standing up. "I see my wife's cousin."

The duke turned to meet Alfred's gaze.

"Radcliff! Here you are. I've been looking everywhere for you."

Remembering the night Alfred had crashed into the Abernathys' ball with bad news for Bonny, Radcliff felt his heart nearly stop. He froze, watching Alfred's forlorn face. Something must have happened to Bonny! "Is my wife...?"

"Bonny?" Alfred glanced pensively at Radcliff. "Oh, there's nothing wrong with her."

Radcliff went limp with relief.

"But I do need to speak to you in private."

Radcliff put his arm around Alfred's shoulder. "Come, we'll have cigars on Mrs. Ferndale's balcony."

Outside, with the glass doors shut behind them, Radcliff offered Alfred a cigar. Radcliff liked Alfred. He wondered how two such nice offspring as Alfred and Emily could have come from that contemptible Lucille Wickham. Then he thought of the woman's mild husband and swelled with pride. It was Lord Landis's blood—Bonny's blood—that determined the sweet nature of the Wickham children.

Taking the cigar, Alfred tapped it and began speaking. "I felt I needed to tell you what horrid lies are being spread about your wife, your grace." He showed Radcliff his raw knuckles. "I became so enraged when Stanley told me those damned lies I fairly well lit into him."

"I am sure my cousin deserved it," Radcliff assured him. "Now, tell me what he told you."

Alfred took a puff of the cigar. "Well, he—Stanley— began by touching me for five quid. Said as how we were all family now. Then he acted sad and said something like how disappointing it was that your marriage to my cousin was going so badly." Alfred stopped, eyeing the duke ruefully. "I regret to say I told Stanley that I was sorry to hear...to hear of you running wild still with the same old bloods you ran with when you were single. That's when he said you and Bonny had an understanding. She had her affair with Dunsford, and you could cavort with any woman you chose. That's when I hit him. I'll not have anyone talk like that of my cousin. Bonny's as true as a saint, I'll vow."

Damn Stanley, Radcliff thought. He would do more than hit him this time. The vile creature persisted to menace what Radcliff valued most. Radcliff had crashed his fist into

Stanley's face when he found him trying to manhandle his wife. He'd told his wretched cousin he would never again be welcome at Radcliff House. He winced as he decided his next recourse.

Radcliff clasped a strong hand on Alfred's shoulder. "It's my fault," he said in a low voice. "My deplorable behavior has given rise to these wild rumors." He took a long puff on the cigar and slowly blew the smoke out into the cool night air. "I thank you for coming to me with this information. My cousin will not slander my wife any-more—thanks to you."

Once her stomach settled, Bonny left the house and rode to the square near Kepple Street. The day before, Duns-ford's page had slipped her a note requesting her to meet him at eleven-thirty.

When she arrived, Bonny saw that Harriet already had her uncle making a cake of himself over her. He met Bonny with smiling eyes as she sat on the carpet next to Dunsford and planted a kiss on top Harriet's fair head. "This must be the last time you beckon me here," Bonny said. "I find deceiving the duke most distasteful."

"I may not have to come here again myself," Lord Dunsford said, throwing the giggling baby in the air and catching her.

Bonny shrieked. "I beg you will not do that again. I am quite terrified you will drop her."

"Nonsense." He nuzzled Harriet's plump neck and pre-tended to blow bubbles against her flesh, causing the baby to giggle anew. "Is she not the most beautiful baby girl ever created? Of course, I expect her mother was just as lovely as a child."

"Then you know who her mother is?"

"Since the night I met Emily, I have known."

"I think you should tell her."

"When the time is right, I will." He tossed Harriet in the air again. Catching her and holding her close, he turned to Bonny. "I called you here to ask your opinion. I'm mad about this baby, and I want her to live with me." He put Harriet down on the carpet and allowed her to crawl. Meeting Bonny's gaze, he said, "I shall admit she is my brother's baby, but that her mother was a Spanish woman who died during her lying-in. That way Harriet would have all the advantages she is due as my brother's child."

"It would be most wonderful for Harriet," Bonny said in a soft voice.

"But?"

"I shall have to break the news to Emily. She will miss her visits with Harriet most dreadfully."

His face clouded. "I hate to hurt Emily. I had not thought of that."

"But I am sure Em would agree that what you propose is in Harriet's best interest." Bonny chewed on her lip. "I shall first have to tell her that I have broken her confidence and told you of the baby." Bonny rose and walked to the window, pulling back the lace curtains and gazing out on the gray day. "She will not be happy to learn you know the truth. She believes herself tainted."

"Tainted indeed! She's everything a man could hope for. Why, she's more beautiful than...." He picked up Harriet again. "Like you are, my pet," he said to the baby.

If only Lord Dunsford knew he was in love with Emily, Bonny thought.

That afternoon Lady Landis welcomed her niece to Wickham House. As much as she wanted to believe the worst of that upstart niece of hers, Lady Landis no longer wanted to repeat Stanley Moncrief's wicked tale about Barbara and that nice Lord Dunsford. And she had told Stanley Moncrief a few nights ago at the Radcliff dinner that his wicked tales about dear Lord Dunsford and her niece were nothing but a pack of lies. Why, anyone with two eyes could tell the earl was besotted with her own lovely Emily. That is, anyone except Emily. Thank the Almighty, her daughter had at least been civil to the peer.

Already, Lady Landis's imagination had run wild. *My daughter, the Countess of Dunsford.* She liked the sound of it.

Now she walked her daughter and her niece to the Radcliff barouche. "I daresay you two never will sit down and have tea with me. Always you must go off together. One would think you were plotting to rob the crown jewels."

"Nonsense, Mama," Emily said, giving her hand to the footman, who assisted her into the coach. "We just like to be together."

Bonny instructed the coachman to take them to Hyde Park. After they were away from Cavendish Square, Bonny asked, "When you were increasing with Harriet, were you allowed to walk, Em?"

Emily's head spun around. "Are you with child?"

Bonny's eyes sparkled. "I think perhaps I am. I'm dreadfully sick every morning. Were you?"

"No. I had a very healthy appetite. I had absolutely no idea I was increasing until I realized I had not had a monthly flow in far too many weeks. So, of course, I walked and did everything as I had before. Then, when Aunt Camille found out, she would not allow me to do anything." Emily took Bonny's hand. "I'm so happy for you. I know how much you love Harriet and how much you have wanted a baby of your own. What does Richard think?"

"I haven't told him yet. I just realized this morning." A contented smile settled on Bonny's face.

"I'm sure he will be delighted."

"Perhaps we had better not walk today. I suppose I need

to save the little energy I have. I haven't been able to have a really good visit with you, since I've been sick every day."

"Poor Bonny. I should have come to visit you."

"Nonsense. I understand you've been spending a good amount of time with Lord Dunsford."

"I had not meant to. It's just that I so enjoy being with him. At first it was because he looked so very much like dear Harold. But now I realize they are quite different. Lord Dunsford is much more reserved than Harold." She averted her gaze and spoke softly. "I like him very much."

Bonny's heart began to hammer at what she was going to say. "Em, I have a confession to make."

Emily gave a little laugh. "A confession? Now you sound like Mama. Have you stolen the crown jewels?"

"No. I told Lord Dunsford about Harriet."

Emily whirled around, her eyes like hot coals. "You what?"

"I confirmed what he already knew. Harold's man had told him that Harold and a woman named Emily had conceived a child."

"Then...Higgins knew," Emily said softly, her eyes brimming with tears. "Tell me everything," she whispered.

"The first night I met Lord Dunsford I made the mistake of telling him a friend of mine knew his brother in Spain. I said my friend was a female. Lord Dunsford knew of you from Harold's letters. After that, Lord Dunsford hounded me. He wanted to know if his brother's child was a girl or boy. He pressed me into allowing him to see Harriet."

"He's seen her?"

Bonny nodded solemnly. "Many times. He's grown very fond of her. He...he loves her very much."

Emily sat dazedly staring in front of her.

"Oh, Em, I'm so sorry, but really, Lord Dunsford needed

to know about his own niece. He's in a position to see that she gets what she is entitled to as the niece of an earl.''

"To bc sure," Emily said distractedly.

Emily turned to Bonny. "I shall never again be able to see him. I should die of shame."

"But all these times he's been with you, he has known, and he thought no less of you. If you ask me, he's falling in love with you."

"I could not look him in the face."

This was not a good time to tell Emily about the earl's scheme to adopt Harriet, thought Bonny. Emily was distraught enough.

Chapter Twenty-Two

Radcliff heard the sound of draperies sliding back and closed his eyes tightly against the sun. "Good God, man, what are you doing?"

"Perhaps your grace has forgotten that your solicitor is to meet you here at one o'clock," Evans said evenly.

Radcliff opened first one eye then another to the harsh sunlight. "What ungodly hour is it, pray tell?"

"Fifteen past twelve, your grace."

"Blast Mr. Willingham." Radcliff attempted to lift his head from the pillow but was overtaken by great pain. "Be a good man, Evans, and bring me a tisane. I'm afraid I'm not feeling quite the thing."

"I already have it, your grace."

His head aching abominably, Radcliff managed to sit up and drink the elixir in one long gulp.

"May I say that it is good to have you home, your grace. In your own bed. It has been quite some time." Humming happily to himself, Evans went to Radcliff's dressing room and came back with a clean shirt and breeches.

"Thank you, Evans. Town was deuced dull last night, and at one time I did remember that I had to meet with Willingham early today." Radcliff threw off his covers and swung his legs over the side of the bed. "Tell me, has her grace had breakfast yet?"

A smirk came over Evans's face. "It has been quite some weeks since her grace has eaten breakfast."

Radcliff shot a quizzing glance at Evans, his brows low. "She doesn't eat breakfast anymore?"

"No, your grace. She appears to be very sick each morning, but her tolerance for food will improve." The valet held out a crisp white shirt.

"How do you know so much about my wife?" Radcliff slid his arm into the shirt Evans held open for him.

"Oh, the whole house knows about the baby, your grace."

"The baby?" Radcliff could not understand what a baby had to do with poor Barbara being sick. And who had a baby around here, anyway? Then, like a shot from a cannon, the meaning hit him. Barbara was with child. The thought made his insides go mushy, a warmth spreading from his heart. He thought of how thin Barbara had been looking, and he ached to think of her being so sick.

And everyone in Radcliff House knew except her husband. He must not let the servants think Barbara had not shared the news with him. He sprang from the bed and threw on his trousers, stalking toward the dressing room that linked with Barbara's room. "I must tend to my wife, Evans. I will dress myself later."

The sight of Bonny sliced into Radcliff's heart. Thin and pale, she lay rigid, several lace-covered pillows propped behind her. Her arms looked like twigs poking from the snow white muslin gown. Shadowy gray circles hung under her tired eyes and her cheeks were hollow.

"You look terrible!"

A wan smile touched her lips. "Thank you, your grace."

Radcliff sat on the bed beside his wife. "I'm told you've been sick for some time."

"I realized yesterday that it might not precisely be sickness. It seems the entire household knows more than I about my own condition." She took Radcliff's hand. "I believe we're going to be parents, Richard." Her face transformed—her eyes no longer tired but lively, a smile playing at her pale lips.

He withdrew his hand. It suddenly occurred to him that the babe might not be his. He had not shared Bonny's bed in months.

"I was very surprised, since we have not been together. Then I remembered that night." Her eyes softened. "Not that I had forgotten it."

That night, Radcliff thought. That night the brandy had numbed his brain and he allowed himself the luxury of sinking into Bonny with a hunger that gnawed at him even now.

Then he thought of Dunsford lying with Bonny, and he wanted to skewer the man on his saber.

He lightly touched his fingertips to her cheeks. It was strange he did not want to kill her. Only Dunsford. Barbara had done everything he asked of her. She had agreed to become his wife. She had opened her body to him completely and without inhibition. She had once even used the word *love*. He would carry to his grave the memory of her meeting his gaze and saying, "Did it never occur to you that I might be in love with you?"

He had known when he asked her to become his wife that she had given her heart to another. He had taken advantage of her mother's condition to force her into marriage.

And she had been a good wife. Except she had not kept her vow to "forsake all others."

He kissed her hand and got to his feet. "I am very sorry that you have been so unwell, my dear, but I must hurry. My solicitor awaits downstairs."

As he walked toward the door, she called to him in a shaky voice, "Are you not happy about the baby, Richard?"

With his back to her, he swallowed and said, "It is just that it is such unexpected news. I daresay it will take me a while before I get used to the idea."

As he descended the broad marble staircase, Radcliff cursed to himself. "Damn her eyes!" No matter how hard he tried to purge Barbara from his thoughts, the image of her long black lashes shading aquamarine eyes, her sensuous mouth beneath the aristocratic nose crowded everything from his mind. Now he thought of her with Dunsford, her lovely ivory body beneath his.

And he recalled the words to the ballad of "Bonny Barbara Allan."

On his deathbed lay
for love of Barbara Allan.

A few blocks away, Dunsford skipped up the steps to Wickham House and rapped on the door.

It was opened by Styles.

"Please tell Lady Emily that Lord Dunsford has arrived to take her riding," Dunsford said cheerily.

"I regret to say her ladyship is not in, my lord."

"But..." Emily had agreed to ride with him in the park at five o'clock today. He pulled his watch from the fob and glanced at it. Five o'clock. She had not sent him a message canceling their meeting. He had just come from his house. Vastly disappointed that he would not get to see her, and concerned over the cancellation, Dunsford handed his card to Styles. "Please leave this for Lady Emily."

Radcliff sat behind his desk and directed his gaze at Jonathan Willingham, the white-haired gentleman who had been solicitor for Radcliff's father before Radcliff succeeded. And Willingham's father before him had served the House of Radcliff since the days of the third duke.

"I have asked you here today, Jonathan, because I do not wish the title to go to my cousin Stanley Moncrief."

Willingham coughed, and his bent-over shoulders straightened. "But, your grace, it is out of my hands. It's the law of the kingdom. Primogeniture. In kindredship, Stanley is the closest male to you in the Moncrief line. The only way to prevent him from succeeding is for you and the duchess to have a male child."

"My good man, we are working on that, but in the absence of my yet-to-be-born son, I desire that you find a way to cut Stanley out."

"Your grace—"

"And while you are working on that, draw up a will that is exceedingly generous to my wife." Radcliff stood up and held out his hand. "Good of you to come, Jonathan."

"Really must go before you win the cravat off my neck." Twigs shot a disappointed glance at Radcliff, threw down his cards and rose from the whist table in the card room at White's.

Old Lord Higby also got to his feet. "What's that you say? Winning a habit with Radcliff? Upon my word, fellow's got devilishly good luck."

Stanley Moncrief was by no means ready to leave. Quite the contrary. He had waited all night to get his cousin alone. When the others were safely out of earshot, he leaned toward the duke and said, "I say, would you have any objections to my calling on the lovely Lady Lynda?"

Radcliff's eyes studied Moncrief with blatant insolence. "You ask that of a newly married man?"

"Well, when I saw your wife with Dunsford the other day, I quite naturally assumed..."

Radcliff did not move an eyelash as his gaze hardened. "You assumed incorrectly."

"Then this marriage of yours is a love match?" Moncrief's spirits sank. If the two loved each other, surely an heir would be produced within the year, cutting his likelihood of succeeding to the dukedom.

"Did you suppose I married Barbara for her dowry?" the duke replied mockingly.

A sly smile curved Moncrief's lip. "It is widely known she had no dowry, your grace, but I thought you might merely want to possess her because she is undoubtedly the most beautiful woman in all of London."

"In all of England," the duke amended, the corners of his mouth lifting slightly. "And I will thank you to keep your hands off her in the future."

"I daresay if I were married to the most beautiful woman in England I would not be sitting at White's tonight, nor all the other nights of late."

The duke leveled cool green eyes at Moncrief. "Your appetite for gossip is not unlike a woman's, Stanley." He leaned toward Moncrief, his gaze brittle, his voice chilling, and said, "The story about the duchess and Dunsford had best not reach my ears again. I would hate to have to call you out."

That said, the duke scooped up his winnings, nodded at his cousin and left.

Though it was a cool night, Moncrief wiped fresh beads of perspiration from his brow. He knew he balanced on a very thin wire between victory and oblivion. He would have to be most careful to avoid vexing his cousin any further. The duke's skill with the sword and with pistols was as well known as his appreciation of beautiful women.

A moment later, Radcliff returned, hat in his hands. "And one more thing, Stanley. The duchess and I are to be parents." He turned on his heel and left.

Chapter Twenty-Three

The sound of violent retching woke Radcliff the next morning. Not accustomed to sleeping in his own bed, he sprang up to see where he was. Who in the bloody hell could hold his liquor no better than a blade in his first season? The warm claret velvets and rich dark woods of his own chamber made him realize where he was. He shuddered as he listened to the waning sounds of his Barbara's agony.

Pulling on the trousers that lay on the floor where he'd left them late the night before, Radcliff went to his wife.

She was alone, slipping from her bed to remove the chamber pot now that she had filled it with yesterday's dinner.

"Here," he said sternly, taking the porcelain bowl from her. "Back to bed, my dear." Turning his back on his surprised wife, he walked to the door, placed the pot in the hallway, came back and plumped up several pillows behind Bonny, then sat on the edge of her bed. His eyes wandered over her pallid face. "How long have you been sick like this?"

She shrugged. "I don't really know. Quite likely two months."

"I am worried about you. How long will this keep up?"

"For many women, about three months. For others, the duration of their confinement."

"How can a baby survive under such circumstances?"

"I do not at all understand, but they do. Already, my shift is too tight. Our baby seems to be thriving." She took Radcliff's hand and placed it on her stomach. "Feel, Richard. He is already growing."

Splaying his fingers over her belly, he felt a hard swell where she had been soft. A lump came to his throat. A tangle of emotions nearly overpowered him. When he gazed back into her pallid face with its great, sad eyes, the urge to encircle her in his protective warmth overcame him. He drew her against him and closed his arms around her.

For some time, he basked in the peace of her, the feel of her hands moving gently over his back, the sweet rose scent of her. He did not want to break the spell with words.

But Marie, coming to check on her mistress, broke the spell.

For once, the duke spoke kindly to the startled abigail. "I appreciate the excellent care you have given the duchess, Marie. I fear I have been very neglectful."

Neglectful did not come close to describing his deplorable treatment of Barbara. He had been so deuced low over his own doubts, he had not considered her. But worry over her now consumed him like a raging fever. Whether or not that babe was his, he could not bear for her to suffer.

"But you did not know, Richard," Bonny said, gazing at her husband with laughing eyes.

He turned back to Marie. "I will see to the duchess's needs this morning, Marie."

Marie curtsied. "Very good, your grace."

With Marie gone, Radcliff directed his attention once again to his wife. He brought a hand to caress her face. "I intend to get the pink back in your cheeks, my love. I believe what you need is a ride in the park.''

"With you?'' she asked hopefully.

"Of course.'' His brows came together. "It is all right for you to ride, is it not?''

"I think it will be the very thing I need.''

Since it was a cool day, Radcliff insisted upon covering Bonny with rugs before he sat beside her and gave instructions to the coachman. He settled back in his seat as he eyed his wife. She wore a black bonnet, tied under her chin, and a black serge pelisse covered her mourning dress. "I would love to see you again in the blue cloak you wore the first time we kissed.''

Bonny thought about the cold day in Milford when she and Radcliff had stood atop the knoll, the wind slicing through them as they surveyed the misty moors below. She remembered her love bringing his mouth to hers, her hood slipping off. And once again she felt the same happiness she had felt that day.

During the short ride to the park, Radcliff took her gloved hand in his.

"Do you realize, sir, this is the first time you have ever taken me to the park in these six months we have been in London?''

"Is that so? I shall have to rectify my neglect of you, my dear.''

"I had come to think you must be ashamed of me.''

"When have I ever given you reason to suspect that I felt anything but extreme pride in you? Have I not said a hundred times how much I wanted to display your loveliness to all of London?''

She lowered her lashes. "To be sure, Richard. It is not your fault I have been in mourning.''

Despite the coolness, throngs of riders, walkers and a

dazzling array of equipages wound through the park, and almost every person they passed seemed to know her husband, Bonny thought. To most of them, he merely nodded, his face—as always—serious.

But with one decidedly frilly old woman, his manner was quite changed. Radcliff actually relaxed his stiffness and issued a warm smile before ordering the coachman to stop so he could chat with the matron of advanced years.

"Radcliff, pray, make me known to this lovely creature. Your wife, I presume."

He nodded. "But, Lady Eggerton, I believe you have met her before. She is Lord Landis's niece, the former Bonny Barbara Allan. I first saw her at your home."

The old woman raised her quizzing glass to her eye and stared at Bonny. "To be sure. I remember her now. All the young bucks swarmed around her. And she had that lovely name…but now I suppose it's the Duchess of Radcliff." Her lively blue eyes met Bonny's.

"How good of you to remember," Bonny said. "And it is very agreeable to see you again."

"The fact that you are in mourning has reached my ears, dear girl."

Bonny bowed her head.

Lady Eggerton turned back to Radcliff. "You have done very well for yourself, Richard. It is too unfortunate your dear mama could not have met your little wife. She is very beautiful. Very delicate looking."

"I fear my wife has been unwell of late."

Countess Eggerton gave a shrewd glance at Bonny. "Do I have the honor of felicitating you on the expansion of your family?"

Bonny blushed and raised her gaze to Radcliff.

"Yes, my lady. We are to become parents," he said.

"How happy you must be."

Radcliff actually smiled again, the skin around his eyes crinkling with the depth of his mirth. "To be sure."

Lady Eggerton nodded to her driver. "It was very good to see you, my dear." She eyed Radcliff. "Take care of her, Richard."

"I most certainly will, my lady."

His coachman flicked the reins and they rode on, Radcliff continuing to curtly nod at passersby.

From the corner of her eye, Bonny saw Twigs enter the lane they traveled on. He perched high on his gig with Cressida beside him and a tiger at the back. "Look, Richard, there's Twigs!"

Radcliff instructed the coachman to approach Twigs's gig.

Twigs pulled up alongside the duke and duchess, and when he perceived that Radcliff was riding with his wife, a wide smile covered his face. "By Jove, good to see you out, Duchess."

"I have missed you most dreadfully since you moved out," Bonny said. "I've yearned for a good game of piquet with you."

"Just have to pop in and play a hand or two," he said shyly, averting his reddened eyes from Bonny.

"Why not tonight?" Radcliff suggested.

"Sounds like a jolly good plan," Twigs said.

Cressida laid a possessive hand on Twigs's arm above his ruffled cuff. "Oh, but Mr. Twickingham, I was so hoping you could escort me to the new play at Drury Lane. You know how abominably bad I am at card games."

"To be sure—" He coughed. "No, no, no, Miss Carlisle. What I mean is—"

Cressida fluttered her lashes and pouted. "Then, you would consider Drury Lane tonight?"

Twigs sniffed and cast a dubious glance at Radcliff. "Well, if you are certain—"

"Then it is settled," said Cressida, patting his arm patronizingly, a smug smile settling on her face.

Once they had said their farewells, Bonny spoke. "Poor Twigs, he's doomed to be totally dominated by that meek-looking Cressida Carlisle."

"How right you are, my love. However, I think she is exactly what he needs. Otherwise, Twigs would die a childless bachelor, for he would never have the nerve to initiate either a romance or a proposal."

Bonny's heart soared. This was the first time her husband had indicated he would be pleased to have a child since he had learned of her expectancy. And he had admitted to Lady Eggerton the baby was due. He must be proud, she thought hopefully.

A short time later, Bonny felt her husband stiffen, and she looked up to see an approaching carriage bearing Stanley Moncrief and Lady Lynda Heffington, properly chaperoned by Lady Lynda's nearly deaf companion, who rode alone in the back seat of the carriage. Bonny could not help but remember Stanley telling her that Lady Lynda was Richard's true love, and she swallowed hard. How would her husband greet his former lover and his cousin?

To Bonny's surprise, Radcliff gave both of them the cut direct. She wanted to ask him about it, but she dared not speak of that odious widow.

When Radcliff spoke, it was not of his cousin or of Lady Lynda but of Bonny's lying-in. "We need to go to Hedley Hall," he said.

She nodded. Her husband did not have to tell her. All the Radcliffs had been born at Hedley Hall. In the same bed. Her heart filled with pride and happiness.

Most of all, she longed to return to the idyllic happiness she had shared with her husband at his boyhood home. Now, all of her misery would be behind her.

* * *

While her husband completed his business in the city, Bonny happily prepared to return to Hedley Hall, thoroughly content with his sudden conversion to domesticity. She relished every dinner at which they faced only each other across the candlelit table, the morning rides with him in the park, and most especially the nights he shared her bed, both of them lulled into sleep after being spent with their frenzied, nearly insatiable passion.

Radcliff had left early this morning to peruse the offerings at Tattersall's but had insisted she rest more, therefore it was nearly noon before Marie entered her mistress's chamber and opened the draperies to rouse Bonny from her slumber.

The sun cast its warmth over the room as Marie assembled Bonny's clothes. "See, Mrs. 'enson's always right as rain. Said ye'd be well in three months, and 'ere ye are with the bloom back in yer cheeks."

Bonny smiled as she watched a robin flit from branch to branch on a tree outside her window. She gave her approval to the outfit Marie selected and sat patiently at her dressing table as Marie fashioned her hair.

Once she was dressed, a rap sounded on her door. It was Mandley. "A caller here to see your grace," he announced. "I told him you were not receiving callers so early, but he insisted upon seeing you."

"He?" Bonny queried.

"The Earl of Dunsford," Mandley said.

The person she least wanted as a visitor. Richard disliked him so excessively. "I cannot see him, Mandley," Bonny said.

"He insisted I was to tell you he needs to see you about your cousin Emily."

Lord Dunsford must want to offer for her, Bonny mused. "In that case I will see him."

Rushing downstairs, Bonny decided she would have to

dispatch him quickly. It wouldn't do at all for Richard to find him here.

When she crossed the drawing room to hold out her hand to Dunsford, he answered her questioning gaze. "Forgive me, your grace, but I had to see you. It's about Emily."

Bonny failed to offer him a seat, nor did she offer him tea.

"She has refused to see me."

"I daresay it is because I imparted to her that you knew of the baby. She is extremely embarrassed to see you now."

As Bonny looked at him and saw the dark circles under bloodshot eyes, she was reminded of the first time she met him, when he had been so forlorn over his brother's death. "Surely she knows I have known all this time and have had no objections."

Bonny only nodded, not wanting to prolong the conversation in any way.

"I have been every day for the past month. Sometimes several times a day, and never is she in to me. Once I watched her house and called immediately after I saw her enter, and still that damned butler told me she was not in."

"I am very sorry, my lord, but I do not see what I can do."

He hung his head in his hands. "I must see her. I have to tell her..."

"That you love her?"

He met Bonny's intense gaze and swallowed. "Yes."

"Are you willing to offer marriage?"

He clenched his fist. "Of course! What do you take me for?"

"I only wanted to gauge your sincerity before I agree to intercede."

Relief washed over his face. "Then you'll...?"

Bonny nodded. "I will talk to Emily and tell her what you have told me."

He stepped toward Bonny and took her hand.

At that precise second, the drawing room door flew open so violently it banged against the wall, chipping the plaster and causing the crystal sconces to clatter.

Bonny turned to face her husband. Not that he looked like her husband at that minute. He looked more like a satyr. His eyes flashed angrily, his brows drew together, his face grew red as he thundered, "Get out of my house, Dunsford!"

Not taking his eyes from Radcliff, Dunsford snatched up his riding crop and wordlessly crossed the room.

When he walked by Radcliff, the duke said, "I would call you out if it would not utterly ruin my wife's character. But let me warn you." His voice shook. "If you ever see my wife again, I will kill you."

"There must be some misunderstanding, Radcliff," Dunsford said, pausing an arm's length away from the angry duke. "I assure you I would do nothing to hurt your wife in any way."

"My wife is no concern of yours."

Dunsford swallowed hard, threw an apologetic glance at Bonny and left the house.

Radcliff's eyes flashed at Bonny, then he kicked his boot against a nearby table and stormed from the room.

Bonny's breath caught. She heard Radcliff order his bay to be brought around, and she ran from the room to try to talk with him.

"Richard, surely you don't think—"

Radcliff cut her off. "Have I given you so many orders that you cannot remember one, Barbara?"

He watched her with cold eyes.

She swallowed. "No, sir, you haven't."

"Yet you allowed that man into my home."

Mandley announced that Radcliff's bay was mounted in front. Radcliff faced Bonny and gave her a hard look. "I have nothing more to say to you."

Chapter Twenty-Four

Evans stood stiffly in front of Bonny. "You called, your grace?"

She put down the embroidery she had hardly touched. "Yes, Evans. I am very concerned about the duke. He hasn't been home in four days. Please tell me if you know where he is."

"I do not know, your grace."

"You most probably would not tell me if you did know, would you?"

He inclined his head. "That is most likely true. As it happens this time, though, I share your concerns. I do not remember when his grace has been absent this many days. And he has no shaving things, nor a change of clothes."

All manner of sordid possibilities had run through her mind, and in each instance, something dreadful had happened to her husband. Nearly convinced his throat had been slashed and his body dumped in the Thames, she had been unable to sleep or eat.

With constricted heart, she had directed the servants to unpack the portmanteaus. It was unlikely they would travel to Hedley Hall. If Radcliff came back that very day, he would hardly welcome a cozy coach journey with his wife, nor a lying-in with no one but her to keep him company.

When he had stormed from the house, Bonny's insides had rocked and trembled like a mastless ship on stormy seas. The malice in his words frightened her. There was more to his fury than a strong dislike of Lord Dunsford. He had threatened the man for seeing her. Then she remembered Lord Dunsford had been holding her hand when her husband walked into the room. Radcliff had given every indication of being in a jealous rage.

She considered this at length and decided he was indeed jealous, but not because he loved her. Proof that he did not love her were the far too frequent nights he stayed away from her. She was merely a possession, and the Duke of Radcliff would not tolerate any man touching his wife.

After she sorted out her thoughts, she lost her anger and turned remorseful. She should have listened to her husband. He had done so much for her and asked so little in return. After Richard had forbidden Lord Dunsford to cross the threshold of Radcliff House, she should have sent the earl away. If only she could turn back the clock.

But she could only cry into her pillow or her embroidered handkerchiefs and lament her sorrowful situation. She prayed for her husband's safety and paced the floor, often stopping to press her face against the window glass to search the streets for signs of him.

"You are at liberty to make inquiries about his grace," Bonny informed the valet.

Evans bowed, and she thought she detected a slight smile.

"Do you know the address of Mr. Twickingham's lodgings?"

"Yes, your grace."

"Perhaps he has seen Richard," Bonny said absently,

her eyes darting to the window at the sound of horses'
hooves.

As Evans left the room, Bonny peered out the window.
She lifted the lace curtain and was once again bitterly disappointed. It was only Lord Sillsby's groom bringing
around his curricle across the square.

She dropped the lace and began to pace again. During
the past four days she had been much too upset to leave
Radcliff House for fear of missing her husband. She needed
to speak to Emily about Lord Dunsford's suit, but Emily
would have to come to her.

Bonny crossed the study to her escritoire and penned a
note asking Emily to call because she herself had been too
unwell to pay calls. After she sealed the envelope, Bonny
called for the page to deliver it to Cavendish Square.

While Twigs lined up four empty Madeira bottles on the
game table, Radcliff glared into the fire.

"I say, Richard," Twigs sniffed, "does Duchess know
you're here?"

"Do not concern yourself, my good man."

"Bloody easy for you to say. Fact is, don't like the way
you treat her."

Radcliff faced Twigs, his eyes hooded. "She cares not."

"The deuce she don't! Of course, you wouldn't know.
Off doing all manner of mischief, but I saw how much she
worried over you. Nearly wore out those lace curtains in
m' room, lifting them to look for you, her sweet face shadowed with worry."

"Then my plan met with some success," Radcliff said
smugly.

"Plan? You planned to make her mad with grief?"

"That is what I hoped."

"'Pon my word, don't understand a thing you utter."

Radcliff picked up the *Gazette*. "It's just as well."

The latest dispatches of the battles in the Peninsula distracted Radcliff. Finally, he turned to Twigs, excitement leaping to his eyes. "Still want to buy colors?"

Twigs eyed his friend suspiciously. "Why?"

"I have a fancy to join you."

Twigs dropped his full cup of coffee. "Can't do that, my good man!"

"Why not?"

"Because you're not a younger son. Everyone knows only younger sons serve in his majesty's army and navy. Besides, you're a duke. Dukes don't rise to arms."

"The first Duke of Radcliff did. That's how he got the title."

"Different thing altogether."

"They're making Wellesley a duke. Says here he's to be called the Duke of Wellington."

"Still altogether different."

"Will you join me?"

"Does Duchess know?"

"Why must you always bring her up?" Radcliff said angrily. Though, truly, his anger was vented as much at himself for giving in to the weakness of loving his duchess too dearly. He really must get away from her. Perhaps then he could cleanse her from his being. And how better could he leave her than under the cloak of patriotism? That way, his honor would be preserved, and she need never know of his weakness.

Perhaps he would be lucky enough to die a hero's death in battle. Anything would be better than the torture of loving a woman whose heart belonged to another.

"You'd leave Duchess alone to have the babe? Why, she don't even have parents to care for her," Twigs said.

Radcliff crushed the newspaper and flung it into the fire. "If you're so bloody worried about Barbara, why don't you go take care of her?"

He stalked from the room, grabbed his hat and coat and began to walk about London aimlessly. Twigs was right to worry about Barbara's confinement. Radcliff himself could not bear to think of her alone in her agony.

But what of his own private agony? How was he to hold another man's babe in his arms and give it his name? His heart wrenched every time he pictured Bonny standing in the drawing room, the sun streaming through the window to highlight her glistening black hair. Then he turned cold when he pictured her taking Dunsford's hands in hers. He would never forget the haggard look on Dunsford's face. Bonny must have been saying goodbye to him before departing for Hedley Hall.

Radcliff knew Barbara's parting with Dunsford would be their last. She was too good to continue such deceit. Although he should be happy he would now have a clear field, the victory was hollow.

For still she carried the baby that very likely might not be his own.

Twigs's man, balancing a tray of empty wine bottles in one hand, opened the door to Evans.

"I say," Evans said, "is my master, the Duke of Radcliff, within?" He counted five empty bottles and winced.

"He left just moments ago."

Still eyeing the evidence of his master's recent occupation with the bottle, Evans asked hopefully, "There was a large group of gentlemen here?"

The valet shook his head. "Only Mr. Twickingham and the duke."

"Has his grace been here these four days?"

"Yes."

Evans lowered his gaze. "I do not suppose that his grace has a fresh suit of clothing?"

The man shook his head.

"Or a shave?"

Another solemn shake of the man's head.

Back on the sidewalk, Evans headed toward Radcliff House, his step slow, his mind a muddle. Wasn't this the life he wanted for his master? The carefree bachelor, running rather wild with other fashionable rakes, leaving brokenhearted women in his wake? Bloody fun his set had always had.

But it no longer seemed so fun. Evans feared the liquor would ruin the young duke. And the thought of how many times of late his master had neglected his rather exceptional appearance quite rattled Evans. Not to mention how the duke's careless grooming would reflect upon himself.

This would never do. The duke was too old to act the rake and too young to mimic a disoriented old man. His grace really should settle down. Got him a wife and a baby on the way. Why, he had no business sleeping in Mr. Twickingham's lodgings when he had his own grand town house. And, God only knows, the duchess was besotted with him. He really should be kinder to her.

Within half an hour, the page returned to Bonny with a note from Emily informing Bonny that she regretted she was unable to leave Wickham House, for she had developed a mild case of spots. The note conveyed Emily's displeasure over her cousin's poor health and promises to come to Radcliff House as soon as her spots cleared.

Bonny quickly wrote a note to Lord Dunsford to inform him that she had been unable to talk to Emily. She absently started to ring for the page, then realized she could not use one of Richard's servants to transport the letter to Dunsford.

Evans knocked on Bonny's study door, then entered the room as she shoved Dunsford's letter into a drawer of the escritoire.

She perceived a flicker of satisfaction on the valet's granite face. "You have located my husband?"

"In a manner of speaking, your grace. He has been at Mr. Twickingham's the past four days but had just departed when I arrived."

Bonny clutched at her breast. "Thank God nothing has happened to him."

"My sentiments exactly."

"Nothing's happened to whom?" Radcliff boomed from the door of his wife's study.

Evans bowed and left the room as Bonny flew to her husband, but instead of throwing her arms around him as she wanted to do, she was startled by his stiff manner. If she did not love him so fiercely she would have been repelled by his appearance. Four days' growth of a cinnamon-colored beard shadowed his craggy face. His clothes were wrinkled, his cravat carelessly tied. He smelled of stale liquor. Something in his eyes, in the grim set of his mouth, filled her with fright. For a flinch of a second she felt he stared death in the face, and her heart caught. Had she made him so miserable he didn't wish to live any longer? She spoke in a soft voice. "I was very much afraid I was a widow, Richard."

"Were you a merry widow, my dear?" he said lightly.

"Not at all, I assure you. I've been dreadfully worried about you."

He strolled into the room and sat down at her desk, running a hand through his disheveled hair. "You worry about everyone, my dear. It seems to be your purpose in life. If you aren't worrying about Emily's failing health or Twigs's mending leg, you're wanting to adopt every street urchin you see. You must try not to worry so much."

Bonny moved to the desk, placed her hands on her hips and spoke in a rising voice. "I am your wife. I am the Duchess of Radcliff, and I deserve the courtesy of you informing me when you *choose* not to come home. I will not live under your roof if you cannot accord me the simple consideration your wife is due.''

His eyes followed her as she stalked across the Aubusson carpet. ''And I am very sorry I allowed Lord Dunsford into *our* house. I shall never do so again.''

He silently studied her for a moment, his face grim. Then his eyes flashed mischievously. ''You look horrid, my dear.''

Bonny burst into tears.

Still angry, he restrained from going to her. Nevertheless, it wounded him considerably to watch her cry.

She started to leave the room, when he addressed her sternly. ''Have you eaten today, Barbara?''

She rounded on him. ''What would you care that I haven't eaten in four days?''

''It does not please me for you to grow thin. I much preferred your body as it was when we married.''

Bonny snatched a nearby book and threw it at him, then left the room.

Radcliff chuckled and rang for Mrs. Henson to take his wife a tray. He planned to stand over her and force her to eat.

After he gave the housekeeper her instructions, he opened Bonny's desk drawer to send a note round informing Twigs he had returned to Radcliff House. There he saw the letter with Dunsford's name penned in his wife's hand. He shoved the drawer back in, toppling a small Roman statue that stood at the desk.

Chapter Twenty-Five

Perhaps it was because she had been in mourning that Richard had not spent time with her, Bonny thought. If she had been free to go to the theater and balls, he might have been content to at least spend his nights with her. During her sleepless night after Richard had finally come home, she had determined to ease back into society. And what better way to begin than by ordering an entire new wardrobe?

Besides, she was still angry with him. She planned to have Madame Deveraux fashion the most positively extravagant gowns that money could buy. She would go to the milliner's, too, and take every expensive head covering and bonnet in the shop. It was her hope that the enormity of the bills for her finery would set Richard's heart into palpitations. He deserved a bit of discomfort for all he had put her through these past months, and especially this last week.

How tormented she had been worrying about his safety, feeling totally inadequate as his wife and bearing the private agony of imagining him in the arms of Lady Lynda Heffington.

But she had to push those thoughts from her mind and

give clear instructions to the French modiste who now stood before her.

"Oh, but, your grace, the sapphire gown was made to be worn by you. You are so very lovely in it."

Bonny stood some distance back from the looking glass and turned first to her right, then to her left. Still it was not obvious that she carried a baby in her womb. At least in this dress. Gentle gathering of the delicate sarcenet under the bodice concealed the thickening of her midsection. "I like it very much," Bonny said decisively. "I shall have another in pink and another in lavender. But you must know I am increasing so you must allow extra room in the front."

Madame Deveraux made the appropriate congratulations on the duchess's announcement before ordering one of her assistants to bring in the turquoise lace gown for the duchess to try on in her private dressing chamber.

Lady Lynda Heffington had not thought to pay a call at Madame Deveraux's today, but as she was riding her barouche to purchase ribbon, she saw a barouche bearing the Radcliff crest outside the modiste's. Her first thought was that Radcliff was there with that young wife of his. She remembered him accompanying her own self to the shop on several occasions. He had particularly instructed Madame Deveraux to clothe his mistress in rich ivory silks and bright red lace. Her heart sank when she thought of how much she had lost to that scheming little country miss.

Then an idea occurred to her. She instructed her coachman to stop.

One of Madame Deveraux's assistants, Miss Clopham, rushed to Lady Heffington when she entered the lavish shop. "Lady Heffington, how good to see you. Madame Deveraux has set aside a rust-colored silk she said would be most *jolie* for the beautiful Lady Heffington."

Lady Heffington flashed a mischievous smile at the sales-woman. "By all means, I must try it on at this very moment." She lowered her voice to a whisper. "Place me in the dressing room adjacent to the duchess's, if you please."

The walls between the two chambers were very thin. Lady Heffington could plainly hear Madame Deveraux complimenting the duchess's beauty. "No other woman in London could do for this gown what you do for it, your grace," Madame Deveraux said.

Lady Heffington fumed. *The exact words she always says to me!*

Of course, she did have to admit the vulgar Bonny Barbara Allan was beautiful. Damned Radcliff. Must he always possess what was the most beautiful?

Miss Clopham hung the rust-colored gown on a brass wall hook and assisted Lady Heffington into it. "How very beautiful you look, Lady Heffington."

Lynda's lips curved into a smile. "Yes, Miss Clopham, this will do very well. Radcliff loves me to wear this color," she said, her voice louder than necessary. Her eyes on the looking glass, she bent forward slightly. "You do not find the neckline a bit too low cut? Radcliff does so glare when other men's eyes alight on my endowments. He is so very jealous! I shouldn't want to make him angry."

Miss Clopman nervously glanced in the direction of Bonny's dressing room and actually turned red.

Not as red as Bonny. Not only did Bonny feel as if her face were on fire, she felt as if a volcano were erupting within her body. Her worst nightmare had come true. All those nights Richard had been away from her, he had been in the arms of his former mistress.

Bonny would never know how she managed to take her leave of Madame Deveraux's establishment without making an utter cake of herself. She held the tears in check and, immediately after overhearing Lady Heffington's conversation, said in a shaking voice, "I will take the dress. Send this and all the others to Radcliff House and send the bills to my husband."

As Madame Deveraux assisted her back into her black muslin dress and pelisse, she thought, *At least I can call Richard my husband. Lady Heffington can never do that!*

Would that she could have his heart rather than his title, she thought as she settled into her barouche and instructed the coachman to take her for a drive through Hyde Park. She would gladly exchange being his duchess for being his lover. To have his love and to share his bed.

How peculiar it was to love a man so desperately she would sink to such a life. Had she no pride? Of course she had pride. Hadn't her pride kept her from tearfully declaring her undying love for Richard on a thousand occasions? At least she had been able to save him from such embarrassing confessions. She was glad, indeed, that she had spared him that and had held on to some semblance of dignity.

But it wasn't dignity that she sought. It was Richard's love. That was all she could ever want.

Yet she assumed it was Lady Heffington who had that.

Why had she ever allowed herself to marry him? Perhaps by now she could have got over this obsessive love for him.

And perhaps by now he could have happily been married to the woman he really loved. She put her head into her hands and sobbed. She had not only ruined her own life. She had ruined his.

Twigs only half listened to the prattle of the pretty Miss Carlisle, who perched beside him in his curricle, riding through Hyde Park on a mild afternoon. What the deuce had come over him lately? He hardly knew himself any longer. He had given up a chance to spar with Jackson this very afternoon in order to escort Cressida for her afternoon jaunt. And last night at the Rowlanders' ball he had very much wanted to box the ears of John Hargrove, who held Miss Carlisle much too closely while waltzing with her.

The delicate lady in question placed a pink-gloved hand on Twigs's arm and said, "Isn't that so, Mr. Arp?"

The silly gel had taken to calling him Mr. Arp after some character in one of those novels she always had her head poked in. Truth be known, Twigs rather fancied her calling him by a special name. "Tell me again, Miss Carlisle, about this Arp chap."

"Oh, he's the most dashing of heroes, I do assure you. He's tall, as you are. And, like you, he is every inch the sportsman. Takes to the hounds, is a noted swordsman and an infamous boxer. At first he takes little notice of the heroine. He's much too interested in his sporting pleasures."

"What changes him?"

"Rosemary—that's the heroine's name—makes him jealous at a ball."

"So then what does he do?"

"He fights a duel for her."

Twigs gulped. "Bloody illegal, they are."

"And glad I am of it. I would simply die if someone I cared about, someone like you, were to jeopardize his life for me."

Twigs sat taller, flicking the ribbons with authority, tilting his head ever so slightly. "If your honor were challenged, I would, of course, have to set things to rights, no matter how great the danger to myself."

Cressida linked her arm through Twigs's and nearly purred with satisfaction. "You are, indeed, my Mr. Arp."

He blushed and glanced about him. "Do wish we'd see Radcliff and Duchess. It would do her good to get out in the fresh air more."

"It's so very good of you to care for the duchess and not feel jealous of her for clamping your best friend in parson's trap. But I suppose you realize it was time Radcliff and the others settle down."

"Quite so."

"You must be envious of the duke."

"Can't say that I am," Twigs said.

"You cannot tell me you don't envy Radcliff. He's got a lovely wife. A fine town house instead of bachelor quarters. And an heir on the way."

"Never thought about it—except for the part about having a little fellow. Always did want a little guy to teach the ropes."

"A little boy! It's the very same with me. How I would love to have a son one day."

He slowed his pace, cast a sideways glance at Cressida and swallowed hard. "Picture you with little golden-haired girls."

"How sweet of you. I would love to bear children of the man I love. A man like you."

He swallowed even harder. "Awfully nice of you."

"Have you given any thought to marriage, dear Mr. Arp?"

Not until the last five minutes, but all of a sudden, the idea of being married to the lovely Miss Cressida Carlisle seemed rather splendid. Not just the part about having a son, either. He particularly favored the idea of this pretty little creature being his wife. Fact is, he'd like to wrap his arms around her and kiss her thoroughly. He blushed again. He would like to do more than kiss her—after they were married, that is. "God's teeth, Cressida, call me Twickingham. If you'll do me the honor, it will be your name, too."

"Oh, Mr. Twickingham," she said breathlessly, "nothing could make me happier."

"James. If you're to be my wife, I expect you should call me James."

"James." She spoke the name reverently. "The name of the hero in *The Secret at the Vicarage*."

He turned off the heavily traveled lane down a little-used path.

Cressida placed a possessive hand on his velvet sleeve. "Are you going to kiss me, dearest?"

He reined his horse, faced his intended and drew her to him. She felt so very tiny in his arms, he was afraid of crushing her. But he had to admit he very much liked the feel of her. He wasn't sure if she found his lips or he hers, but he did know he found her soft lips even more to his liking.

This marriage business might just be the ticket!

In the week that followed her visit to Madame Deveraux's, Bonny knew a despair a thousand times greater than she had experienced when her father had suddenly died and she had been bereft of the most tender love she had ever known. She could neither sleep nor eat. Her days were an agony of regrets and misery. She thought death would be a blessed relief from her wretched existence. But she was too religious to contemplate suicide. And, besides, she had to remember the baby. If she couldn't have Richard, at least she could have *his* child.

She stood before the painting of Hedley Hall that hung in her husband's library. The artist had painted it as it looked when Bonny first set eyes on it in the golden glow of the late afternoon sun. The centuries-old building presided over acres and acres of land that had been in the Moncrief family for generations. The tall fir trees recalled to her the day she and Radcliff had gone fishing, of how close they had been. If only they were back where they had been so happy, Bonny thought, longing to return to the shelter of the place where Richard had sprung to life like a desert flower after spring rains.

No renewal of her husband's desire to travel to Kent for the birth of their child had been forthcoming. In fact, she thought grimly, he had not renewed any of the activities that had made her so happy less than a month ago. No more rides in the park. No more solicitous inquiries about her health. No more nights enfolded in his loving arms.

Though Radcliff had spent more time at Radcliff House since her scolding of him, he might as well have been in Bombay for all the company he was to her. Hardly a word had passed between them. He shut himself up in his library for hours on end. While part of her wanted to beg his forgiveness for allowing Lord Dunsford into their house, another part of her knew that Radcliff's hostility masked something much deeper than his dislike of Dunsford. It was obvious he regretted his hasty marriage. He wanted only to be with Lady Heffington and the rakes he had run with before his marriage.

She supposed she should hate him for trifling with her heart and fathering a child on a whim and later regretting it, but she preferred to remember him when he had been loving and selfless.

It had been more than a week since her husband had mentioned the baby. It was hard for her to remember that Richard had ever been enthusiastic about her pregnancy. Judging from the way he acted now, he must regret the impending birth that—in his own words—had ruined his wife's body.

Sickened over his shallowness in loving only her looks, Bonny patted the swell that was their baby and had no regrets. Even if his own father no longer acknowledged his offspring, Bonny knew she would love the baby. She swallowed over the thick lump in her throat. Would the baby look like Richard? Despite his deplorable conduct, she loved him with unwavering potence and would until her dying day. She would always have the child, their child, to remember the tender moments when their love for each other had burned steady and powerful.

Coming to a decision, she turned away from the painting. She had made her husband's life miserable. For she was persuaded that his misery resulted from his loveless marriage. Of late he had talked about joining forces in the Peninsula. He would rather be dead than be married to her. The thought of him seriously injured or—much worse— dead was a blow to her heart. If he were that unhappy, there was only one recourse. She would have to leave him. To restore his freedom.

The door to the library opened and she turned to face Mandley.

"Mr. Twickingham to see you, your grace."

"Show him in, Mandley."

Twigs limped into the room, leaning on his silver-handled cane, his face redder than usual from the outdoors.

A wide smile on her face, Bonny took his hand. "So very good to see you, Twigs. You haven't come for piquet, have you?"

He nodded solemnly and sniffed. "Much as I would love it, no, Duchess. Fact is, I need your help."

She continued to press his bony hand within hers, a look of concern on her face. "Come, let's sit down." She led him to a pair of cozy wing chairs near the fireplace. "Would you like a drink?"

He swallowed, accentuating his prominent Adam's apple. "Am a bit thirsty."

"Madeira or brandy?"

"Brandy, a capital idea."

Bonny tugged the bellpull and, when Mandley entered, requested two glasses of brandy. "Now, how can I help you?"

"You may have noticed I spend a great deal of time with Miss Carlisle."

"I would be blind not to have."

"Well, Cres—Miss Carlisle has impressed upon me that one who is four and thirty needs to be settling down, and I realized if I were to settle down, who better to make an offer to than one as pretty as Cres—Miss Carlisle."

"So you made her an offer."

"Quite so."

Bonny had to credit Cressida. She could skillfully manipulate Twigs.

"My…" He sniffed and cleared his throat before continuing. "My intended tells me it is my responsibility to place an announcement in the newspapers. Can't credit it. Bound to make a big blunder. Need you to help me."

Through all this, Bonny was able to determine the purpose of Twigs's visit. "Would you like me to write the announcement for you?"

"Capital idea, Duchess. Can't let Cressy know I'm no good at that sort of thing."

Mandley reentered the room carrying a tray with a fresh bottle of brandy and two snifters.

Twigs took his glass and downed a third of its contents before Mandley left the room.

Bonny got up and went to her husband's desk for a piece of vellum. "I will be happy to compose the announcement. Have you set a date for the nuptials?"

"The what?"

"The ceremony."

"Cressy said May would be a good time. She's to arrange everything with her vicar."

"Very good." Bonny took up the pen, dipped it and began writing. "Forgive me for asking, Twigs, but what is your proper first name?"

"James. Family calls me James Edward."

She nodded and took up the pen to write with haste until she had filled a page. When she finished, she put the pen down and held the paper at arm's length and read it to him, observing a look of sheer admiration on his face. "That's all there is to it, Twigs."

"Sounds very professional."

The library door opened, and Radcliff said, "What sounds professional?"

Bonny squarely met her husband's demanding gaze. "The notice I wrote to the newspapers announcing the forthcoming nuptials between Mr. Twickingham of St. Dennis Meade and Miss Cressida Carlisle."

The corners of Radcliff's mouth lifted. "This calls for a celebration. Shall I ring for champagne or cognac?"

"We're drinking brandy," Bonny said, "but, of course, an announcement such as this does call for a toast."

Radcliff eyed the nearly full bottle of brandy on his desk. "I'll just ring for an extra glass." Observing Twigs's nearly empty glass, Radcliff said, "More brandy, Twigs?"

"Capital idea."

"So when's the wedding?" Radcliff asked Twigs.

"May."

Mandley entered the room, a single brandy snifter on a tray.

"Very good of you to anticipate me, Mandley." Radcliff poured a glass. After the butler left the room, Radcliff turned to Twigs. "How agreeable it is that you should be waiting here in our library. I have been looking for you. I went round to your lodgings this hour past."

"Fate," Twigs uttered. "Cressy would say it was fate."

Radcliff looked at Bonny with eyes less cold than they had been of late; in fact, there was even an amused look on his face.

Bonny returned his bemused smile. "Would you two care to speak privately?"

"Whatever I have to say can be said in front of you." Radcliff's face inscrutable, he placed a hand on her shoulder and walked her to where Twigs sat, lifting his glass for a toast. "Stay seated," he commanded Twigs.

Twigs and Bonny swung their glasses to meet Radcliff's.

"May your union be satisfying in every way," Radcliff toasted, no mirth in his voice. He thought of how utterly unsatisfying his own marriage was.

Following the toast, Radcliff sat down on a sofa near Twigs's chair and motioned for Bonny to sit next to him.

His jaw tightened as he watched his frail-looking wife. She had again grown pale and seemed to be getting thinner except for the small mound in her lap.

He couldn't call it their baby. It couldn't be. She had told him it had been that night…that one night when he had almost forced her, when he'd been enraged with repressed, mind-numbing desire. But it was not likely that a babe was conceived that night when they had failed to conceive all those other nights that he had come into her over and over again.

It was too much of a coincidence that the baby was conceived at a time when he knew her to be enjoying Dunsford's company regularly at the house on Kepple Street.

He fisted his hands. The more he thought of it, the more convinced Radcliff became that the baby had to be Dunsford's. But he was also convinced Bonny was no longer seeing the earl. The letter must have put an end to the illicit relationship.

Radcliff thought back to the letter he had seen in her desk drawer. When he discovered it gone the next day, he had known she had sent it. The letter had been written just before he and Bonny were to have left London for Kent. Of course she would be sending her farewells, but Radcliff felt sure the letter had been more than an announcement of itinerary. It was surely Bonny's final break with Dunsford.

Having decided to return to Hedley Hall and give birth in the Radcliff ancestral bed, Bonny would have determined to sever all links with her lover in order to finally give in to being the Duchess of Radcliff, mother of the future Duke of Radcliff.

But as much as Radcliff desired to remove Bonny from London and harbored the hope of recapturing that magical intimacy they had shared at Hedley Hall, he could not allow Dunsford's baby to be born there.

Damned if he knew what he wanted. No, that wasn't precisely true. He still wanted Barbara with all his heart. But he kept telling himself it was a sign of weakness to be so besotted with a cheating woman that he would accept her, knowing she was enlarged with another man's seed. And how could he be in love with a woman so wicked she would break their marriage vows? He had valued honesty and family and had thought his vicar's-daughter wife did, also. What a paradox his wife was. Such a sense of what was always proper in all cases except where that monster Dunsford was concerned. If he hadn't seen her with Dunsford himself, he would never have believed her capable of such deceit.

His initial plan to win her by his absence was now his answer for ridding himself of her debilitating hold over him. He had to regain command of his life.

He rued the night he had first beheld Bonny Barbara Allan.

His eyes swept over her. She was not drinking. She looked so weak. So young and helpless. And still so very beautiful. "You're looking pale, my dear." He could not let her know how it tugged on his heart to see her like this. He wanted nothing so much as to take her in his arms and to love her to completion. But he had to be strong. He had to conquer his overwhelming thirst for her. He was as addicted to her as some men were to opium.

She lifted her chin and glared at him with cold eyes. "I daresay it's because I no longer get fresh air since you discontinued our rides in the park."

He touched her cheek with a light finger. "Don't let my absence keep you from the outdoors. Did you not used to ride with Emily?"

She turned to Twigs. "Do you see how shabbily Richard treats me? Trying to push me off on Emily. Always too busy for me. I do hope you never treat Cressida as Richard does me."

"I have been very busy, my dear," Radcliff said.

"Doing what?" she asked challengingly.

"If you must know, I have been looking into military affairs."

She inhaled sharply. "To go to the Peninsula?"

"Yes."

"I beg of you not to," Bonny said softly.

He ignored her and looked at Twigs. "That's why I wanted to have a word with you. Wanted to persuade you to join me. Didn't you fancy the redcoats not too many weeks past?"

Twigs's eyes darted from Radcliff to Bonny as her eyes moistened and her face went white.

She sprang to her feet, grabbed a Sevres urn from over the fireplace and ran toward the door, retching into it as she left.

Concern on his face, Radcliff followed her.

In the hallway, she had emptied the contents of her stomach into the urn, which she still held with shaking hands.

Radcliff stalked over to her, removed the urn and placed it on the stairway to the basement. He walked back to Bonny, who braced herself on a side table. He pushed back loose tendrils of dampened hair from her cheeks. "I knew you were looking unwell," he said chidingly.

She stroked his arm and spoke in a quavering voice. "It's

the army talk. You will be killed if you go, and I could not bear it.''

He caught his breath. He wanted to believe her words a declaration of love. But, then, he thought again. Could she mean that she would blame herself if anything happened to him because she had driven him away?

His arms encircled her, drawing her close, so close he could smell her floral perfume. ''Drive such foolish notions from your beautiful head.'' His gentle hands moved over her back until he knew she no longer cried. ''Come, my love, let me get you to bed.''

Marie was in Bonny's room. ''If you will, Marie, get the duchess into bed. She is unwell.''

Marie curtsied. ''Yes, your grace.'' Turning to Bonny, she soothed, ''Come now, poor thing.''

Overwhelming emotion washed over Radcliff when he caught sight of his forlorn-looking wife and remembered her words. *You will be killed...and I could not bear it.* He strode up to her and brushed her pale cheeks with his lips, then suddenly left the room.

Bonny sat, dazed and quiet, as Marie removed her half boots and stockings. For a brief moment, she had thought Richard would stay with her, and her heart had rejoiced. She had hoped to duplicate some of the tender intimacy they had shared in this very room. But now he was gone, and her crippling melancholy returned. She silently lay atop her bed in her muslin day dress and turned her face toward the window so Marie would not see the tears in her eyes.

Back in the library, Radcliff refilled his and Twigs's glasses and returned to his seat on the settee.

''See what that army talk does to the poor duchess,'' Twigs scolded. He turned the snifter in his hands. ''Know you all find me a tad dull-witted, but a raving idiot could see how much she loves you.''

How utterly disappointed Radcliff was that he could not believe Twigs's words. "She's taken a notion that I'll be killed if I purchase my commission."

"'Pon my word, she could be right."

Radcliff drew on his drink. "Perhaps I no longer wish to live."

"Don't say that, Richard. Think of the babe. He'll need a father. Think of the duchess. Not a soul to take care of her. Can't leave her alone to have the baby."

While he had no desire to be around when Dunsford's child came into this world, Radcliff could not bear the thought of Bonny going through it alone. Since the first time he held her in his arms during the waltz, she had evoked in him a deep sense of protectiveness. "You're quite right, my dear Twigs. I must take better care of my wife." He placed a firm hand on his friend's shoulder. "Good of you to care. She has no other champions in her own home."

Chapter Twenty-Six

Neither sleep nor peace came to Bonny as visions of Richard dying at the hands of French soldiers intruded on her every thought. Underlying the disturbing reverie was guilt that she was the cause of his misery. He had become so unhappy being married, he saw service to his majesty as the only gentlemanly way of leaving her. The sooner she liberated him, the better.

At midnight she heard Richard speaking softly to Evans in the dressing room. She knew the likelihood of him sharing her bed was as great as Lord Byron staying celibate, and when the voices faded away, the sound of the door to Radcliff's chamber closing was as melancholy as a death knell.

Just before dawn, she got up, dressed in an old black serge gown and packed a small valise. All the fine mourning wear Madame Deveraux had fashioned would stay here at Radcliff House. There would be no need for such finery in Milford.

Then she sat down and wrote a letter to Richard. When she finished, she hesitated over how to sign it. Every closing that came to mind had the word *love*, a word they never shared. She hadn't said it; she had shown it. As much as she wanted to tell him that she loved him to the depth of her breaking heart, she stopped herself. She must not do anything to make him feel compelled to come after her. He must feel no guilt over her leaving, only joy over his release.

None of the servants were above stairs at this hour, only Cook in the basement kitchen. Marie would not bring up a tray before noon, and even then she would not know Bonny was not coming back. Marie would likely suppose she had merely taken a morning walk as she had frequently explained when she used to go to Kepple Street.

Bonny walked to the door of her chamber and turned back to look at the room of Richard's wife. She wanted to remember everything clearly. Her gaze moved to the bed, the bed where their baby had been conceived. The ivory silks surrounding the bed. The rich lace of the pillows. The gilded vanity. The Carrara fireplace. Taking a deep breath, she clutched the door knob and left.

No one was in the hall. The soft Persian hall runners muffled the sound of her footsteps. When she got to the top of the stairs, she stood still and listened for any sound from the ground floor. All she heard was a distant clanging of pots in the kitchen far below.

She proceeded down the stairs and across the broad marble floor to the front door and quietly let herself out.

Rousing the groom to deliver her to Emily's house could easily have been done, but Bonny wanted to avoid leaving a trail for Radcliff. He would be honor-bound to follow. Besides, walking the few blocks from Berkeley Square to Cavendish Square was something Bonny Barbara Allan would readily have done. She had to forget now that she was the Duchess of Radcliff. Forever.

The night was yawning into day, its smoky light settling over the city. She pulled her cloak tightly around her to protect against the cold. There were no lights inside the foggy windows she passed. She had never been on the streets of London alone at this hour. Indeed, no other gently bred people were about. Only ill-dressed laborers with sooty faces and the occasional hay cart or milk cart clopping along. Bonny was very glad she had chosen not to dress in her duchess finery. Dressed as she was, she would draw little attention.

In ten minutes she was in Cavendish Square, looking up at Wickham House. All the windows were shut, and there were no signs of life within. Setting down her valise in the park area, Bonny decided to sit on a bench and wait another hour or so before waking Emily.

At the first signs of life in Wickham House, she presented herself at the door to a placid Styles. "Allow me to go up to Lady Emily's room, Styles," Bonny said with the full air of a duchess.

He moved aside, swept the door back and bowed—all seemingly in one swift movement. "Your grace."

She handed him her valise. "Put this aside for me, if you please, Styles."

"Very good, your grace."

Once in Emily's room, Bonny found her cousin hard to wake. "Go away, Martha," she barked.

"It's not Martha. It's me, Bonny."

Emily rubbed her eyes and sat up, groggily gazing into Bonny's fresh face. "Whatever time is it?"

"It's very early in the morning, but I had to leave before Richard or anyone in the house woke up, for I am leaving Richard and returning to Milford."

Emily jerked up, fully awake. "You cannot mean that!"

Bonny nodded.

"But you can't. You two love each other."

Bonny took Emily's hand and squeezed it, her eyes shining with unshed tears. "Trust me in this. Richard does not love me. He has grown to regret that he married me."

"I will never believe that! One has only to look at him when he is with you."

"There was…an attraction in the beginning, but it has waned."

Emily gazed deep into Bonny's troubled eyes. "Can you tell me your love for him has cooled?"

Bonny shook her head. "But in the seven months we have been in London, he has chosen to share my bed fewer nights than there are in a single week."

Neither spoke for a moment.

Bonny opened her reticule and took out the letter. "I have written this letter to Richard. I want you to give it to him should he inquire about me. And if he doesn't, send it to him next week. I don't want you to tell him where I'm going, though I daresay he will likely guess I have gone to Milford. Where else could I live so cheaply?"

"As the Duchess of Radcliff, I should think you could afford to live anywhere in the world you wished."

"That is if I wished to infringe upon Richard's generosity, which I do not wish to do."

"But, Bonny, he's richer than a nabob. What would he care if you asked for a few hundred pounds a year? Or even a thousand?"

Bonny's lips were a straight line. "I wish nothing from him."

"What about his child?"

"I am persuaded that Richard does not care about the baby."

Emily pushed the stray blond hair from her face. "You cannot be describing the same duke I know. He could never be so insensitive."

"I find it difficult to countenance myself, but he has greatly changed since coming to London. If only we had never come. Things were so wonderful at Hedley Hall. I almost believed him…"

"In love with you?"

Bonny nodded solemnly.

"I cannot believe any of this about Radcliff."

The tears in Bonny's eyes now spilled. "Believe it. If there were any hope, I would never leave, but it's leave him or allow him to kill himself. He is so unhappy with me he is ready to sacrifice himself in service to his majesty and the Wellesley general in order to get away from me."

Emily got up and placed Bonny's letter in a desk drawer. "I suppose I must believe you."

"There is another matter that brings me to you," Bonny said.

Emily came back and sat on the bed beside Bonny, lifting her brows.

"I have talked to Lord Dunsford."

Emily thrust out her chin. "I would prefer that you didn't."

"Since you have not received him these dozens of times he has called on you, he came to see me. He is very distressed over not seeing you." Bonny watched Emily's face for a reaction, but her cousin's expression remained inscrutable. "He has been most unhappy since you refused him your company."

"I am sorry that he is unhappy, for he is a fine man."

"He's also in love with you."

"Pray, do not say such things," Emily begged, her voice shaking.

"I am not imagining it. He told me himself he is in love with you."

Emily's eyes widened. "Was this before he knew that I am not pure?"

"He has always known about you. Because you loved Harry, he looked favorably upon you since the beginning. Then he fell in love with you." Bonny reached for her cousin's hand. "He wants to make you his wife."

A look of stark grief passed over Emily's face.

"Em, just think! You two could marry, and Lord Dunsford would adopt Harriet. The three of you could be so happy."

"How would he explain Harriet?"

"He would say that Harry married a Spanish woman, who died during her lying-in with Harriet. Naturally, Lord Dunsford would be the baby's guardian."

"Nothing could be more wonderful," Emily said softly, "but I cannot allow him to throw himself away on me."

"I am persuaded if you don't accept his suit, he would most likely do away with himself. He is very deeply in love with you."

"But how can he be?"

"Why wouldn't he be? In his eyes, you've done nothing wrong. You loved the only person in the world he loved. Because of you, part of Harry lives still through Harriet. For that, I think he loves you even more."

"But I'm not pure."

Tears slid from Bonny's eyes. "Richard always told me that nothing that happens between two people who love each other could ever be impure."

Emily's face brightened. "But don't you see, Bonny, if Radcliff said that, it means he loves you."

"He never once said, 'I love you.'"

"Did you?" Emily's eyes held rebuke.

Bonny bit her lip and shook her head.

"Why can't you just talk to Radcliff before leaving? Tell him how you feel."

"He is too much the gentleman not to feel obliged to pretend an attachment to me."

"There is no pretending to it, you idiot."

"I pray that you believe me when I say he desperately seeks to remove himself from my presence."

* * *

A light rap sounded at the door to Radcliff's library. He put down his ledgers. "Come in."

Marie, her head bowed, slowly entered the room and quietly closed the door behind her. Curtsying, she asked, "Does yer grace have another post for me while 'er grace is away?"

Radcliff's brows lowered. "Her grace away? What are you talking about, woman?"

"Then ye didn't know no more about her leaving than I did?"

"What do you mean?" Radcliff snapped. "What makes you believe my wife has gone away?"

"She wasn't there when I took up her breakfast this morning, nor 'as she returned all day."

"Most likely she is spending the day with her cousin."

"Why would she need a valise to visit Lady Emily?"

Radcliff's heart stopped. "Her valise is gone?"

Marie nodded.

"What else is missing?"

"Not one of her new gowns from Madame Frenchy. Best I can figure, she's wearin' that old black dress she arrived in at 'edley 'all. The black serge. The former duchess's pretty jewels is still 'ere. And the new duchess's pretty nightgowns, too. But 'er old ones is all gone."

Radcliff leapt to his feet, stormed from the room and up the stairs, leaving Marie standing in the library staring after him.

In Bonny's room he went straight to the wardrobe, flinging aside the gowns Madame Deveraux had fashioned. The blue cloak—his Barbara's old blue cloak—was not there. He slammed the door and stalked to the dressing table. On the center of its glass top rested her wedding ring. Had one of his own limbs been severed and served up there, he could not have hurt any deeper.

He fell into her chair. Though he had lost her long before

this day, he had had the satisfaction of knowing she was his wife. He had had the torturous pleasure of gazing upon her. Now he had nothing. He had allowed Dunsford to win. Why hadn't he fought harder for her? His heartless treatment of her had only made it easier for her to leave. A lump formed in his hollow chest.

And for the first time since his mother died, he buried his head in his hands and wept.

From outside in the hall, Evans listened to the duke's deep, racking sobs. He was most alarmed but restrained himself from going to his master. How painful it would be for the rugged duke, a leader among his peers, to let his valet see him crying like a woman.

Evans knew his grace's state of distress was intrinsically linked to the duchess's disappearance. His first reaction to her absence was disbelief. The woman was far too much in love with his grace to leave him.

A pity for both of them, Radcliff did not realize that.

As surprised as he was that the besotted duchess could leave her husband, Evans was more surprised over his master's reaction to her departure. Radcliff had sadly neglected his wife—to such an extent that Evans had grown to believe the duke was no longer in love with her.

But the broken man sitting in his wife's empty room was most assuredly a man in love. And most assuredly thoroughly miserable.

As a father hurts for his wounded son, so Evans hurt for Radcliff.

That fool woman. Why did she have to go off and leave? She deuced well loved the duke—as he did himself. It was that very affection, their mutual love for Radcliff, that had just recently forged a solid bond between the duchess and himself.

And didn't she know a woman in her condition was not

supposed to lift things like valises? She might jeopardize the future duke.

Perhaps it was too late to win her love, but it wasn't too late to claim what was lawfully his. Radcliff would be dead before he would let Dunsford take possession of his wife. He should have called out the earl long before, but always he had wanted to keep Bonny's reputation unblemished.

Now she had chosen to tarnish her name and the House of Radcliff. For that, he would blow off the smirking head of the Earl of Dunsford. Or die trying.

He would start at Dunsford House on Half Moon Street. Of course the earl would not be there, but a few quid properly dispersed should sufficiently loosen the servants' tongues as to their master's destination.

Radcliff wondered if Dunsford would be off to his country seat. He did not even know where it was. Perhaps the earl had carried Bonny aboard a ship bound for the Continent. If that were the case, Radcliff might have to employ Bow Street runners to aid in his search.

At Dunsford House, Radcliff dismounted from his stallion, giving the reins to a footman. Handing his card to another footman, Radcliff said, "Announce to your master that the Duke of Radcliff wishes to speak to him."

"I am sorry, your grace, but Lord Dunsford is not in."

Radcliff raised an eyebrow. "Left London, has he?"

"No, your grace."

He's lying. Dunsford, naturally, would have instructed his staff not to divulge his whereabouts. "I am interested in purchasing his barouche. Could you direct me to the stables so that I might examine it?"

"His lordship's equipage is stabled just around the corner," the middle-aged footman said, pointing to his left.

To Radcliff's surprise, Dunsford's barouche was, indeed,

stabled around the corner. He sought out the groom. "What mount did Lord Dunsford take today?"

"'E's riding 'is gray," the lad said.

"How long ago did he leave?"

"Noon straight up."

Now Radcliff was more baffled than ever. Clearly, Bonny had left around dawn. And if Dunsford were on a single horse, he could hardly be spiriting off a pregnant woman.

Radcliff walked off, looking up at the blackening sky.

Chapter Twenty-Seven

The man beside Bonny in the crowded stagecoach stank of onions and several weeks without bathing. She wasn't so sure now she had done the right thing by not taking a cheap seat on top of the stage, but when they ran into torrents of rain along the way, she held her breath and gave thanks for a dry seat.

When she had boarded the stage at Piccadilly, Bonny had tried to cover her belly so no one would know she was pregnant. Those who held to the old ways might have refused to seat her had they known of her condition. Old wives' tales had it that coach rides would jostle the baby out prematurely, but Emily had assured her these suspicions were totally unfounded.

"Why, I traveled from Badajoz up the Pyrenees not a month before Harriet was born," Emily had said. "And you have seen for yourself how perfectly she turned out."

Now confident that she would not jeopardize her baby, Bonny took a cue from the shapeless flower sellers at Covent Garden and wore most of the clothes she possessed on her back. This disguised her maternity quite well. She planned to do embroidery during the trip to keep something over her lap to hide the roundness that was her child, but gazing at the tiny pattern made her feel sick. It would not do to be sick on her fellow passengers, she decided.

It tore at her heart to remember the last time she had left London. The night she sat beside Richard for the first time. Even now her breathing quickened when she remembered him offering his shoulder for her sleepy head. Tears sprang to her eyes. She ached with a deep emptiness, an over-whelming urge to feel him next to her right now. She would trade all her tomorrows for that one yesterday.

She remembered those raw stirrings that Richard had aroused from the first time she saw him. What could she have done to earn his love?

Many times throughout the long days of the journey, she fought the lulling caused by the monotony of the road. She tried to force herself to stay awake but would find her head drooping as she dozed.

Looking at the odious men on either side of her, Bonny thought how repulsed she would be if either of them offered her his shoulder to sleep upon. But it was as if they sensed something highborn in her. And they knew their place.

Had Richard been attracted to her that first night? Is that why he had offered his shoulder? She remembered when she apologized for robbing him of sleep. With warmth spreading over her like a woolen blanket, she recalled his words that hazy dawn. *I don't know when I've ever been more comfortable,* he had said.

It was those little reflections that would sustain her in the years to come in Milford.

While Emily had spurned him, refusing to see him, Dunsford took consolation in the fact her mother had been especially fond of him. Of course, he could see through her like fine crystal. The woman clearly wanted an earl to court her daughter.

So the scheming Lady Landis would become his ally.

By now Dunsford had become familiar with the routines of everyone at Wickham House. Lord Landis left at precisely one every afternoon on his gelding. Lady Landis entertained callers at noon and frequently left Wickham House at two. Emily, since he had began stalking her, had left the house less and less.

On this day, Dunsford timed his arrival at Wickham House to coincide with Lady Landis's leaving. As she descended the steps, a liveried footman holding a parasol over her to repel the sprinkling rain, Dunsford stood at the bottom step and extended his greetings.

"Why, Lord Dunsford," a beaming Lady Landis said. "Such a pleasure to see you. Such a stranger you've been lately."

He gave her a sweeping bow. "Not by choice, I assure you, my lady. In fact, I wish to appeal to you today. Can you contrive to help me have a private audience with your daughter?" He wasn't sure if Lady Landis's eyes squinted from the sun or from undiluted pleasure.

"Pray, my lord, come ride with me. I am sure we can devise a plan to get you two together."

Like his heart, the day had been so wretchedly black Radcliff could scarcely tell when night began to fall. He turned his mount off Piccadilly onto Berkeley. He would have to get out of these wet clothes, dress for the evening and begin again his search for Dunsford. Thus far, his queries had proved futile. The earl had not been to Jackson's, Radcliff had learned after a casual inquiry there. A trip to Tattersall's also yielded no information on the whereabouts of Lord Dunsford. Radcliff had even gone to Brook's where being a duke afforded him admittance, although Radcliff was not a member of Dunsford's club. But Radcliff's offhand inquiries there about Dunsford had also proven fruitless.

Handing his bay to a hostler, the duke scurried up the steps to Radcliff House, shed his drenched coat and handed it to Mandley. It felt good to be within a warm house. He shivered through every limb. But he must not get too comfortable. He could not stop until he found Dunsford. Even if it took all night.

On the way to his chamber, Radcliff passed Bonny's door and his heart caught. He paused, then knocked on the wistful hope that she had returned. Only black silence answered. He opened the door and stepped into her room. It was in total darkness. Not even a fire in the hearth. How quickly word of the duchess's departure had reached the servants, he thought grimly, stalking through her chamber to the dressing room.

He did not know if it were his imagination or reality that scented the room with her floral fragrance. He thought of lying with her in this very room, surrounded by the dark stillness he now felt. But then he had had the comforting beat of her heart. And now there was nothing.

With that bitter reminder blackening his mood, he opened the door to his dressing room, which was lit by a brace of candles. And there he faced Evans.

"Your grace!" Evans exclaimed. "You will surely take a lung infection. Come, let me help you into dry clothes."

"I regret to say it would be no great loss were I to take a lung infection and depart this world, Evans."

"Do not say such things, your grace," Evans said, removing Radcliff's shirt. "A great many people would grieve exceedingly if anything should happen to your grace."

A pity that his Barbara was not one of those people. Radcliff sat on a sturdy chair and allowed Evans to take off his boots. Good boots they must be, he reflected. His stockings were the only dry article on his body.

"Your grace must have spent a great deal of time outdoors today to have got so wet."

"Yes, I've been searching for someone all day."

"And have your efforts met with good fortune?"

"No, but I shall renew my quest tonight."

"You will have the good judgment to take the barouche tonight, will you not, your grace?"

"How diplomatically you scold, Evans, but you do have a capital idea. I'm damned tired of being wet." Sliding into dry breeches, Radcliff met Evans's gaze squarely. "Tell me, why is there no fire nor candles in the duchess's room?"

"But...we were given to understand the duchess has left."

"From whom did you receive this information?"

"All of the servants understood from Marie that the duchess—"

"Say no more! You will instruct *my* household to keep the duchess's room in perfect order for her return."

"Her return?"

"My wife will be coming back shortly," Radcliff said as he grabbed a coat and stalked from the dressing room.

"A pity it is raining tonight," Lady Landis said as she entered their box at the Drury Lane Theatre. "I had so wanted to go to Vauxhall Gardens, but I am given to understand that tonight's play is very entertaining."

Lord and Lady Landis sat in the front row, then Lady Landis turned around and gazed affectionately at her two offspring. "By the way, dear," she said to Emily, "leave a seat between yourself and your brother. A friend of Alfred's will be joining us."

Emily did as her mother instructed, then began to read the program. Despite being in London the past seven months, she had been very little in society. Pleas of ill health had spared her from many of her mother's efforts to marry her off to a wealthy husband. But no protests had spared her from tonight's activities. No doubt, she thought bitterly, Alfred's "friend" would be yet another prospective husband.

When the curtain rustled open behind her, she did not even turn her head. The young gentleman moved to the seat beside her, and Emily turned to give him a stiff greeting. And she froze. It was Lord Dunsford. How she wished for a magic potion to make her disappear. She felt her face coloring and her chest rumbling from a torrent of emotions, not the least of which was pure embarrassment. She knew she should give him a greeting, but she could not find her voice. She faced him, her eyes downcast.

He gave friendly greetings to Lord and Lady Landis and to Alfred, then he turned his full attention on Emily. Bowing, he reached for her hand, and she gave it to him. "Lady Emily," he said, kissing her hand. "How very good it is to see you again." He sat next to her and inquired, "I trust your good health has returned?"

"Yes, my lord," she said shakily.

The curtain opened, and the comedy commenced. Emily could not say if it were entertaining or not. She could think of nothing save the handsome man who sat beside her, recalling the things Bonny had told her that morning. It was very hard indeed to believe that he knew of her shame and still sought her out. Could it be that what Bonny said was true? Could the earl truly be in love with her, despite her past? Could he really wish to marry her?

As the first act played on, her discomfort ebbed. Somehow, Lord Dunsford's closeness was reassuring. He did not care about her past. He had met Harriet. Bonny said he was quite attached to Harriet, and a liquid comfort spread through her at the thought. And he was here. Beside her. Could she dare hope he would be there always for her?

At intermission, Lady Landis sprang to her feet and announced, "David and I simply must speak to Lady Smitherton, my dear."

As she and Lord Landis left the box, Alfred said, "Must have a smoke." He did not ask Lord Dunsford to join him.

When there were just the two of them left in the dimly lit box, Dunsford turned to Emily. "You may have guessed that your family knows I particularly wished to speak to you alone."

Her heart hammering rapidly, Emily met Dunsford's serious gaze. "Yes, my lord."

He took her gloved hand and placed it within both of his. "Surely you know I wish to make you my wife."

She would have to speak of that which she had never thought to utter. It was as if his handclasp passed his strength to her, giving her the courage to speak her fears. "Considering what you know about me, my lord?"

He ran a loving hand across her cheek. "Especially knowing you. I love everything about you."

She saw the love in his eyes and wanted more than anything on earth to return that love tenfold. "But would I not cause you embarrassment?"

"You could never give me anything but happiness, Emily. But I love you too deeply to allow society to think ill of you. What happened on the Peninsula should remain a secret only you and I and Bonny share. But that doesn't mean that we can't be parents to Harriet and make a home for the three of us."

"Oh, Henry! You are the kindest man in the world."

"I don't want to be the kindest man in the world. I want you to make me the happiest. Say you will marry me."

A slow smile crossed her face. "I will marry you."

He scooped her into his arms and kissed her. The kiss captured all the tenderness in her being, and when it was through, he drew away and gave her a glowing look of love. "I had hoped for your love, and now you have answered me."

She chuckled contentedly, kissed his cheek and said, "I love you very much, my lord."

What a bloody waste this night had been, Radcliff thought as he trudged up the dimly lit staircase of Radcliff House. He had been to every blasted gaming establishment in the city but had not found Dunsford. The closest he had come was at midnight, when Thomas Squires told him he had seen Dunsford driving his curricle near Bow Street—alone—at around eight that evening. That, at least, had been good news. Dunsford was not with Bonny.

At Madam Chassay's, Radcliff had not even inquired after Dunsford because Stanley was there. Radcliff would be damned before he would allow Stanley to know he sought the earl who had been keeping company with his wife. He gave his cousin the cut and left.

Instead of going to his library and sulking with brandy as he normally did, Radcliff went to Bonny's chamber. He knew she wouldn't be there, but he longed for her so badly he was drawn to her room.

Now it was warm from a fire in the hearth. A candle glowed beside her bed. Her torchères were lit, too. He sat in the slipper chair beside the fireplace and heard a soft knock from the dressing room.

"Your grace?" Evans questioned.

"Yes."

Evans opened the adjoining door. "I thought perhaps you would like me to bring you some brandy."

Suddenly, Radcliff despised what he had become. The man who had driven Barbara away with his sulkiness and drinking. He had no taste for liquor tonight. He wanted only to keep a clear head, to determine how he could find Barbara and bring her back. "I want nothing that is in your power to give me, Evans."

"Would you like me to help you get ready for bed, your grace?"

Radcliff shook his head. "I do not plan to sleep until the duchess returns."

"But, your grace—"

"You are dismissed."

Radcliff walked to Bonny's dressing table and picked up her wedding ring. Even if she did not want to be married to him, he would not let her go. He would find her if he had to spend every shilling he owned. And he would bring her back. He would take her back to Hedley Hall and proceed with his initial plan of enveloping her in so much love she would have to love him in return. And even if she could never love him, he would never stop loving her. It would be easier to stop drawing breath.

He realized that it no longer mattered if she was in love with him. He did not have to have her love. He had only to have her. To never look upon her again would be worse than death. No longer did he want to die.

But how could he find her? Who besides Dunsford might know her whereabouts? Emily. By Jove, he would visit Emily in the morning. She was bound to know where to find Bonny.

Radcliff was not the only one who could not sleep since Bonny's departure. Evans, too, found himself lying awake. He kept remembering his grace's deep, racking sobs when he learned the duchess had left. Then, earlier in the evening, Radcliff had talked as if he wanted to die. Talking about taking lung fever. God forbid that something should happen to him.

Would that he could restore his master to happiness. But,

as the duke had so morosely informed him, there was nothing in his power that could bring the duchess back.

But the broken man of the last two days was most assuredly a man in love.

In the morning, Evans let himself into the duchess's gilded chamber. The duke, in the wrinkled clothing he had worn the night before, stood with his back to him, looking out the window onto the square.

"Your grace," Evans said boldly, "it is my opinion you have driven away the duchess by your neglect of her."

Radcliff gave his valet a startled look. "I know that, man, but there are…other factors. Things you don't know about."

"I know that she loved you, your grace."

The duke gave a mirthless laugh. "It sounds as if you are defending her, Evans. I could have sworn that you held the duchess in dislike."

Evans hung his head. "I have done her grace a great disservice and have grown to regret my treatment of her."

"As have I."

"If there is anything I can do—"

Radcliff placed a hand on Evans's shoulder. "Thank you, Evans."

"There is one other matter, your grace, about the missing jewels."

"The Radcliff Jewels?" Radcliff asked.

Evans nodded. "I have learned that your cousin, Stanley, took them the night of that first dinner party."

Radcliff smiled. "And how did you learn of this?"

Taken aback by his master's unexpected good humor, Evans almost whispered, "I would rather not say, your grace."

"Very well," Radcliff said cheerfully. "Assist me into clean clothes. I shall visit Wickham House this morning."

Chapter Twenty-Eight

Pale sunlight gleamed through the cloud cover as Radcliff's horse cantered toward Cavendish Square. Since Evans had revealed that Stanley—and not the duchess—had stolen the Radcliff Jewels, Radcliff's spirits had soared. And each step closer he came to Wickham House, the closer he came to finding Barbara.

Evans's revelation did indeed put a different perspective on things. Not to mention that there were now two men in London whom the duke wished to call out. It was while he took an almost pleasant surge from the thought of running a sword through Dunsford that he beheld the sight of the lean earl mounting the steps to Wickham House.

"Dunsford!" Radcliff called in a commanding voice. "A word with you, if you please."

The earl whirled around, his brows plunging together and a scowl of displeasure sweeping across his face when he recognized the duke. But, ever the gentleman, he did as he was bid, freezing in his step as he watched Radcliff leap from his mount and tie it up. He gave a stiff bow as Radcliff walked up to him.

Radcliff, his eyes like cold jade, stiffened and spoke with

malice. "May I ask what brings you to my relatives' home today?"

Ignoring the duke's steely tone, Dunsford gave him a shaky smile. "Your grace's will be the first ears to hear my wondrous news. You, Radcliff, will soon be my kinsman."

That the earl could smile at him completely stunned Radcliff. It was clearly not the action of a man who had stolen his wife. And what did he mean, they would soon be kinsmen? "Whatever are you speaking of, Dunsford?" Radcliff snapped.

"Of my upcoming nuptials."

The words struck Radcliff a paralyzing blow.

"Lady Emily," Dunsford continued, "has done me the honor of agreeing to be my wife."

Radcliff was more stunned than ever. Could it be possible that the earl loved Emily and not Barbara? "But...why is it you have been meeting my wife at Number 17 Kepple Street?"

The earl's face clouded. "Those meetings were of a private nature."

Radcliff grabbed the earl by the lapels of his morning coat. "Nothing that concerns my wife shall be private to you, Dunsford."

Dunsford's eyes softened. "It is not what you think, Radcliff. Your wife is completely devoted to you. In no way has she ever compromised her marriage vows."

"Then why, pray tell, was she meeting you on Kepple Street?"

"I cannot say, your grace. I can only tell you that the duchess in no way has sullied your good name."

His face inflamed, Radcliff shook Dunsford and spit out his anger in even harsher tones. "You will tell me, or we shall speak through our seconds."

Dunsford's eyes rounded. "But, your grace..." He hung

his head. "Very well. Since you are family, I will tell you what no one knows, save my dear Emily and the duchess." He stopped and his voice softened. "I have been paying visits to Number 17 Kepple Street to see Emily's baby."

"Emily's baby?" Radcliff exclaimed.

Dunsford nodded solemnly.

"Your babe?"

Dunsford shook his head. "My brother's. He died before he could wed Emily. The duchess—before she was a duchess, of course—was the one who came to Emily's assistance. She took her small legacy from her grandmother to set up a home for the baby."

God in heaven, Radcliff thought, he had done Barbara such an injustice. All the while she had been as true as the North Star. She obviously had vowed to her cousin never to tell anyone about the baby, hence the reason for such secrecy.

He had also done Dunsford a disservice. "My good man," Radcliff said to the earl, "may I offer you my apologies as well as my felicitations?"

"Thank you, your grace."

Radcliff placed his arm around Dunsford's shoulders and began to skip up the steps to Wickham House. "Allow me to make it up to you for my uncharitable behavior. Do me the goodness to compute the sum of your gaming debts, and I will settle them as a wedding present to you and my cousin."

. "You are all kindness, your grace."

Radcliff rapped at the door of Wickham House. "Not at all, Dunsford. I was thinking of my wife and how happy she will be if you and Lady Emily are in a state of bliss unmarred by financial worries. For, as you know, the duchess and her cousin are extremely close."

"Quite so."

When Styles opened the door, Radcliff said, "Please announce to Lady Emily that her betrothed and the Duke of Radcliff wish to see her.''

Not betraying the slightest surprise over the announcement of Emily's ''betrothed'', Styles showed in the two gentlemen.

Emily stood at the top of the stairway. Radcliff could see that she clutched a piece of folded paper in her hand. She looked at her intended first and started down the stairs. ''I trust you slept well, my lord.''

Dunsford moved to her side and clasped her hand. ''How can one sleep when complete bliss is so near at hand?''

A smile played at her lips and her fingers brushed across her fiancé's cheek, then she turned her attention to Radcliff. ''Bonny said you would come. I was to wait a week before I gave you the letter.''

Radcliff stepped closer. ''But you and I both know you are going to give it to me today, even if it's been only three days. Three long, horrible days.''

Emily's eyes twinkled. ''So you do love her.''

''Of course I love her. She's my wife.''

''Did you tell her?''

Radcliff gave Emily a puzzled look. Then he understood so much. If only he could turn back the clock. He held out his hand. ''May I have the letter?''

She handed it to him, and he tore it open with shaking hands and began to read.

My dear Richard,
By the time you read this, I shall be gone and you will have your freedom. It was a noble sacrifice you made by marrying me, and I will always be grateful for your generosity to me and to my mother. I will remember your many acts of kindness. I will remember, too, the tenderness we shared, particularly at Hedley Hall, and I have no regrets. My only regret is that

you were so utterly unhappy in London. It is obvious you did not want to be married to me.

I take nothing with me that I did not bring to our marriage, and it is my intention to get along without your financial assistance. Since I don't plan to return to London, perhaps you could explain my absence by allowing people to assume I died in childbirth.

I leave you with two requests. First, I beg that you do not worry about me. I will get on tolerably well. Secondly, I implore you to give up all notions of becoming a soldier.

His stomach still plummeting from the thought of her dying in childbirth, he noted the absence of a signature. Had she been in a dilemma over how to close the letter without using the word *love?*

He looked up at Emily, his eyes brimming. "Where is she?" he asked in a trembling voice.

"Milford."

He nodded and left.

Throwing open the door to his dressing room, Radcliff smiled and told Evans, "Help me into my riding clothes and pack my things, Evans. I go to my wife."

"May I inquire her whereabouts, your grace?" The valet took off his master's velvet waistcoat.

"She goes to Milford."

"Does your grace know by what means she is being conveyed?"

"I regret to say by the stagecoach."

"If I might be so bold as to make a suggestion, your grace, it is my opinion you could travel much better were you not fatigued from lack of sleep. Remember, the duchess will have many stops along the way. With yourself fresh and good horses, you could leave tomorrow and still arrive at approximately the same time her grace will arrive in Milford.''

Radcliff paused, nodding. "I believe you are correct, Evans. Besides, there is another matter I would like to settle before I depart London." Glancing at Evans, who was unbuttoning a buff coat, Radcliff said, "I will no longer require riding clothes after all, but I shall need them in the morning. Very early in the morning. And I would like you to instruct my household to ready the traveling coaches for the trip to Milford. Only the best carriage will do to convey the duchess to Hedley Hall. My child shall be born there.''

My child. Something stirred deep within him at the words. A pride as great as acknowledging that Bonny Barbara Allan was his wife.

"Evans," Radcliff said, "have Marie pack everything the duchess will need for her lying-in.''

A slow smile spread across Evans's solemn face. "With pleasure, your grace.''

On the last two occasions he had seen his cousin, Radcliff had given Stanley the cut direct. But not today. He sought him out at his lodgings on Marylebone.

"Richard," Stanley greeted him in a puzzled tone. "What a pleasure it is to see you.''

"This is not a pleasant visit, Stanley." He refused to take a seat in the chair Stanley indicated but stood facing his cousin, so close he could smell the liquor on his breath. "Do not protest what I am going to say, cousin, for I shall never again believe you. You are a liar. You are vile. And you are a thief.''

Stanley started to argue, but Radcliff silenced him. "I know with certainty you have stolen the Radcliff Jewels. I also know your pockets are full since this is the beginning of the quarter. You will restore the jewels to Radcliff House by tonight, or suffer the consequences.''

Stanley's cold, hate-filled eyes met Radcliff's, but he only nodded.

"And," Radcliff ordered, "you will leave England within the week. It grows tedious meeting you in society, cousin."

"But, Richard, we share the same blood. There's only the two of us left."

"A pity it would be to see my own cousin's head on Tower Bridge, the same as that of a common thief."

"You have made your point, cousin," Stanley said through gritted teeth.

Chapter Twenty-Nine

Radcliff would surely win a wager that no one could ever reach Milford from London in less time than he. He had taken his best horse and would have ridden it day and night without stopping, had only the horse no need to rest. So great was his haste to see Bonny that he slept but a few hours at each coaching inn before pressing onward, his thirst to see her driving him like a rushing avalanche.

During the countless hours of his lonely ride he phrased what he would say to Bonny in hundreds of ways. Through misty mornings and blustering winds, over rugged glens and along soggy lanes, his thoughts remained constant. Always, it was how he would tell her how much he loved her. Confess how cruel and jealous he had been. Beg her to come back to him.

The last three-quarters of a year he had been such a fool. He hated his damned pride, pride that had prevented him from telling Bonny from the beginning that he loved her with a fierceness that was frightening. And it was his same, bloody pride that had kept him from confronting her when he saw her with Dunsford at the house on Kepple Street. If only he had not been so blasted proud. Why had he not laid bare his wounds so Bonny could have soothed them with the truth?

All the problems in their marriage had arisen over his inability to communicate with his wife. Now he was determined to open his heart to her and let her know how dearly he loved her.

Though he feared her rejection more than ever, he told himself that he had nothing more to lose. What pain could be greater than that which he had already suffered?

And another growing fear gnawed at him. He worried that the journey had been too much for Bonny in her condition. He worried, too, about their child. He prayed that his Barbara would be safe and well, and their baby thriving.

No muscle in his body was free from the aching of several days of heavy riding. The bitter northern cold had settled in his lungs, leaving him with a rumble in his chest and a deep, racking cough. And he was certain now he had taken a fever.

As night began to fall, pains stabbed his every limb and his head felt as if a hammer were slamming into it. He shivered though sweat poured from his body, and his wet hair clung to his forehead. Radcliff was seized with a permeating chill that no amount of heavy clothing could slake. Feeling as if he were spinning into oblivion, he slowed his mount to a trot.

As he began to slide from the horse, his last foggy thoughts were of Barbara. His beautiful Barbara, whom he would never again see.

How foolish she had been to think she could purge Richard from her thoughts by removing herself from his presence, Bonny thought as she braced against the blustery North Country wind. She had wanted to recapture the happiness she had always known within the comforting walls of the old cottage, enveloped in the potent and unselfish love of her parents. But now she knew an ever greater love.

This land, this rugged hill she trod over, seemed steeped with his presence. Her eyes stung not from the winds but from the memories of the last time she had walked this overgrown path with Richard at her side. How fortunate she had been then. Perhaps she had not possessed his love, but she had had him.

What could she have done to have made him happy to be her husband? she wondered for the thousandth time. But she knew the power over his happiness lay in giving him his freedom. By her suffering, she had restored his well-being.

She pictured him as he had looked the first time he kissed her, so tall and strong, the wind whipping his honeyed hair, his greatcoat flapping behind him. His voice reassuring. Warmth spread through her as she remembered the sweetness of his kiss. She would trade her eternity to have those moments back.

Pulling her cloak more tightly about her, she climbed higher toward the place where she had first kissed him. She must have been mad to think she could be content now in the little cottage where she had once known so much love. Without Richard, contentment was as unattainable as the stars. The cottage—like her life—offered nothing but emptiness. An emptiness that could never be filled.

At the top of the knoll, she came to a stop. Despite the cold, this was where she felt warmest, for this place, more than any other, evoked his presence. God in heaven, would she ever lose her obsession over him?

Not as long as she remained here, where the very winds carried memories of Richard. Turning away, she sauntered down the slope. She knew what she had to do. The church had been wanting to purchase the old cottage. She would sell it and move to another village where she could free herself from the invisible chains of Richard's possession.

Days later, Richard woke to the feel of a gentle hand on his brow. "Barbara? Barbara?" he feebly repeated.

"No, my lord, it is I, the wife of the farmer who found you lying near death in the mud," said the kindly voice of an old woman.

He struggled to sit up in the clean bed, looking first at the plump woman in her simple dress and cap, then at the small stuccoed room. "How long have I been here?" he asked.

She gathered up the bleeding bowl and said, "A week. All's ye needed was a warm bed and a little doctoring. Dr. Haygood said ye'll be good as new this time next week."

But Radcliff was not about to wait another week before seeing Barbara. The next day, cleanly shaven and having given hardy thanks—as well as a handful of gold sovereigns—to the farmer and his wife, Radcliff set off once again for Milford.

Late in the afternoon two days later, he rode up to the old parsonage where Barbara had grown up, a light mist beginning to fall.

He dismounted, then knocked loud and long at the weathered door, but no one answered, giving rise to his mounting gloom. Turning back to the afternoon's gray fog, he looked toward the knoll where he had stood with Barbara on that long-ago day she had agreed to be his wife. And his heartbeat accelerated.

Wearing her old blue cloak, his lovely Barbara walked along the same small hill, silhouetted against the darkening skies, their unborn baby rounding into her cloak. His heart caught.

Radcliff began the climb toward her. Her back was to

him, and she appeared so deep in thought she had not noticed that someone was intruding on her solitude.

As he got closer, she must have heard his footsteps, for she turned suddenly and faced him, her mouth opening as if to say something. But no words came.

A lump formed in his throat. He started to tell her how lovely she was, but he stopped. She had never seemed pleased over his praises of her beauty. Instead, he spoke his heart. "I was thinking you look just as you did on the day you made me the happiest man on earth."

Her lashes lowered. "I then surely made you the unhappiest."

He did not disagree. "I was very unhappy because I loved you too deeply."

She lowered her head and spoke in a soft voice. "It is noble of you to feign such an attachment, Richard, but your preference for other company over mine speaks more truly than your words."

He stepped toward her. "I feign nothing where you are concerned. It shames me to admit that my unhappiness was the result of my mistaken belief that you were in love with another man."

"Another man?" She gazed at him, her eyes filling with tears. "There's never been anyone else for me since the first time I beheld you."

"I have done you an unpardonable injustice, Barbara. I believed you to be in love with Dunsford."

She tossed her head back and laughed. "Lord Dunsford! What a very peculiar notion." She took a step toward him. "Did I not give myself to you completely, Richard?"

He quivered at the thought of how sweetly compliant she had always been in his arms. "The blame for my blind jealousy does not lie with you, my love. I happened to see you leaving Number 17 Kepple Street with Lord Dunsford, then, remembering you dispatch a letter to him that night we left for Milford, I deduced that you had given your heart to him before you pledged your life to mine.''

''My visits to Kepple Street were not at all what you thought, sir.''

''Yes, I know,'' he whispered throatily. ''I've had a talk with Dunsford. I know all about your cousin's secret.''

She looked at him squarely and declared, ''I'll have no more secrets from you.''

''And I will no longer be so bloody proud I fail to tell you how dearly I love you. And our baby.''

He stepped closer to her, stroking her cloak where their baby grew, a melancholy gaze transforming his handsome face.

Had she dwelt so much on her own misery that she had failed to consider Richard's feelings? Bonny wondered. If only she had paid more heed to her husband. Why hadn't she delved into the reason for his great dislike of Lord Dunsford? Why hadn't she shared Emily's dark secret with her own husband? And why had she not told him how deeply she loved him?

Did he truly love her as she loved him? Had he been torn apart as she had, imagining her in Dunsford's arms as she had thought of him lying with Lady Heffington? Could he possibly have been bleeding inside as she had? She had only to look into his tortured face to know the answer to her question.

Almost weakened by the heady realization that it was within her power to provide balm to Richard's wounds, Bonny gently trailed her cool hand over his warm forehead as her eyes raked over him—the golden hair swept back by the North Country winds, his sun-parched skin and reddened nose, the grim set of his mouth, the cleft furrowed into his square chin.

''My poor, beloved Richard. I am sorry to have caused you such pain. I should have been more honest with you.''

Her arms circled him, her head resting softly against his chest.

He drew her to him and held her close for a long while, afraid to release her, to sever his lifeline. "Then you do not hate me?"

She looked up at him, and her hood slid off. "I have ached with my deep love for you. I could not tell you because I did not want to force a false declaration." She swallowed. "I never could imagine that you loved me. I thought you the noblest man alive to offer for me."

He crushed her against him, softly kissing her hair. "Twice now on this very spot," he said throatily, "your words have given me utter happiness."

*   *   *   *   *

Coming in March 1998
from *New York Times* bestselling author

Jennifer Blake

**The truth means everything to Kane Benedict.
Telling it could destroy Regina Dalton's son.**

Down in Louisiana, family comes first—that's the rule
the Benedicts live by. So when a beautiful redhead starts
paying a little bit too much attention to his grandfather,
Kane decides to find out what the woman really wants.

But Regina's not about to tell Kane the truth—that she's
being blackmailed and the extortionist wants Kane's
grandfather's business...or that the life of her son is
now at stake.

Available where books are sold.

**The Brightest Stars
in Women's Fiction.™**

MJB429

Take 4 bestselling love stories FREE

Plus get a FREE surprise gift!

Available in March
from *New York Times* bestselling author

ELIZABETH LOWELL

Carlson Raven had no choice but to rescue Janna Morgan—
the beautiful, courageous woman who struggled against the
stormy sea. When he pulled her from the choppy waters and
revived her with the heat of his body, his yearning was as
unexpected as it was enduring.

But Carlson was as untamed and enigmatic as the sea he
loved. Would Janna be the woman to capture his wild and
lonely heart?

LOVE SONG FOR A RAVEN

Available in March 1998
wherever books are sold.

DEBBIE MACOMBER

invites you to the

HEART OF TEXAS

Join Debbie Macomber as she brings you the lives
and loves of the folks in the ranching community
of Promise, Texas.

If you loved Midnight Sons—don't miss
Heart of Texas! A brand-new six-book series
from Debbie Macomber.

Available in February 1998
at your favorite retail store.

Heart of Texas by Debbie Macomber

Lonesome Cowboy	February '98
Texas Two-Step	March '98
Caroline's Child	April '98
Dr. Texas	May '98
Nell's Cowboy	June '98
Lone Star Baby	July '98

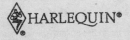

HARLEQUIN®

HPHRT1

New York Times bestselling author

LINDA LAEL MILLER

Nathan McKendrick—world famous, devastatingly handsome, undeniably passionate... Was it any wonder half of America was in love with him? And Mallory O'Connor McKendrick was just as successful in her own right. Their storybook marriage had defied the odds...as well as the rumors.

They believed that they were different, that their love was something special. But suddenly, inexplicably, the marriage was crumbling. What could destroy such a strong bond and what could they do to save it?

SNOWFLAKES ON THE SEA

Available in March 1998 wherever books are sold.

Welcome to *Love Inspired*™

A brand-new series of contemporary inspirational love stories.

Join men and women as they learn valuable lessons about facing the challenges of today's world and about life, love and faith.

Look for the following March 1998 Love Inspired™ titles:

CHILD OF HER HEART
by Irene Brand

A FATHER'S LOVE
by Cheryl Wolverton

WITH BABY IN MIND
by Arlene James

Available in retail outlets in February 1998.

LIFT YOUR SPIRITS AND GLADDEN YOUR HEART
with *Love Inspired!*™

Steeple
Hill™

LI398

**Look for these titles—
available at your favorite retail outlet!**

January 1998
Renegade Son **by Lisa Jackson**
Danielle Summers had problems: a rebellious child
and unscrupulous enemies. In addition, her Montana
ranch was slowly being sabotaged. And then there was
Chase McEnroe—who admired her land and desired her
body. But Danielle feared he would invade more than just
her property—he'd trespass on her heart.

February 1998
The Heart's Yearning **by Ginna Gray**
Fourteen years ago Laura gave her baby up for adoption,
and not one day had passed that she didn't think about
him and agonize over her choice—so she finally followed
her heart to Texas to see her child. But the plan to watch
her son from afar doesn't quite happen that way, once the
boy's sexy—*single*—father takes a decided interest in *her*.

March 1998
First Things Last **by Dixie Browning**
One look into Chandler Harrington's dark eyes and
Belinda Massey could refuse the Virginia millionaire nothing.
So how could the no-nonsense nanny believe the rumors that
he had kidnapped his nephew—an adorable, healthy little boy
who crawled as easily into her heart as he did into her lap?

**BORN IN THE USA: Love, marriage—
and the pursuit of family!**

 HARLEQUIN®   **Silhouette®**

Look us up on-line at: http://www.romance.net   BUSA4